Perfect Cadence

Hari C. Barnes

Perfect Cadence

Hari C. Barnes

Cover art by Geoff Diego Litherland.

This novel is entirely a work of fiction. The names, characters
and incidents portrayed in it are the work of the author's
imagination. Any resemblance to actual persons, living or dead,
events or localities is entirely coincidental.

First Edition

ISBN: 1544899343
ISBN-13: 978-1544899343

www.perfect-cadence.com

for Rebecca

The impediment to action advances action.
What stands in the way becomes the way.

Marcus Aurelius

Two Weeks Before

◆

Sam West stepped into the hallway and called out for his father, the drone of west London's evening rush hour was replaced by an eerie silence. After ten years, the smell of leather-bound books infused with antique furniture was immediately familiar, plunging Sam back amongst almost two decades of intertwining, childhood memories. In all that time the front door had never been left ajar.

Sam called out again. Through the darkness he went, the only sound from his leather soles on the tiled floor, punctuating his deepening breaths. He passed the staircase on his left and he reached for the lamp he remembered was on the side table against the wall opposite. Desperately he tried the switch – *on/off/on/off/on*… Still darkness. His fingers searched beneath the lampshade but only discovered two metal contacts where the light bulb should have been.

"Dad, it's Sam!" His voice echoed about the stairwells climbing the two floors above him.

Further into the black he went until the music stopped him. He focused every part of himself on the faint, gentle sound coming from downstairs. His father would often play records in his study, the small room backing onto the garden, behind the basement kitchen.

He gripped both rails, taking one step at a time, and followed the music down into the heart of the enveloping darkness. The air grew warmer and with it the spicy scent of Indian food from the kitchen, reminding Sam how hungry he was.

Stepping off the last step a shaft of orange light cut through the darkness of the kitchen, from below the study door; Sam groped for the light switch, his hand brushing fruitlessly back and forth over the smooth, painted wall. Down the length of the kitchen he continued, drawn to the light. He clattered a dining chair and clipped his ankle against the dresser, but he was now close enough to recognise the melancholic final bars of the opening aria of Bach's *Goldberg Variations*. He reached for the handle to the study door and landed it at the first attempt.

He took a deep breath. He hadn't expected his reunion with his father to start like this. Why had his father suddenly arranged this meeting?

He turned the handle and opened the door.

The gentle aria was replaced by the spritely *Variation One* swirling around the room. The immediate glare of the light flooded Sam's eyes. He winced but saw enough to register his father slumped in his armchair, legs unnaturally far out in front of him, chin flat on his chest and eyes closed.

He was too late.

The colour of life had gone from his father's cheeks. The stature, the gravitas, the wisdom had all vanished, leaving behind a poorly crafted, grey waxwork of the man that Sam remembered.

Sam struggled to lift him upright, his hands pulling the weight of his father's large, once intimidating frame from beneath his armpits.

A bead of sweat rolled down Sam's forehead and stung as it mixed with the tears in his eyes. He dropped to his knees, rested his head on his father's lap and squeezed his right hand.

Bach filled the room.

Variation Two became *Variation Three*, became *'Four*…

Sam fought against his shaking legs to get to his feet. Slipping his hand free of his father's stone grip he noticed a scrap of paper in the palm of his ashen hand; only an inch and a half wide by an inch tall along its two straight sides, it was the torn corner of a larger piece of writing paper. Sam dried his tears on his sleeve and turned away from his father, towards the lamp. Upon the paper was a single word written in black ink, in a neat, traditionally cursive, unfamiliar hand. The first character was just about legible despite the frayed tear across its top edge; the size, swirl and angle of the writing meant it was certainly part of the signature at the end of a letter.

Sam read the word over and over… The word *Frost*.

Day One

07:00

Gema Bank's trading floor was already buzzing. Sam clicked *Compose* and addressed the email to his boss, Jerry Hart.

Subject: Resignation.

He typed *Dear Jerry,* when his dealer board lit up and a phone call came through.

It was Jerry's secretary, Tanya.

"Jerry wants to see you now," said Tanya. Her voice flat and emotionless as always.

"On my way." Sam hung up, put his jacket back on and straightened his tie.

The air was thick with the smell of coffee and pastries as he walked through the long, narrow banks of desks. The guys trading Asia were in full swing, shouting down their phones in front of the stream of numbers and graphs across their six screen arrays. The European market traders were huddled in groups of three and four receiving instructions from their sales team on client flows and overnight orders. Economists and researchers gave their morning briefs over blaring speaker phones. Black and red digital tickers suspended from the ceiling scrolled commodity prices, foreign exchange rates and stock market prices for the *FTSE*, *Dax*, *CAC* and *NIKKEI*. Along the dozens of pillars in this football pitch sized room hung flat screen televisions silently broadcasting *CNN*, *Fox*, *BBC World*, *ABC* and *Bloomberg News*. The floor was flanked by management offices – glass boxes guarded by officious, bottle-blonde secretaries wearing too much makeup. The only natural light came from a few stingy windows at the far end of the floor. The air-con was blowing hard to chill the two hundred or so occupants and their technology.

Sam walked along the aisle of foreign exchange – FX – traders. A fat guy wearing yellow braces screamed out "What's the big figure on cable?" to nobody in particular. A bell rang out as a client hit a bid, followed by a whoop of excitement from a couple of boyish looking traders. Sam used to find this so exciting but even now, his first day back in the office for two weeks since his father died, it felt pointless and childish. Jerry's office was at the end of the floor.

Tanya looked up from her screen as Sam approached and jumped out of her chair to block his path. "Wait here, I'll see if Jerry is ready for you." Tanya span on her stilettos and gave a perfunctory knock before opening the heavy door to Jerry's office. She stepped aside and waved Sam over the threshold.

Sam didn't acknowledge her as he walked through her haze of sickly-sweet perfume, and left behind the clean, modern lines of the trading floor, for the oak panelling and deep pile carpet of Jerry's giant office. The office was big enough to seat twenty traders – boardroom proportions: The building's top office for the firm's top man.

Jerry sat perched on the edge of his desk with his arms crossed. He smiled broadly as he shook Sam's hand, "Sam, good to see you back. Do take a seat."

Jerry waved to the left-hand of the two chairs in front of his desk but Sam remembered his mistake from the last time he'd been in and took the other: Six months ago, when Jerry had given him his annual bonus, he had taken the left-hand seat, directly in front of the photographs of Jerry's wife Janie. Jerry had four individual, chronologically arranged, photo frames on one side of his enormous antique, mahogany desk: One of Janie and Jerry on their wedding day, taken at least thirty five years ago – the young, good looking couple in their mid-twenties. The next two of her alone on beach holidays – demur, bright and beautiful. The fourth photograph had been taken more recently, after the horse riding accident that had left her severely paralysed, requiring round-the-clock care. Sam had been unable to forget the image of her in that wheelchair, her hair a mess, that lifeless expression with lopsided smile and dim eyes – the Janie that Jerry had married gone forever. The handicapped and disabled made Sam feel uncomfortable – filling him with a dread that some disastrous event was awaiting him just around the corner. He wondered whether that photograph was another one of Jerry's power games. Another tactic to soften and disarm.

Jerry sat down behind his desk. The panoramic London skyline behind him – St Paul's Cathedral and the Shard over his left shoulder. "Can I ask Tanya to get you a drink?"

"No thanks, Jerry."

"Good, good. Well Sam, I wanted to start by saying how very sorry I am – we all are – to hear about James's death. He was a great man. You know he and I did a lot of work together back in the day? It's a real shame."

"Thanks Jerry, I really appreciate it and thanks for letting me have the last couple of weeks off." Sam saw his chance; the longer he spent in here the more anxious he felt. This was his opportunity to tell Jerry he was leaving. "In fact I've been thinking about things."

"Yes, yes thinking is good. That's your strength isn't it Sam," interrupted Jerry. He got up and walked round to join Sam in the chair next to him. "You've a bloody great mind, just like James." Jerry adjusted the chair so he faced Sam directly, their knees only a few inches apart. He leaned in and continued, "Tell me something, what do the guys out there think about me?" He gestured at the venetian blinds that shut out the trading floor from his office.

Sam pulled back as far as he could in his chair. "Jerry?"

"Come on. I know they all think I'm some old duffer... An... um... What's the word?..." Jerry searched the heavens.

All part of his act, thought Sam.

"... Anachronism," said Jerry finally.

"I wouldn't say that."

"Ha! Come on. Tell me what's the first thing that strikes you when you come in here?" Jerry stared keenly with his grey-green eyes at Sam.

Sam stared back as he pondered his answer, before deciding to play along. "You don't have a computer."

Jerry's eyes lit up with delight, "Precisely. Can't stand the things. Can't use the things. You see I'm from another time. I know that's what they all think out there. They all wonder when I'll be given my gold watch and a kick up the arse. You all ask each other, what value does old Jerry add?" Jerry leant in even further, the hundreds of fine wrinkles running through his tanned skin illuminated in the sunlight, "But you get it, Sam. You know what I stand for, don't you?"

Sam just wanted to tell Jerry that he'd had enough of this job. But something intrigued him about Jerry's mood. Sam did what he did best and thought laterally before answering, "Well, I suppose the real value you add in a corporate hierarchy like this one is to inspire the rest of us. You're the carrot. I mean, what better inspiration is there than a boss who's long past it yet makes ten times more money than anyone else in the firm? There's no better reason to continue working your balls off because one day you could – *should* – be just like Jerry Hart in his ginormous office with the great view and his feet up on the desk."

Jerry was frozen, staring hard into Sam's eyes.

Sam wondered whether he had overstepped the line of candour and misread the point of Jerry's question. But before he could say anything to rectify the situation Jerry erupted into another roar of laughter and slapped him on the thigh.

"You see. You're different Sam. You get it. You really get this whole game. That's what marks you out. I know you're damn good at your job. Your year-to-date P&L is off the charts again. And that's why I want to give you more."

So this was Jerry's game; a pre-emptive strike before Sam had chance to resign. Out of touch maybe but Jerry didn't get to the top without understanding people. But Sam wasn't going to let him win. "Jerry, I say that..."

"Hold on. I haven't finished." Jerry's face switched in an instant and a sharp, seriousness took over. He sat back in his chair and crossed his legs. "What do you know about Charles Frost?"

The word hit Sam like a smash in the face. Unable to hold Jerry's intense stare, he gazed out of the window at nothing in particular, battling to maintain his composure. That word, *Frost*, had plagued him for the last two weeks. Was this just a coincidence?

"Is anything the matter?" Jerry tilted his head to regain Sam's attention.

Sam ran his hand through his hair and inhaled deeply, contracting his diaphragm tight to fill his lungs, before exhaling slowly through his nose. He told himself to play it cool. "No, I don't think I recognise the name. Why?" He regained eye contact with Jerry.

Jerry frowned, "You surprise me, Sam. Charles Frost is a billionaire, one of the richest men on the planet. Our wealth management team have been trying to win his business for as long as I can remember but he's notoriously hard to get hold of. He's a recluse. Never seen in public. We understand he made his fortune mining in Africa."

Sam knew of the name Charles Frost, from gossip columns in the financial press. "I've heard he doesn't exist at all," Sam shrugged.

"Well he does exist. And I have some news for you boy. Charles Frost wants to work with Gema Bank and he wants to deal with you personally." Jerry rubbed his hands together as if he were suddenly cold.

Sam stared out of the window once more, his thoughts on the last time he had heard his father's voice – the phone call at seven on Sunday evening, after ten years of not seeing or speaking to one another, inviting him over for a take away curry the following evening. *'I need to see you Sam. There's so much I need to explain to you.'* His father was a particular man, everything done for a reason, no whims, no fancies. A knot formed in Sam's gut. He took another deep breath, forcing his attention back to Jerry, "Me?"

"Yes, you. Frost contacted us last week. It must be off the back of that *StarzHotel* trade you did last month. Bloody good bet. Two hundred and fifty million reasons to like that one." Jerry's face was still serious now he was talking business. "Mr Frost has bought an old stately home. He wants to turn it into a hotel. He's asked for you personally to check it out. See whether it's a goer."

That word… That name… This was no coincidence. The knot pulled tight. Sam had to know what more Jerry knew. "Just because I knew *StarzHotel* was going to sell to the Japanese doesn't make me an expert on hotels. I think Frost needs an estate agent not a banker."

"I don't have to point out to you how important a client like Charles Frost would be to Gema Bank, do I Sam?" Jerry uncrossed his legs and sat up straight. "And I would of course ensure you were very, very well looked after. All you need to do is get yourself up to Scotland, have a look around this house, talk to a few people and write up a report. The fresh Highland air will do you some good... After..." He paused again and touched his nose. "...Everything you've been through."

Was Jerry hiding something? Sam knew he wouldn't get anything more out of him now. There was only one way to find out: "When do you want me to leave?"

Jerry's expression softened once more and his smile returned. Business was over. "Excellent. First thing tomorrow morning. Tanya has all the details. But remember, mum's the word. As I said, our client does like his privacy." Jerry got up and walked towards his door and opened it. The cacophony of the trading floor flooded into the office. The meeting was adjourned. Sam got up and walked over to the door. Jerry extended a hand and the two men shook hands firmly. Sam tried to let go but Jerry maintained his strong grip. "You said you knew *StarzHotel* were going to sell to the Japanese. There's nothing I don't want to know is there, Sam?"

Sam smiled for the first time. Like a magician forced to reveal the secret behind his trick, he reluctantly explained, "I spent the last bank holiday weekend in the *Starz* lobby drinking tea and eating their delicious sandwiches and cakes. For three days I watched Mrs Takashi come and go, laden with shopping from Bond Street, *Harvey Nic's* and *Harrods*, before indulging in the hotel spa and beauty salon. She was having a whale of a time, falling in love with London and falling in love with the *Starz*, while her husband was upstairs locked in negotiations to buy the place. Each evening around seven Mr T would come down looking weary, while Mrs T was quite the opposite. The two of them would then have a meal in the double *Michelin* starred restaurant while I looked on from a table close by –

fantastic wine list I should add. By the end of the night, Mr and Mrs T would be laughing and joking their way back up to their complementary penthouse suite like a couple of teenagers – you'd have had no idea Takashi was Japan's most ruthless businessman. This went on for three nights. The market said the deal was off; *Starz* hadn't made a profit for two years, their share price was tanking. Nobody believed the prudent Mr Takashi would buy them out. But seeing the effect the place had on his wife and the influence she had on her husband, I was convinced the deal was on. By close of business Tuesday, Gema Bank had a sizeable long exposure to *Starz*. By day five the papers were reporting the second biggest hotel takeover in history."

Jerry let go of Sam's hand. "That's one hell of a story."

"I have the expense claims from the *Starz* to prove it – you'll be getting them soon enough," said Sam with a grin.

Jerry roared with laughter once more and slapped Sam on the back, "Now bugger-off to Scotland."

07:28

When Sam returned to his desk he found a cardboard document wallet waiting for him on his keyboard. Jerry must have instructed Tanya to deliver it while he was in the office. He picked it up and slid it inside a copy of *The FT*. The other three traders from his team were now in; no doubt having watched Sam come out of Jerry's office – every trader had half an eye on Jerry's office, no matter what the market was doing.

"Good holiday?" one of them asked. Sam hadn't told anyone except Jerry that he was off for the last fortnight grieving his father's death.

Sam nodded, "Fantastic. Jerry wants me to go away on business for a few days."

And that was that, the three traders turned back to their screens and continued to watch the markets. Sam slipped the newspaper under his arm and found an empty conference room. He closed the venetian blind and sat down in one of the twelve *Eames* chairs. There were three pages in the folder. Page one: His travel itinerary – a chauffeur at four tomorrow morning would collect him from home and drive him to City Airport, for the six o'clock flight to Inverness, Scotland. There another car would be waiting to drive him to the port where he would be taken to the Isle of Aul by boat. There was no ETA. No return trip details. Sam had never been beyond Edinburgh before and he'd never heard of Aul.

He pulled out his phone and searched 'Isle of Aul'. A website about tweed fabrics topped the list, explaining Aul was a tiny, privately owned island in the Inner Hebrides, the ancestral home of the Laird of Aul. Most of the one hundred and fifty islanders were sheep farmers and fishermen but in the nineteenth century it was renowned for its fine tweed-making wool. Page two: A grainy, black and white photograph of a large stone building. Sam figured this was the place Frost had bought. It was certainly big enough and grand enough to be a hotel. The building was a peculiar mix of castle – turrets with battlements, portcullis and large arch-shaped windows – but also house, with gabled roof and suburban chimney stacks. It was surrounded by ancient pines and rolling hills. Page three: A handwritten note from Tanya, 'Take plenty of cash. *Amex* unlikely to be accepted up there. Enjoy!'

He spent the next half an hour on his phone searching the internet for information on Charles Frost. But as he expected there was very little fact. The man was an enigma. No date or place of birth. The only consistent thread was a connection to mining in Kenya in the late nineteen-fifties and his philanthropic work through the *Frost Foundation* that had donated over a billion dollars to malaria research. A few gossip sites and blogs perpetuating the myth that Charles Frost didn't exist and never had existed. Instead, Charles Frost was a marketing ploy – a *Mr Kipling* or *Betty Crocker* – the acceptable face of a secret society of billionaires and corporations who pooled their wealth and collective cunning for their own evil means. The more Sam read the more confused he got. He was getting up to leave the conference room when his phone rang, the screen said CALLER UNKNOWN. Sam answered.

"It's Tanya. There's a change of plan on the Scotland trip. Jerry says you're to meet the client at his club in Mayfair this evening. A car will collect you from your house at seven."

"Okay," said Sam. He hung up and shook his head. He had an appointment at five with his father's solicitor to hear the reading of his will. Plus, he'd have to pack for the trip. He didn't bother to return to his desk; instead he went straight for the lifts and left the office.

Outside the City was already warm, bathed in the July sun. Streams of commuters charged along the pavement on their way to the office. Sam ducked into a coffee shop and ordered a double espresso macchiato. He sat in the window watching the taxis and buses make slow progress through the heavy traffic; miserable looking City workers repeating the same journey they made every weekday morning trudged past. Most wore headphones to escape the monotony and to shut-out the chants of the group of anti-capitalism protesters who could offer little more of a solution to the world's problems than to block the pavement at rush-hour.

Just like most of the people in this scene, this wasn't what Sam had planned for himself. But for the last ten years it had been his life. Seven a.m. to seven p.m. five, sometimes six, days a week. Trapped by the gilded cage of the City along with thousands of other would-be doctors, engineers, inventors and artisans. Now, at thirty he didn't need the money anymore – his last three bonuses had taken care of that. He didn't need to impress his successful father anymore.

Sam ordered another coffee at the counter and returned to his seat in the window. He replayed that evening two Mondays ago in his mind:

As arranged on their call the evening before, Sam left a client event in the City at eight thirty and took a cab to his father's house in Marylebone, arriving no later than five minutes past nine. That was when he discovered the front door ajar. He had found his father's body at about quarter past nine. By ten o'clock the doctor had arrived and put the time of death at about nine o'clock. The cause of death was a massive heart attack. The police were called by the doctor on account of Sam having found the front door open. But the police found no signs of forced entry or stolen property. On Sam's insistence they interviewed the owner of the Indian restaurant his father had ordered the takeaway from. They confirmed that the order had been placed at seven that evening. The delivery driver had noticed nothing untoward about the customer who paid cash and tipped generously for his curries, at the pre-arranged time of eight forty-five. The police had concluded that, at this point, his father had failed to close the door properly, speculating that the beginnings of the heart attack most likely distracted him. The doctor concurred that light headedness and a shortness of breath would have preceded the heart attack. He'd then gone downstairs, left the food on the kitchen table and sat in the armchair in his study before the cardiac arrest killed him almost instantly.

Sam took out his wallet and from it the scrap of paper he had found in his father's hand. He hadn't told the police about it. He hadn't thought it was important then even though he had fruitlessly searched the house for the rest of the letter to which the fragment belonged. He stared at the black ink and pictured the potential, complete signature – *Charles Frost*. What had been written on the letter? Where was the letter now? Had the letter been pulled from his father's hand? Was it Charles Frost who had written the letter? Why did Charles Frost want to meet *him* now?

It was just after nine. The pavements were quiet once more as the City went to work until lunchtime. Sam stepped out into the street and lit a cigarette. He was immediately disappointed for breaking his promise to himself to only smoke after dark. But the rush of nicotine to his brain felt so good. He smoked half and hailed a cab trundling down the opposite side of the road.

"How about a fag, matey?"

Sam could almost smell the anti-capitalism protestor before he saw him. The man's hand, replete with blackened finger nails, was already out-stretched, with an ironic sense of entitlement.

Sam smiled, "Here, have the pack."

The cab pulled up and Sam got in.

"Hey, you're alright, mate. You're alright!" called the protestor.

Sam closed his eyes, lost in his thoughts as the cab pulled away from the curb.

09:54

The cab stopped at the end of Ridge Mews and Sam got out. Cabbies avoided driving down the narrow cobbled street as it meant having to reverse back out or risk a scrape attempting to turn around in the cul-de-sac. This was precisely why Sam bought his stable conversion on the edge of Hyde Park. This tiny mews of only eight houses had no through traffic and brought a piece of tranquillity in the hubbub of London's west end. These stables were some of the last to be converted to homes in the sixties. Sam's house still had the original stable doors within which a more practical front door had been cut. He picked off a bit of the peeling bottle-green paint that gave the place a shabby chic feel, before turning the key and going inside.

The ground floor was one large space dominated by his mother's *Steinway* grand piano. In the back right-hand corner industrial stainless steel units and a free standing butcher's block marked the kitchen area. A pale white breakfast table with one original Shaker chair was pushed up beneath a small window that looked into the walled courtyard garden. The living area was marked by a single armchair in front of a large *Anglepoise* floor lamp that peered over the top of the chair, positioned to illuminate him as he read. Next to the chair, upon a worn Persian rug, was a pile of dog-eared paperback novels and a thin-line laptop. Cube speakers hung discretely from the exposed brick walls. There was no television. The room was immaculately clean and sparse. He spent a lot of time and money making the place appear an inexpensive afterthought.

His phone chirped and vibrated in his pocket. Sam checked the screen, pressed the silence button and left it to buzz itself still on top of the piano.

He climbed the spiral staircase to the mezzanine level where two bedrooms and a bathroom overlooked the ground floor. He changed out of his suit and put on a plain white t-shirt, black shorts, white socks and a pair of gel-cushioned running shoes. He emptied his pockets, took off his *Patek Philippe Nautilus* watch and placed it on the squat table next to his imported futon bed. He folded a twenty pound note three times and slid it into his right sock and unclipped his front door key from the bunch and tucked it into his left sock.

Downstairs his phone chimed again, this time it was a voicemail. Sam dialled his mailbox and let the message play through speaker from the piano while he went into the kitchen area.

'*Sam, it's Dr Carter. I read the obituaries in the Times today. Now I know why you've missed our last two sessions. I'm very sorry Sam. While it's obviously always your choice,*' There was a long pause, '*I really think we need to meet soon. Seeing as your father has been the topic of most of our sessions for all these years–*'

Sam turned the tap on full bore and gulped mouthfuls of water direct from the tap. The voicemail was finished before he had quenched his thirst. Stepping out into Ridge Mews he walked a few paces over the cobbles and stretched out his calves before breaking into a jog.

Soon Sam was crossing the Bayswater Road and into Hyde Park. The park was quiet despite the hot summer sunshine. He ran hard and fast, over the Serpentine and into Exhibition Road, following south to Fulham Road and then the river.

Covered in sweat, Sam stood hunched over, his hands on his knees, gasping for breath. He took the note from his sock and wandered up to the flower stall. He picked up a mixed bunch and told the florist to keep the change. Still a little breathless he went through the gate and walked slowly along the path. The temperature dropped in the shade of the tall oak trees. The noise of the traffic along the Magdalen Road faded away with every step.

Sam unwrapped the flowers from their cellophane and split the bunch in two. He knelt slowly and placed them against the gravestones that stood side by side. Ten years of weathering had faded one of the stones; green moss grew along its northern face. The other was only a week old, its black reflective granite gleamed in the sunshine. He remained on one knee, motionless, reading the names on the stones until tears blurred his vision. His parents were gone.

For the first time in his life he acknowledged his loneliness.

14:30

Sam stepped out of the shower. He dried himself in his bedroom. At the foot of his bed was a tan, leather weekend bag; next to it a matching suit carrier packed with two suits and a light-weight sports jacket – enough for three days. He made a mental note to call Tanya to confirm the details for his return journey back to London.

Sam shaved and styled his thick brown hair with wax. He splashed on a little aftershave and returned to his bedroom to dress for the evening. He couldn't quite believe he was meeting a multi-billionaire. He'd met plenty of multi-millionaires – he worked with many – but a billionaire was different. He remembered a statistic his father had told him when he was a young boy: A million seconds is eleven days; a billion seconds is nearly thirty-two years. He looked in the mirror and studied his reflection. At thirty he wasn't yet a billion seconds old. Charles Frost had earned many pounds for every second he had been alive. Sam didn't like the fact this impressed him. The rational side of his brain told him Frost was just another man like everyone else but a larger, more powerful side of his brain was deeply in awe of his gratuitous wealth. Sam pulled out his favourite, bespoke Savile Row suit. The luxury dark blue wool was a little too thick for this time of year but the cut was perfect for his tall, slim frame. He matched the suit with a made-to-measure white shirt from Jermyn Street and a black handmade slim line tie. A pair of black Oxford shoes brought a sobering banker feel to his otherwise contemporary look.

Downstairs he made a call to Morris Forster, his father's solicitor. The answering machine picked up straight away. Sam left a message: "Morris, it's Sam West. We have an appointment at five this evening. I'd like to do it at three thirty instead. Call my mobile if this is a problem." Sam spelt out his number twice and hung up. He had thirty five minutes before he needed to be there. He sat down at his piano and looked at the photograph of him and his mother, which he kept on the music rack. He remembered when it was taken, he was thirteen; his father had come in with his new camera and snapped the two of them while she was giving Sam a lesson. Almost all of Sam's memories of her were at the piano. Next to the photograph was the manuscript for Beethoven's *Moonlight* sonata. He played the opening bars but stopped after fumbling a couple of notes. He closed the lid and got up. He checked he had his mobile, wallet and keys and went to the front door. Stepping out into the sunlight his vision was suddenly filled with the unmistakable blue hair of Mrs Price, his neighbour.

"Aw, you look nice. Got a date tonight?" she asked.

Sam closed the front door behind him as she tried to peer inside. She frowned through her crude, almost pantomime dame, makeup.

"Mrs Price," said Sam, looking at her skinny black jeggings and over-sized vest.

"So who's the lucky lady?"

Sam noticed lipstick on her top row of teeth as she smiled. Mrs Price had lived in the mews since the sixties, originally squatting before her and her husband bought up one side of the cul-de-sac from the council. Sam had bought his place from her three years ago after Mr Price died. She lived alone with her Siamese cat and a potter's wheel. Sam suspected she still had a key for his house – every now and again he'd get home and notice a book out of place or cat fur in his armchair. But it didn't bother him, it was good having someone keep an eye on the place while he was away – she was as harmless as she was eccentric.

"I'm seeing a client if you must know."

"Shame. When are you going to find a girlfriend? I don't think I've ever seen you..."

"I'm going away tomorrow morning for a few days. If you wouldn't mind keeping an eye on the place until I'm back."

"Well, I'm busy you know. But I'll keep an eye open." She gave an unconvincing, nonchalant shrug.

"Thanks, Mrs P. I'd give you a key but I don't have a spare."

Sam watched her cheeks redden through her thick makeup.

"Well, I'll do my best. Have a lovely time. I must get a drink for Lucian," she said as she disappeared through her front door, whistling and calling for her cat.

In the cab to Ludgate Circus Sam felt anxious. The reading of the will was the final act of his father's death. It puzzled him that he felt this way. He distracted himself by sending an email to Tanya, asking her to confirm the details of his return journey from Scotland. Travelling along the Strand, Sam opened the window to let in some air. The cabbie was saying something but Sam ignored him and closed his eyes, trying his best to focus on the stream of warm air blowing over his face.

Morris Forster's office was in Bride Court, a narrow passageway in the shadow of St Bride's Church and its tiered wedding cake spire. Sam pushed the buzzer next to the anonymous blue door.

"Yes?" croaked a voice through the intercom.

"Morris, it's Sam West."

A few moments later the door was opened by a man in his seventies. His cheap black suit hung from him as if he had lost three stone overnight. His greasy white hair had deposited a generous dusting of dandruff over his shoulders.

"Sam, you're early," said Forster with surprise.

"I left a message on your machine."

Forster looked perturbed but waved Sam in and up the stairs into his pokey office where he had worked for the last fifty or so years. The room was littered with papers and boxes stacked four and five high. A three foot high oxygen cylinder leant against a tower of boxes closest to his desk, a clear plastic tube attached to a face mask was wrapped several times around the valve. Forster had battled emphysema for a while but to Sam this looked like one of Morris's better days, his skin had overcome the unhealthy pallor of the funeral last week and his breathing was absent its rattley wheeze. Sam admired Forster's ability to find solace in his work.

Sam took a seat and Forster almost folded into his chair behind his desk, hunched over his paperwork. How different this scene was to Jerry's office this morning, thought Sam.

Forster put on his gold, half-moon reading glasses. Without looking up from his papers he said, "That was a lovely speech you gave at the wake, Sam."

Sam felt embarrassed. It triggered more uneasiness inside him. The memory of writing the speech and having to give it to the thirty guests made him more restless. "Thanks and thank you for writing the wonderful obituary in today's *Times*. A great piece. You knew him much better than me." Sam hadn't read it and couldn't bring himself to even buy the newspaper.

Forster gave a deferential nod. "You've caught me unprepared but there's a fast way and a slow way to do these things. I prefer the fast way if you don't mind?"

Forster looked over his glasses through his small inquisitive eyes, still hunched over his papers.

"Suits me."

"Good. Well, as you know you are the last surviving member of the West family so to you goes your father's entire estate, minus taxes and some small amounts left to the *Law Society* and a few charities."

This was just as Sam had expected. He stood up. "Sell everything."

Forster got to his feet as quickly as his stiff old frame would let him, "Yes certainly, Sam. But there is one more thing." He patted his chest with both hands eventually pulling a key from his waistcoat. He looked at Sam before shuffling across the frayed carpet to the floor-to-ceiling sized cupboard. "As I said, I'm a little unprepared." There was panic in Forster's voice. "If you'd take a seat."

"I can't stay."

Forster looked over his shoulder, "Please sit down, it will take me a minute to open this old thing." Sam noticed the slight quiver in Forster's hand as he attempted to insert the key into the lock. It took a few attempts before he successfully turned the key.

Sam was already growing impatient, "Actually, Morris. There is something I would like to ask you." He returned to his seat.

Forster looked back at Sam, "Oh yes, what's that?"

"Who is Charles Frost?"

Forster stopped what he was doing and turned to face Sam, his back against the cupboard doors. "Who, Sam?"

"Charles Frost. What's his link to my father?" Sam stood up.

Forster's eyes rolled around in their tiny sockets as he also rested the back of his head against the door, his cheeks flushed with a tinge of crimson. "Why do you ask?"

"So you recognise the name then?" Sam moved around the desk.

Forster was flustered, his cheeks puffed out in unconvincing incredulity, "I didn't say that. Look, I don't understand what this has to do with me."

"What has *what* to do with you?" Sam spoke through half a smile to release the obvious tension Forster was feeling. He was now stood next to the bedraggled solicitor.

Forster glanced at his watch, "Sam, I have another appointment now. As I said, you've caught me somewhat by surprise coming so early."

"You said there was one more thing." Sam looked at the cupboard.

Forster turned to face the cupboard and shuffled a little to his right, blocking Sam's line of sight of the brass handle on one of the two doors. Forster looked back at Sam once more before trying the handle. It squeaked as it turned and Forster pulled but the door didn't budge. He tried again. Still no movement. He gasped as he pulled with as much effort as his scrawny arms could manage but it was useless. "It's not opening."

"Here, let me help."

Forster span around and blocked Sam's path to the cupboard. "It's painted shut. I'll get it sorted out. We can arrange another appointment."

Sam looked at the door. It hadn't been painted in years. The thought of having to come back was a definite no so he stepped around Forster and tried the handle.

"Sam, this is highly irregular. I have confidential..."

But before he could finish, Sam had pulled the door ajar. Forster's arm reached across and Sam felt his dry hand touch his own on the door handle. Sam let go and took half a step back, instinctively craning his head around Forster to take a look inside the cupboard. But Forster was already closing the door as he leant inside to pull out a red briefcase. Sam caught a glimpse of something of the same red colour next to where Forster had taken the briefcase but the door closed before he could see anything more. Forster leant his back against the door and used his free hand to find the key and lock the cupboard.

Sam diffused the awkwardness by returning to his seat on the other side of the desk. Forster regained his composure, pressing his hair into a semblance of style before sitting.

"Your father wanted you to have this," said Forster as he pushed the briefcase across the desk.

Sam took it and rested it on his lap. The case was light and slim, solidly made with hand stitching along its tapered sides. The red leather was bright but not garish. It looked old yet not well used, nearly as good as new. Sam had never seen the briefcase before and couldn't remember seeing his father with it. He pressed both of the gold catches with his thumbs in unison but they didn't move. Locked. A four digit combination lock, set to 0000, sat between the catches, in line with the centre of the handle.

"What's the combination?" asked Sam.

Forster was unwinding the plastic tube from the oxygen cylinder, his breathing laboured. "I don't know."

"When did he give you this? Did he say whose it was or why he wanted me to have it?" Sam had shifted the combination lock to his father's year of birth, 1952, but that didn't work.

The hiss of the oxygen tank filled the room. "All I can say is your father wanted you to have the briefcase. Client confidentiality, you see." The elastic on the face mask made a snapping sound against Forster's cheeks. He took long hard breaths of the oxygen, his face a few shades redder than healthy.

Sam knew this was his prompt to leave. He'd rattled Forster but now wasn't the time to press further. "Do you need help there Morris? Should I call a doctor?"

Forster dismissed the idea with the wave of his free hand, the other pulling the mask from his face to allow himself to speak, his wheeze had returned, "No, no. I'll be quite alright in a moment. Now, you'll have to sign a few things before you leave…" He took another deep breath of the gas, "And promise me you'll take care, Sam."

16:30

Sam left Forster's office carrying his new briefcase. He crossed between the traffic queuing up Ludgate Hill. A motorcycle with a passenger riding pillion, both dressed in black leathers and helmets, cut up the inside, brushing Sam's arm as it sped past him. Sam's curse was drowned out by the bike's overcooked throttle as it headed up towards the shimmering white Portland stone of St Paul's Cathedral.

Sam caught his reflection in a bookshop window, he looked a lot older carrying a briefcase but at the same time he liked what he saw; a certain gravitas and self-assuredness.

He stopped for a sandwich and a coffee in Paternoster Square, outside the *London Stock Exchange* building. He got a table in the shade and, for the second time that day, broke his smoking curfew. He checked his emails but still no word from Tanya. Sam was uneasy with his lack of control. He didn't want to go up to some remote Scottish island with no idea of when or how he'd be getting back to London. This wasn't how he ran his life.

He put a twenty pound note under the ashtray. He stared at the briefcase in the chair opposite to him, wondering how best to open it. He didn't want to prize it open and risk damaging it. The combination lock had four digits, each numbered zero to nine, so ten thousand possible options. If he went through them systematically, 0000 to 9999, at a rate of one per second that was approximately two hours and forty five minutes to crack. Sam settled for this option, as soon as he had the time.

As he stood up to leave there was that familiar, shrill serge of motorcycle revs but the sound was far too close to be right in this pedestrianised piazza. A heavy push in his back sent Sam face down into the table, his plate and cup smashing on the cobblestones. The smell of hot oil filled his nose as the motorcycle stopped inches from his face, the noise of the engine overwhelming. The passenger on the back had the briefcase before Sam could get back to his feet. Away across the square, under Temple Bar and through the crowds of tourists in front of St Paul's, the thieves were gone before anybody knew what had happened.

Waiters and fellow diners surrounded Sam as he tried in vain to wipe food and coffee from his ruined tie. He ignored the fuss around him and ran half-heartedly after the thieves, hoping that maybe they had got caught in the traffic or better still stopped by the police. But he knew it was hopeless. As he reached the steps of St Paul's and looked back down Ludgate Hill he saw his aggressors were already halfway up Fleet Street. Sam was breathless, his heart pounding against his chest. He stood still catching his breath, watching the motorcycle disappear between two buses. The crowds around him had returned to normal, enjoying photo opportunities in the hot sun. Sam took off his tie and threw it in a bin. He had half a dozen more ties hanging next to his desk at Gema Bank, only a few minutes' walk away. He'd call the police from there as well as talk to Jerry about exactly who Charles Frost was and what this was really about.

The traffic was beginning to build as five o'clock approached. The noise of the City was once more on the ascendency. Again Sam caught his reflection, this time in the revolving glass door into Gema Bank HQ and this time with no briefcase or tie, replaced by a bubbling rage and a determination to get answers from Jerry. He approached the turnstile, reaching into his jacket pocket for his wallet; he pulled it out and pressed it over the sensor to let him through – the same automatic motion he'd repeated thousands of times before. The turnstile didn't release and he was brought to a sudden, painful halt as his thighs crashed against the steel barrier. Sam tried his wallet over the sensor again but still nothing. A security guard watched him from the doorway with suspicion. Sam stepped back out of the turnstile and opened his wallet to find his Gema Bank ID card but it wasn't there.

"Can I help you, sir?" queried the security guard. The guard now stood next to Sam. He was in his late fifties, tall and hard looking.

"I must have left my ID at home. Strange, I had it this morning." He retraced his steps in his mind, attempting to recall the last time he had seen the card. The last time he used it was to swipe out of the building this morning.

"Sir, if you would step aside, please." The security guard placed a hand on Sam's shoulder.

Sam immediately recoiled, pulling his body away from the guard's reach. A surge of adrenaline shot through him. "Don't touch me." The words came out louder than they should have. Immediately he felt stupid and awkward.

The security guard frowned and stepped closer to Sam, his broad shoulders raised a couple of inches taller, "Could you please step aside, you are blocking the exit. If you are an employee the receptionist can help you," he said in a calm voice, pointing Sam in the direction of the reception desk on the other side of the cavernous lobby.

Sam looked around him and saw the queue of Gema Bank employees on the other side of the turnstile waiting to leave for the day. He walked over to the reception desk. His heart raced. The security guard returned to his position by the door. Sam remembered emptying his pockets before getting changed for his run; he decided the ID must have fallen out of his wallet then. In ten years he'd never forgotten or lost his ID.

A receptionist smiled through bright red lipstick as he approached the desk. Sam explained he had left his ID at home.

"Someone will have to sign you in then. Who shall I call?" she asked.

"Jerry Hart's PA, Tanya."

The receptionist typed the name into her computer, found the internal extension number and dialled. There was no answer.

"Anyone else I can try?" she asked, hanging up on Tanya's number.

Sam gave the names of each of his three teammates. Each time the receptionist dutifully looked up their extension and dialled. Each time the same outcome – "I'm sorry there's nobody there."

Sam couldn't understand, there had to be at least one of his team watching the markets. This wasn't right.

"Keep trying," he said.

The receptionist tried the numbers again but still nobody answered. Sam used his phone to email them all individually. An anxious feeling grew in his stomach as he wondered what was going on upstairs. Had Jerry called them all into a meeting? What were they talking about? Were they talking about him? Was one of his trades going wrong? Were they working on a secret trade without him?

"If you want to take a seat, I'll keep trying for you," said the receptionist.

Sam ignored her as he paced around the lobby, hitting *refresh* on his phone, desperately awaiting a response to one of his emails. His hands were clammy with sweat. It was now nearly half past five and a constant stream of

Gema Bank employees flowed through the turnstiles and out into the evening sunshine. Sam watched carefully for someone who could sign him in. But all he saw were hundreds of anonymous faces. He knew none of his team would be leaving until after six, probably closer to seven. With still no email response from anyone he approached the reception desk once more. The receptionist shrugged as she hung up the phone.

"Can't I get a new ID? I have my driving licence for identification and you can find my name on the system," said Sam.

"Yes you can but I'll still need somebody with a valid Gema Bank ID to vouch for you."

"This is fucking ridiculous. Do you have any idea how much money this could cost? I need to get to my desk." Sam slammed his fist down on the reception desk.

The receptionist jumped in her chair and her cheeks went the colour of her lipstick. She looked past Sam at the security guard who was already on his way over.

"Sorry sir, it's been like this since September Eleventh," she said, pressing her hands over her lap.

"I'm going to have to ask you to leave the building." It was the security guard behind Sam's shoulder.

Sam shook his head and let out a deep sigh. The security guard shadowed him across the lobby. Sam had a cigarette in his mouth before he reached the revolving doors. In the warm sunshine he took long drags to calm himself down. His heart was still racing as his mind ran wild with paranoid thoughts and conspiracy theories.

18:28

Sam finished his second whisky and ginger with a large gulp. He swirled around the ice cubes with a wristy, circular motion before placing the tumbler back down on the bar. The alcohol had taken the edge off his bad mood. The televisions above the long bar alternated between tennis and *Bloomberg News*. He checked his phone for a response but still nothing back from Tanya or his team. He left the bar opposite the Gema Bank office. He wanted to go back to the reception but he knew he didn't have time. He'd given up on calling the police too, after all what would they do? His was just another robbery in London; the police didn't have the resources to do anything more than take his statement which would likely take hours to process. Right now his priority was Charles Frost – his driver was collecting him at seven.

The traffic was too heavy for a cab so he walked to St Paul's tube station. He picked up a copy of the *Evening Standard* before descending the stairs to the ticket hall. The front page had been hijacked by the summer's biggest West End play, *Route 60 Hicks* – a svelte, Hollywood actress barely out of her teens, who Sam recognised but could not name, lay totally naked upon the flag of the United States of America, with only her arms and hands for cover.

The west-bound Central Line was crammed with weary City workers and summertime tourists. The heat and smell of body odour was oppressive. Sam held his newspaper under one arm and clung to the rail with the other, flanked by two spotty, Spanish teenagers wearing yellow rucksacks on their stomachs like fat-suits. Yet more adverts for *Route 60 Hicks*, the same naked girl and her stars and stripes but this time above the heads of the passengers along both sides of the carriage. A defective train ahead delayed them at Holborn. Sam's shirt stuck to his skin – he regretted wearing a woollen jacket. Eventually they made the seven stops to Lancaster Gate. He ran up the escalator and into the Bayswater Road, striding with purpose around the evening strollers looking for a place to dine. As he reached Ridge Mews he was red-faced and breathless. He stopped at the corner to check the time: Seven o'clock precisely.

Stepping onto the cobbled street his path was blocked by the *Flying Lady* of a black *Rolls Royce Phantom*. Sam rocked back onto the pavement. The car glided silently to a stop in front of him, blocking the entrance to the mews. He noted the extended wheel-base – bigger and more expensive than the rest – and admired the high-gloss paintwork sparkling in the hazy west London sunshine. The windows were like mirrors, preventing Sam from seeing into the passenger side front-seat. Instead, he used his reflection to flick his hair into shape. He was also reminded that he didn't have a tie – he could grab one from his house. The driver's door opened on the opposite side of the car. A blonde haired man rose until his tall, thin frame towered above the black roof of the vehicle. His head was bowed as he walked around the front of the car with the sombre grace of an undertaker leading a funeral procession, before raising his eyes to face Sam on the pavement. Sam was immediately struck by his face – his cadaverous, hollow cheeks and ashen skin were completely at odds with the bluest and brightest eyes he had ever seen. They were the round, inquisitive eyes of a baby boy planted in the sullen, sockets of an older man. His tightly cropped hair was thick and neatly parted. The man smiled to reveal a set of perfectly straight, brilliant white teeth.

"Good evening, sir," said the man.

"How do you know you're here to collect me?"

The man's eyes dropped once more before he said, "You don't want to miss tonight, sir." The driver opened the rear passenger door of the car and stood attentively beside it.

Sam looked inside at the sumptuous white leather and walnut, more luxurious than any first class aeroplane cabin he'd ever seen. He stepped inside and the door closed behind him. He sank into the soft leather and stretched his legs over the thick pile carpet. The air was chilled and there was no sound from the traffic on the Bayswater Road. The cadaverous driver appeared in the seat diagonally ahead of him and the car pulled away without a sound.

The ride was smooth and easy. The traffic through central London seemed to flow faster than Sam had ever noticed before. Red traffic lights turned to green as they approached. The traffic ahead dutifully turned off to clear a path for them. The world from a billionaire's car was simpler, more convenient, better. They reached Piccadilly in what felt like seconds before they turned up Dover Street and into Mayfair. Sam caught sight of those bright blue eyes in the driver's rear view mirror. The car stopped and the driver got out. Sam took one last deep breath of the rich leather scented air before the door opened and he stepped out into the Georgian square. He stood in front of a huge white stucco fronted mansion house, five-stories high and eight windows wide. The grand house took over one corner of the square, along with scattered – not neatly parked – *Lamborghinis*, *Ferraris* and *Bentleys*. Two muscle-ripped doormen in black tuxedos stood at the doorway, both had fiery-red hair, one short and spiky and the other grown down to his shoulders.

Short and Spiky saw Sam and came forth to greet him on the pavement. The badge on his lapel said *Clive*. "Good Evening, sir. Can I see your membership card, please."

"I'm not a member. I'm here on business."

"It's members only."

"I'm here to see Charles Frost."

Clive's expression turned sour and the bulging skin around his collar appeared to expand. "Look, piss off. We don't want any more fucking journalists in here."

The long-haired doorman waddled towards them, his badge read *Clyde* and Sam realised they were identical twins.

"I'm not a journalist. You can ask his chauffeur," said Sam. He looked back towards the road but the car and driver were gone.

"This guy reckons he's here to see Charles Frost," said Clive to his brother.

"Yeah, and I'm here to see Lord fucking Lucan," said Clyde.

Both men laughed.

"It's alright," came a voice from behind the twins.

Clive and Clyde parted and looked back to the front door.

Sam stared through the gap between them. In the doorway a woman in a short, black cocktail dress leant against the frame.

"He's with me," she said. Her accent unmistakably American deep south.

"Your lucky night, sir," said Clive. "Enjoy your evening."

Sam did his best to look calm and unsurprised as he squeezed between the doormen, towards the woman in the doorway. She was expressionless as she turned back into the hallway and into the crowds of tuxedos and designer dresses in the grand entrance hall. Sam caught a glimpse of her bare back before she disappeared into the mass of beautiful people. He had been expecting a stuffy, old club with geriatric pipe smokers and copies of yesterday's

Telegraph but instead the scene was like a society party from *Tatler*. There were about fifty people filling the entrance space, all engrossed in conversation and laughter. Everyone was drinking champagne. The air was filled with a mix of perfume and flowers. A swinging jazz band played from somewhere deeper into the house. It was still early on a Monday evening but it seemed to Sam that the party had been going on all day and that these weren't just members of a club but that there was a shared purpose to their being here, a common bond that had brought them together, like a wedding or christening for somebody with whom they were all close. He felt awkward standing alone on the black and white tiles beneath the huge crystal chandelier that sparkled above them. He pulled his phone out to give his hands something to do but he had no reception at all. A waiter carrying a tray of champagne worked his way through the crowd, Sam watched him until he was close enough to reach. He took the last two flutes, downed the first in two gulps and placed it back on the tray. The waiter did not flinch. With the alcohol easing through his brain and a glass of champagne in his hand, Sam casually made his way around the hall in search of the American from the front door.

The crowd was a mix of young and old couples; most matched for age but a fair number of big-breasted girls in their early twenties hung from the arms of tanned, balding men three times their senior. In groups of six and eight they mingled and networked in a host of different languages. But they all had one thing in common to Sam – they had that self assured, contentedness that Sam admired – envied – in the super-rich. Their laughter was deeper and more satisfying than his; their anecdotes more enthralling. They were in control of their lives and the world they lived in. The world revolved around them just as it was meant to.

The music grew louder as Sam reached the back of the entrance hall and he passed through a set of double doors into a ballroom packed with another hundred or so people. The triple height ceiling was punctuated by six more huge crystal chandeliers along its length. At the far end a four-piece band with trumpet, bass, piano and drums kicked out the sound of the 1920s, both relaxing and invigorating in the way that only jazz can do. Sam instinctively locked into the beat and nodded his head. Couples danced and bopped. Down the left-hand side were long tables of food attended to by a dozen waiters in white uniforms. Sam scanned his eyes for the short black dress as he made his way through the crowd.

"Sam." It was the woman from the front door. She stood next to him with her left hand on her hip and an empty glass in her right. "You going to get me a drink?"

Sam reached out to shake her hand but she was already leaning in to kiss him on the cheek. She was much shorter than him and his hand brushed her stomach before he pulled it away.

She smiled at his awkwardness.

Sam looked away as her confidence and elegance disarmed him. He followed her into a smaller side room, all the while focused on the smooth lines of her naked back. The room was set up in a Prohibition speakeasy style. At the circular bar in the middle of the room a barman mixed cocktails; two couples sat on high stools drinking martinis. Around the outside were red velvet booths, each with their own gold table. The black, wood panelled room had no windows, the only light from the bar and a small candle on each table. She waved at the barman and led Sam to a booth in the back corner. They sat opposite each other, with the orange light flickering off their faces. Sam urged himself to say something.

"I'm sorry, I'm afraid I don't know your name."

"George."

"George, it's a pleasure to meet you." Sam scolded himself for the banal small talk. His eyes adjusted to the dim light and he noticed the brown birthmark covering the right side of her neck, just below the jaw line, wrapping around behind her ear. It was almost symmetrical, like a Rorschach inkblot.

The waiter arrived with a bottle of champagne and two glasses. He poured them a glass each, left the bottle in an ice-bucket at the end of the table and took the half-filled glass Sam had brought in with him away. All the while George smiled at Sam.

Sam raised his glass, "Cheers."

"Cheers," she said, chinking her glass with his, "to Charles Frost."

19:58

Sam took a small sip of his champagne. George stared over her glass as she drank, her round green eyes curious as a toddler. Sam spoke to cut the tension.

"Do you work for Mr Frost?" he said.

Still holding her glass in her left hand, George rested both her forearms on the table. Sam noticed her chunky, digital watch.

"You could say that." She glanced around the room and back towards the door they had entered by, "We *all* work for Mr Frost."

"What do you mean?" Sam looked around the room to see if there was anyone in particular she had been referring to but he only saw the same tuxedos and dresses laughing over their cocktails.

"Yes. Everyone here either works for Frost or is working on working for Frost. Just like you." She emptied her glass in a single mouthful.

"It's Mr Frost that wants to work with *me*, if you must know."

George smiled, "You must be very special."

The waiter came over and topped up her glass. He gestured to Sam with the bottle but Sam covered his glass with his hand.

"What's wrong, had enough already?" said George.

"I'm *working* remember. Now are you going to tell me what's going on? I should be meeting Frost tonight."

George leant into her seat and rolled back her shoulders; the large red velvet booth-seat accentuated her petiteness.

She looked up at the ceiling before closing her eyes. She had cut her hair short so that it required clips to keep it tucked behind her ears, leaving her prominent birthmark fully exposed. He thought it curious that she didn't cover it up with longer hair. Her self-assuredness impressed him.

"Mr Frost is a man of his word. If he said he'll meet you tonight then that's exactly what he'll do. And no – before you ask – I can't take you to him because I don't know where he is."

"And all these people," Sam pointed over his shoulder back to the ballroom, "they're all here to see Frost tonight?"

"If they're lucky." George opened her eyes once more, returning her inquisitive, green-eyed stare back at him. The gentle candle light flickered over her round, dimpled cheeks.

"So this is an average Monday night for a billionaire?" Sam took another small sip to disguise his genuine curiosity.

"No two days are the same for a man like Frost."

"So what next?"

"Next we stop talking about Charles and talk about you. Then we dance."

Sam sank back in his seat and puffed out his cheeks.

"Don't like dancing?"

"Nor do I like talking about myself."

George smiled and put her glass down. She slid to her right and rose to her feet. She took Sam's hand and pulled him out of the booth. Sam offered no resistance. He savoured the gentleness of her small, soft hand in his as they walked out of the bar and back into the ballroom and the jazz. The floor was heaving. They weaved in and out of the dancing couples, George always half a step ahead of him. Sam watched the exhilarated, beautiful faces glistening under the light. The heat grew all the time, as they made their way to the middle of the room. They stopped between a short guy in a white tuxedo, dancing with a girl in a canary yellow maxi-dress and a couple of teenagers who looked like they had been dressed by their parents, dancing with the coldness of siblings. George span on her toes and wrapped her arm around Sam's back and danced. Sam stood motionless for a moment before finding the beat and forcing himself to move. He felt horribly self-conscious. She closed her eyes and her face went blank as it became lost to the music. Sam watched her as they moved. All the time she maintained contact with him – a hand, an arm or her back against his. He wanted to hold her but he couldn't find the courage. He did his best to focus on the music. Occasionally she'd open her eyes and stare vacantly at him, her face serious yet absent, belonging to the music.

They danced to five tunes before George took Sam's hand and guided them to the edge of the room. They picked up a couple of glasses of champagne from a tray and returned to their booth in the side-bar. They sat in their same seats in silence as they caught their breath. Sam felt the sweat and heat rise from under his collar. He noticed a light sheen over George's forehead and her cheeks were flushed with blood.

Sam felt euphoric as the endorphins produced by the dancing mixed with the booze.

"You're a great dancer," said George.

Nobody had said that to him before. "Thanks, you too."

"You like music?"

"Music's the one thing in life I'm certain I like." Sam took a large swig of his champagne.

"Why's that?"

He undid another button on his shirt, the release of heat felt so good. "Because music's the one constant in my life. I've played the piano since I was three and its always been there. I've always loved playing and listening. I always will."

"I hated my piano lessons." George held up her hands in front of her, palms facing Sam, and wiggled her fingers. "Fat fingers."

Sam laughed, "You've got great piano fingers."

George winked. "I bet you say that to all the girls."

He ran his hand through his hair. "You're American?"

"Wow, how *did* you guess?" She hammed up her accent.

"It was the watch. Only an American would wear a watch like that with a cocktail dress." Sam slid along the cushion and leant against the wall, swinging his legs up onto the booth-seat in front of him.

George used a serviette to wipe the face of her rubber-strapped watch. She held her wrist out in front of her and admired her watch. "Why thank you. I spent ages trying to decide between this and my fluorescent green Glastonbury wristband."

"You're weird."

"Brits always think Americans are weird." She poked her tongue out at him.

"Particularly kooky girls from Atlanta." Sam flicked his eyes at hers, keen to catch her reaction.

She stopped drinking and raised her eyebrows. "You *are* clever, no wonder Mr Frost wants to work with you."

Sam felt a thrill at his gamble paying off. "So George is short for Georgia?"

"Yep. Named by my mamma after my glorious state. You?"

"Me? Sam is short for Samson. But I never use that. I don't think I'm named after anyone or anywhere in particular."

"Do you ever wish you could be somebody else?"

"How do you mean?"

"I mean become somebody new. Be precisely the person you want to be all of the time. To be free from all the crap you've accumulated in your life until now." George watched him carefully.

The day's events flashed through Sam's mind, from his botched attempt to resign, to kneeling in front of his parent's graves, to the mugging and the turnstiles at Gema Bank. He sighed, "It's a real shame that's not possible."

"So you do! Yeah, I feel like that too. I guess that's what everyone here is looking for." George swept a hand out in the direction of the door back into the ballroom. "But hey, grass ain't always greener as my ma says." She curled her legs up onto the cushion.

"My mum used to say that, before she died." Sam picked at the paper napkin under his glass.

"I'm sorry, Sam."

"It's okay. My father died two weeks ago today, too. Death is what we Wests do best."

George stopped drinking, her glass suspended in the air.

"No, please. It was stupid of me to say that." He ran both hands through his hair, "I don't know why I'm telling you any of this."

"Say what you like. It must be terrible. I remember when my dad died. I was a mess. My mum was worse. But the worst thing was having to deal with my two brothers and the relatives – having to be strong for everyone else."

Sam put up a hand to the barman; he in turn nodded and signalled to a waiter on the other side of the room.

"That's the thing. I'm an only child. My mum was an only child. My dad had a brother, Richard, who died when I was a baby. There is nobody else. I'm the last of the Wests." Sam raised his glass, "A toast: To death."

"To death," said George.

They finished their drinks as the waiter arrived.

Sam pushed his glass across the table at the man. "Another champagne and a large whisky and ginger for me."

The crash of a gong rang out from the ballroom, prompting a sudden hush. The music stopped mid-tune and everyone ceased their chatter and laughter. Sam looked up from his third whisky at George. She shook through his drunken eyes. But he could tell her expression had transformed once more, this time to one of resignation or even frustration; she bit down on her bottom lip.

"What is it?" Sam whispered.

"It's time for me to go. I'll see you around." She stood up and walked off without another look.

Sam wobbled as he raised himself up – the drunken delay between brain and legs.

"Wait," he called. His voice rang out across the silent room.

George carried on, out of the bar. Sam ignored the gasps and pointing of the other guests as he moved as quickly as he could after her. He staggered into the ballroom where the scores of once dancing couples now stood in silence, in two lines along the length of the room. Sam pushed his way through the dresses and tuxedos looking for George. He searched frantically, calling out her name between the suntanned faces and big hairdos. Somebody pushed him in the back and he fell out of the line, into the middle of the room. His face hit the cold, wooden floor. His nose stung and his eyes streamed. He got to his knees as quickly as the booze would allow. The room span around him and the horrible sound of laughter buffeted about his ears. Eventually he got to his feet, swaying as his weight shifted from one foot to the other. The mocking laughter got louder and louder. The band began to play a terrible, whining tune. Sam couldn't focus through his blurry eyes. He rubbed frantically at his face to clear his vision, only to notice the blood from his nose all over his hands. He felt like throwing up. His mind went blank. He stumbled around the floor towards the frenzy of spiteful faces, contorted in hysterical laughter. The terrible music...

"George!" he shouted, "George!"

A shadow descended upon him. A streak of red hair. Sam raised an arm to cover his face. The blow to his right cheek killed the laughter, the music and the light.

Day Two

01:31

The headlights of the Night Bus stung Sam's eyes as he awoke in a travel agent's doorway. He touched his nose and felt his aching cheek. The bleeding had stopped but his head pounded worse than any hangover. *Fortnum's* clock on the opposite side of the road told him he'd lost the last ninety minutes. He climbed to his feet and took small comfort that he still had his wallet, phone, keys and watch. Piccadilly was deserted in the cold night. He pulled out his phone and dialled 999 but nothing happened. The battery was flat. He looked up and down the road for a cab or police car but there was no one. He slowly walked west and cut up north, back towards the club. His heart raced with rage. Like a dog chasing a car he had no idea what he'd do when he got there but he had to find that ginger bastard that hit him. He thought of George; the dancing; the crash of the gong and the sickening laughter.

Under a street light he saw his reflection in a car window. His shirt and jacket were stained with blood. His right cheekbone raised beyond his swollen eye. None of this bothered him now. He picked up pace through the narrow Mayfair streets, striding with real purpose. He turned into the square and cut diagonally across its central lawned garden towards the club. But as he emerged from the darkness into the white light in front of the building he knew he had wasted his time. Gone were the sports cars. No more music. The front door closed and unmanned. Not a single light shone from the many windows. He beat at the large black door with his fists until they hurt.

"Open up you fucking bastards," he screamed. His words echoed around the deserted square.

Sam walked back through Shepherd Market onto Park Lane, all the time looking for a cab or police car. Along the edge of Hyde Park he shivered in the clear, chilly night. The cold numbed his thoughts. The shock of it all sobering him up with every step. He made the last quarter of a mile through the park. The rustling of the leaves and branches put him on edge as his senses returned. A fear began to take hold as he processed the events of the evening. He lit a cigarette with a shaky hand. But the smoke made his nausea worse, so he flicked it away into a flower bed.

He came out of the park about a hundred yards west of Ridge Mews. He crossed the Bayswater Road and squeezed between a parked van and motorbike to get onto the pavement. A crowd of people were congregated ahead of him. Sam slowed his pace as he approached. Then he noticed something wasn't right; they were all dressed in their nightwear – dressing gowns over pyjamas, vests and shorts; a couple were barefoot, obviously disturbed from their slumber. Conscious of the mess he was in, he wiped his face on his sleeve and pulled up his collar. He joined the back of the crowd, keeping his head down and listening to what they were saying.

"Do you know who it is?" A woman's voice asked.

"No idea. Don't see why they had to close off the street," said another woman.

Sam edged around the back of the crowd. It was then he saw the blue light pulsating from within the mews. Yellow police tape prevented entry onto the cobbled street. Two police cars and an ambulance were parked inside the cordon, their blue lights flashing in silence. Sam shuffled around some more, peering through the light.

Two policewomen came out of one of the houses, both of them speaking into the radios clipped to their lapels. The policewomen were followed by two paramedics carrying a body on a stretcher. The body was covered by a blanket.

Something moved in the shadows to Sam's left, under the awning of the hair salon on the corner of Ridge Mews and Bayswater Road. Sam crouched down and Lucian, Mrs Price's cat, skipped into the street light and rubbed his cheek against Sam's leg. Sam stroked Lucian's head and gently picked him up, holding his warm, blue-grey fur close to his chest. Lucian purred contently. Sam feared the worst; Lucian was never out of Mrs P's sight never mind out of the house. He stood up to get a better view of the body on the stretcher.

"The body came from Sam's house!" gasped one of his neighbours in the crowd.

Sam's eyes shot up and he strained to confirm this. They were right. The body had come from *his* house. His heart thumped against his chest.

"Yes, it's Sam West's house," said another, "Where is Sam?"

The crowd began to move as everyone looked about one and other for Sam, their neighbour. The policewomen approached the yellow tape. "I regret to inform you that there's been a suspicious death here tonight. We have to treat this as a murder scene. You'll all need to be interviewed."

Sam began to panic. He didn't know what to do. He rejoined the back of the crowd and singling out a woman he didn't recognise he thrust Lucian into her arms.

"Take good care of him," said Sam.

"Hey!" shouted the woman, left holding the cat.

Sam was already walking away from her. He looked down at the blood on his hands and shirt. He dropped his shoulders, turned away into the shadows and walked back down the Bayswater Road. His mouth went dry and he could feel the eyes of the crowd behind him searing holes into the back of his head. He picked up his pace; bloodied hands buried deep into his trouser pockets.

"There's Sam!" shouted a man's voice from the crowd.

Sam broke into a run.

"Police. Quick. Police!" shouted the man.

Sam stepped behind the parked van he had passed just a few minutes earlier and leant against its cold doors. Breathless. He tried to think. But he found nothing. His brain was a scrambled mess, overwhelmed by fear and confusion. He could hear the quick footsteps of his neighbours getting closer and closer.

"He's down here!" came a woman's voice only a few feet away from him.

Sam ran his hands through his hair and covered his eyes. His throat began to contract and tears burst from his sore eyes.

"Sam. Get in."

Sam recognised the voice. He looked to his right. A red *Mini* had pulled up next to him, the passenger-side door open and inside, behind the wheel, was George.

"Get in," she ordered.

He jumped in and the car was away before he had closed his door.

02:3b

George sped through the West End, not stopping for red lights. Sam sat in silence with one eye on the wing-mirror and the other on George's profile. She had changed out of her cocktail dress, into a pair of dark blue jeans and a black pullover. She wore oversized black framed glasses that made her look a lot older. Even in this small car she had her seat pushed as far forward as it could go, only just able to see over the steering wheel. They reached Parliament Square in a few minutes and onto the Embankment, following the Thames east. No police cars were following them. Sam began to calm a little but his head was wild with questions and confusion.

"What the fuck is going on?" he said.

"We can't talk here." George didn't take her eyes off the road.

"No. You tell me now or I'm getting out of this car and going straight to the police."

"You *don't* want to do that."

Sam placed his hand on his door handle, "Stop the car, George."

The car sped up.

"What happened back at my house? What happened to Mrs Price?"

George floored the accelerator. Sam pulled his hand away. She was confident driving at speed – doing over double the limit at times. Sam sighed. He pulled out a cigarette, as much to calm himself down as it was to annoy

George. But still she showed no emotion and said nothing as the small car filled with smoke.

They followed the Thames through Limehouse and into the Isle of Dogs. She took them through several run-down council estates before rejoining the river. Finally, she stopped outside the gates of a smart Victorian warehouse building overlooking the water. She pulled a remote control from the *Mini's* central console and pointed it at the windscreen. The gates opened. She drove into the courtyard and down into an underground parking area big enough for ten cars. The *Mini* was the only car down there. George parked in the space nearest the exit. Sam checked his watch; it was five minutes to three.

They got out of the car and walked across the underground car park to a steel door. George pulled out a bunch of keys from her jeans and unlocked it. The door slid open to reveal a small service elevator. Inside, George turned another key in a lock on the control panel and they ascended several floors, precisely how many Sam couldn't tell. They were forced to stand close together in the confined space; Sam could smell her perfume mixed with the stench of tobacco on his clothes. The elevator slid open to reveal another steel door which George unlocked with a third key.

Her rubber soles squeaked in the darkness. Sam hung back. Suddenly the room lit up.

"Close the door," said George.

Sam looked about him. They were in an open-plan warehouse apartment. There was only a brown leather sofa and a coffee table in the living area – few other signs that anyone actually lived here. George was already over in the kitchen, looking through the fridge.

"Here, we don't have a lot of time." She handed Sam a plastic bottle of mineral water and a tray of ice cubes. "The ice is for your face." She pointed Sam to the sofa near the window. Canary Wharf and the cluster of bank skyscrapers dominated the view. Sam sat down and swigged the cold water. George perched on the coffee table opposite him.

"Sam, I need you to listen very carefully."

He screwed the lid back on the water bottle and tossed it onto the cushion next to him. He pressed the ice to his aching cheek. "No, George. You listen to me. Tell me who the fuck you really are. What the hell is going on?"

She stood up and went to the window. "I'm Agent Georgia Hall."

"You're a spook?" Sam's eyes stung as he rubbed them, "CIA or something?"

"You could say I'm a product of our governments' special relationship."

"I don't say." He stood up.

"Sam, please sit down. I've been working undercover for several months in Charles Frost's..." she paused for a moment to find the word she was looking for, "*world*."

"Who the fuck is Frost?"

"That's a good question. For months I've been searching for evidence to corroborate our intelligence but I've made little headway."

"What intelligence?"

"Sit down and I'll tell you."

Sam sat on the arm of the sofa, facing towards the door, away from George.

She continued, "Everything I'm about to tell you is subject to the Official Secrets Act. That means it stays between you and me." She stared directly at him, her green eyes emotionless and serious.

Sam put the ice on the coffee table and wiped the condensation off his cheek with the back of his hand. He lit another cigarette, his hand still trembling a little. "Actually, fuck it, you can keep your secret to yourself. This has nothing to do with me or my neighbour, I'm calling the police."

George sat back down on the edge of the coffee table and rested a hand on Sam's knee.

Sam flinched.

"This has everything to do with you. Where were you between midnight and two this morning?" George's voice was raised slightly for the first time; her drawly accent suddenly crisp and staccato.

"You tell me. One minute I'm dancing and drinking with you. The next I'm waking up in a doorway on Piccadilly. It's *you* who should be telling me what happened because that's two hours of my life I can't remember."

"From where I'm sitting you're a man covered in blood – too much blood for a bloodied nose – with a dead body in his house and no alibi. I'm certain the post-mortem will pinpoint the time of death between twelve and two."

Sam stubbed his cigarette out in the ice tray. He looked down at his shirt and hands. The suggestion that this wasn't his own blood repulsed him. He stood up and pulled off his jacket and dropped it on the sofa. He tore off his shirt and threw it on to the floor, as he rushed to the kitchen. He stood topless at the sink scrubbing his hands under the mixer-tap.

"That's bullshit. You're fucking with me and you know it. I'm calling the police," said Sam from the sink.

George came over to join him. She handed him a tea towel to dry his hands and face. "Sam, I'm not accusing you of murder. I'm just telling you what you already know. If you go to the police that's how they're going to read this. Why don't you have a shower? I'll get you a fresh shirt. We don't have a lot of time."

"Why do you keep saying that. Time for what?"

"Your flight to Scotland leaves in less than three hours."

"You think I'm going to work after all of this?" Sam laughed. "To think I tried to resign less than twenty four hours ago."

"*Resign*?" George looked surprised.

"Yes. Quit. I've had enough."

"It's too late." George filled the kettle at the sink and set it to boil. She spoke as she prepared two cups of instant coffee. "My partner," she paused to correct herself, "my ex-partner, Tom, was deep undercover in Frost's world before me. He managed to accumulate a lot of intelligence."

"Ex-partner?"

"Yes, he's gone missing. Presumed dead for the last eighteen months." George handed Sam his mug of black coffee. She pulled herself up onto the counter next to the sink, her heels kicking at the kitchen cupboard.

The clattering noise annoyed Sam. "What kind of intelligence did Tom gather. *Weapons of mass destruction* in Frost's basement?" He sneered. He noticed George's eyes light-up. He regretted making his quip – for humouring her.

"Over the last five years Frost's bought controlling stakes in major corporations all over the world. He's done this through a complex set of shell-companies and intermediaries to hide his actions."

"So what? If I had his money I'd have done the same thing. Has it ever occurred to you that over the last five years, while the world has been in a state of irrational fear and panic, stock prices have been *irrationally cheap*? Be greedy when others are fearful."

George placed her cup on the counter, still tapping her heels against the cabinet door.

Sam stood in silence and drank his coffee.

"Tom was onto something. Before he died he gave me a list of the companies Frost had secretly bought control of:

Oil companies, power stations, airlines, pharmaceuticals, supermarkets, insurance companies, banks, you name it."

"Sounds like we should have called a regulator not the Secret Service."

"That's not funny. Tom was killed for what he knew."

"You said *presumed* dead."

George ignored him and continued, "Then strange things started to happen to many of the firms on the list. Fires would wipe out major production facilities. Industrial action would halt mining for months. Secret drug R&D would be leaked onto the internet. It was as if Frost was destroying the firms from the inside."

Sam felt goose bumps over his chest and back. He walked to the window in the living area and felt the radiator beneath it for warmth but the steel pipes were stone-cold. George followed him and sat on the coffee table.

"We also believe he's shorting stocks on the companies he owns just before he sabotages them." She put her hands on her hips.

"Betting on the stock price to drop when you have insider information. It doesn't sound like crime of the century."

"It is when done on the scale Frost is attempting. The depth and breadth of his secret portfolio touches every sector in every economy across the globe. He's not only defrauding the financial markets but he risks the stability of entire economies. We're already seeing erratic commodity prices – energy and food supplies disrupted and prices spiralling up and away from billions of innocent people."

"Tonight I was beaten up and a woman *murdered*. That's nothing to do with greed."

"So, here's the thing. I've worked at Frost's club for six months. I've never met him or even got close. So I got desperate and started cross-checking the names of the companies Frost was controlling through other Agency investigations. Then bingo! Many of these companies were also being investigated for money laundering. And not just fraud or even drugs, Sam. We're talking terrorists – nasty bastards like *Al-Qaeda*. Frost is a *terrorist*. And he's not content with getting rich off killing kids in London and Madrid but he's doubling down and rigging the financial markets too." She folded her arms, rubbing her biceps with her finger tips.

Sam just listened. George looked like a librarian scolding a noisy school boy. She got up and approached him. He turned around and looked out of the window. The Thames was calm, reflecting the lights from Canary Wharf. The last twenty four hours ran through his mind.

"We need your help," said George, now stood next to him, also peering out of the window.

"What are you expecting *me* to do?"

"Head up to Isle of Aul and do exactly as Frost has asked. While you're there you only need to gather information on companies and names associated with Frost. One link and we can get him. Just one shred of evidence that proves he's breached the law or a regulation and we can expose him, before it's too late."

"There's nothing in Aul. It's just some house he wants to convert to a hotel."

"I don't believe it, Sam. Tom went missing on Aul. There's more going on there than the house."

Sam rested his forehead against the cool window pane. His breath misted up the glass and he tried to think. "Well it's already too late for Tom. How do I know that's not going to be me next?"

"We've got your back, Sam. We won't lose another agent again."

"I'm not an agent." He returned to his shirt and picked it up from the floor.

"Sam, you're working with us now."

"Fuck you. I'm not working for you. I'm not working for Frost. And in a few hours I'll no longer be working for Gema Bank." He sat down on the sofa and finished his coffee.

"All you need to do is spend a few days in Aul. If you don't find anything then come back to London. Either way, when you return the misunderstanding at your house will have been cleared up."

Sam laughed. "A woman has just been murdered in my house and you call that a misunderstanding. Can you hear yourself?"

"Sam, I still don't know the exact details about what happened at your house tonight but I assure you that if you cooperate then it will all work out for you."

Sam put his fist to his mouth and bit on his knuckle. His cheek was aching and he felt the muscles around his swollen eye stiffen up. "I'll tell you what happened. One of Frost's guys went snooping around my house while I was at the club. He was disturbed by my lonely, nosey neighbour. So he did what any deranged thug would do, he killed her. Just like he'll do to me. Finish the job they started tonight." Sam pointed to his swollen cheek. A tinge of purple bruising now formed below his eye.

"Tonight wasn't Frost." George bit her bottom lip, just as she had done after the gong.

Sam stared at her. He ran his hands through his hair and thought. "Oh I see, tonight was about setting me up. So you could frame me for Mrs Price's murder. To give me no choice but to cooperate. Is that it?"

"I'm sorry but this is bigger than you and I." George didn't look at him as she used her thumb to rub at the lipstick marks on her coffee cup.

Sam went to the kitchen and filled his cup with water from the tap. He stood in silence at the sink and drank slowly. A police siren came and went in the distance. He rinsed his mug out and placed it upside down on the draining board.

"Three days is all you have. Then I want to be back in London. And I never want to see or hear from any of you again," he said.

George smiled. "I'll get a towel. You need that shower."

03:49

George showed Sam to the en-suite off the larger of the two bedrooms.

"Ten minutes, then we have to leave. I'll find you something to wear," she said as she closed the door, leaving Sam alone in the windowless white tiled bathroom.

He locked the door, stripped off and set the shower above the bath running. While the water warmed up he tried to connect the dots between everything he'd just learnt about Frost and his father. What was the link? Is this why his father was suddenly so desperate to meet; had he discovered the truth about Frost too or, worse, was he in trouble? The thought that Frost was linked to his father's death flashed across his mind, Sam dismissed it as quickly as it came. No, there was no proof of murder, the cause of death had been heart attack. Sam decided not to mention any of this to George unless she raised it first. He also decided that there were no coincidences here, there was something going on that meant he and his father were linked to Frost and he wouldn't stop looking until he found out what it was.

The extractor fan worked overtime in vain. The small room soon filled with steam. There was no shampoo, just a chemical smelling bar of soap which he used over his hair and body. But he was grateful for the soothing power of the hot water. He stood facing the jet, allowing it to pound his chest and spray up into his face. He closed his eyes, almost asleep on his feet.

George was waiting for him in the bedroom. She had taken her glasses off and touched up her lipstick. She looked much more like the woman he'd met at the club but her face was still intense and serious. She was holding two bags, in her left a black bin liner and in the other an olive coloured canvas holdall. Sam checked his towel was firmly fastened around his waist. George dropped the bin liner on the floor and placed the holdall on the bed.

"Everything except your underwear, socks and shoes needs to go in here." She pointed to the bin liner.

Sam noticed she'd already thrown his jacket and shirt inside the black plastic bag; his favourite and most expensive suit screwed up and ready for the dustbin. He wanted to protest, tell her she was bang out of order, but at the same time he didn't want to give her the satisfaction of pissing him off again.

"What am I going to wear?"

She unzipped the holdall and pulled out a pair of beige chinos and a navy blue hooded top. "They were Tom's. They're a little big but they'll get you to the airport. Two minutes." She left the bedroom.

Sam dried off and put Tom's clothes on. They smelt like they'd been recently laundered. The trousers were a couple of inches too big around the waist but the length was fine. The top was baggy. Sam transferred the belt from his suit trousers and used it to just about hold up the chinos. He threw his suit trousers in the bin liner. He put his socks and shoes on and looked at his reflection in the full length mirror of the cheap MDF wardrobe in the corner. The soap had left his hair dry and fluffy, the best he could do was sweep it over into a sophomore style side parting. A light stubble shaded his cheeks and chin, framing his tired, bloodshot eyes – one of which had now formed a blue-purple-yellow bruise beneath it. The borrowed clothes were of a middle aged man who had given up on fashion and his appearance. The man he saw wasn't himself. He sat on the bed and held his head in his hands, his heavy eyelids closed.

"Sam?" queried George on the other side of the door. She opened the door but didn't come in. "Your flight leaves from City at five past six." She walked away as she spoke, her words echoing about the hallway, "We need to go."

Sam checked his watch, it was almost four. He looked inside the holdall next to him on the bed. It was empty. He picked it up, as well as the bin liner, and carried them to the living area. George was in the kitchen, writing something on a piece of blue paper. The halogen lights made her birthmark look more prominent than ever. She didn't look up as she spoke, "Have you put everything in the bag?"

"Yes."

"Your wallet, phone, keys. All in the bag."

"What the fuck for?"

George stopped writing, glanced at her watch and then up at Sam. "We don't have time. We can do this in the car." She folded up the blue piece of paper and squeezed it into the tight back pocket of her jeans and switched the kitchen lights off. She came over to Sam and held out a hand to take the holdall from him. Then Sam remembered – the holdall in his hand triggered the memory of holding the briefcase.

"*Shit,*" he said.

"What?" George looked genuinely concerned.

"My briefcase. Did you have anything to do with my briefcase being stolen?" A sick anxiety rushed through him. Of everything that had happened this disappointed him the most. How could he have been so careless, leaving it out of reach on the chair?

George looked puzzled before saying, "No, I know nothing about any briefcase. Do you want me to look into it? Tell me what happened."

Sam told her about the motorbike and the robbery in Paternoster Square, excluding any of the details about Morris Forster and his father's will.

George said she'd see if CCTV footage could be checked and investigated by somebody back at base but she didn't hold out much hope as this was really police jurisdiction. Then she took both bags from Sam and held them in one hand. She used her free hand to pull a bunch of keys from her front pocket and went to the front door, flicking the lights off as it swung open, leaving Sam stood in darkness.

The creak of the hinges preceded a yellow light from the service elevator that awaited them. Sam passively followed, still thinking about the briefcase. He closed his eyes as they travelled down the lift. He felt awkward standing so close to George after everything that had happened in the apartment, being dressed the way he was didn't help either – bereft of what little confidence he had around women.

The lift door wobbled in its runners as it opened. George stepped out first. There was nobody in the car park and it occurred to Sam that he could make a run for it. He could find a police station and explain everything just as it had happened; tell them the *truth* – he was the victim, after all. But the doubt held him back. The fear that the truth now stood for nothing.

George looked back at Sam through her bookish glasses. Sam picked up speed and joined her at the *Mini*. She unlocked the doors and threw the bags on the back seat. They got in. George leant across him and opened the glove box in front of his knees. She pulled out a blue envelope – the same colour blue as the paper she was writing on in the kitchen. She handed it to Sam and pulled away, up the steep slope and out of the underground car park. The tyres screeched as she gave the car more throttle than necessary. She pointed the remote control at the gates, timing her approach perfectly as the iron railings parted, and they were away onto the empty east London streets. The Thames stayed on their right as they followed its hairpin curve through Mudchute and into Cubitt Town. The sun was starting to grow stronger than the darkness.

"Aren't you going to look in the envelope?" said George.

Sam was curious but didn't want to be more cooperative than he had to be. The envelope wasn't sealed, he lifted the flap and looked inside. It was full of cash.

"There's enough in there for you to live off for the next three or four days," she said.

"You're too kind."

"Remember, you're a fugitive. You can't use your bank cards or cell phone. They need to go in the trash bag."

Her matter of fact tone shocked Sam. "I thought you were looking after me. I thought I was working *with* you now."

"You are. We're running interference with Scotland Yard but you need to take precautions." She rushed her words as road signs for the airport marked their route.

"Precaution number one: Don't fly." Sam unclipped his seatbelt. An electric bleeping sound rang out. He twisted himself around, leant into the backseat and rummaged through the bin liner.

"What are you doing?" said George.

Sam returned to his forward facing position with his cigarettes and a lighter. He lit up and put his seatbelt back on. The bleeping stopped. George opened both their windows a few inches.

"Inside the envelope you'll find a driving licence. It's an internal flight so that's all you'll need to get you through security."

He held his cigarette between his lips and opened the envelope a little wider. He fingered through the notes, a mixture of English and Scottish. There, between two twenties, was a UK driving licence.

"You bitch," he mumbled out of the corner of his mouth.

"I know this is all a surprise."

Sam held the pink plastic card in front of him and studied the photograph. It was him. It was his photo lifted from his Gema Bank ID pass. Next to it the name FALCORRS SETH.

He sucked hard on his cigarette and threw the remainder out of his window. "How did you get this?" But Sam knew the answer before it came.

"We took it from your house while you were jogging yesterday afternoon."

"You..." Sam was lost for words. The anger and tiredness mixing into nothing. "... Whoever you are. You make me sick."

"Sam, I know how you feel."

"No you don't. Who is Seth Falcorrs anyway?"

"It's pronounced, *Fal-corr,* the s is silent. He's clean and his ID works for you, that's all you need to know. Until you arrive in Aul, you are Seth Falcorrs. Got it?"

Sam examined the licence. It was in every way *real*. The holograms over his photograph flickered in the light. The date of birth was within a few days of his own. The card, although only forged in the last few hours, had all the wear and tear of an eight year old licence as its issue date suggested.

"You need to leave all signs of Sam West in this car. Your wallet, phone and keys. You can get them back when you're back in London." George stopped at a set of traffic lights next to the entrance to the Blackwall Tunnel. She looked at Sam, "And your watch too."

"Why my watch?"

"It's too distinctive. There aren't many guys in their early thirties wandering around with a watch like that." She pulled up her sleeve and un-did the strap on her chunky digital. "I'll swap you." She smiled her cheeky dimple smile.

Sam unfastened the clasp on his *Patek Philippe* and they exchanged. The lights turned to green and the *Mini* pulled away. The cheap, ugly digital was at least in keeping with the rest of his outfit. He admired his watch hanging loosely on her delicate wrist. Or perhaps it was her wrist he admired. He'd bought the watch with his first proper bonus at the bank and although he'd worn it every day since, he didn't mind seeing her wear it.

"The airport's a few minutes away. Use the self-serve machines to check yourself in. Once you make it to Departures buy the things you need for your trip. You won't have long so I've done you a list." She felt around her back pocket and produced the blue paper she'd been writing on in the kitchen."

Sam unfolded it and read it to himself. She'd listed everything from a toothbrush and razor to new socks and boots. He scrunched the paper in his fist and defiantly shoved it into his trouser pocket, glancing at George for a reaction.

But she didn't bite, "Use the holdall in the back," she said.

Sam pulled the bag from the backseat. "I'm not sure about this. There's police all over the airport. How do you know they haven't already found me on the flight manifest?" He dropped the bag in the foot well between his legs.

"At seven yesterday evening Gema Bank was contacted by Frost's office, with instructions for a new rendezvous point in Hong Kong. Sam West left Heathrow on the Cathay Pacific flight to Hong Kong International Airport at 22:35 last night." She passed Sam her phone that had been resting on the dashboard in front of the *Mini's* oversized tachometer.

Sam scrolled through an email trail that started at 14:17 yesterday.

From: communications@cadencelifeholdings.com
To: TheOfficeOfJerryHart@gemabank.com
Dear Jerry,
Change of plan. Hope your top man is permitted to travel a little further afield than Mayfair. Hong Kong instead. Leave flight CX238, 22:35 Terminal 3, Heathrow.
Yours,
Cadence Life Holdings

The reply came at 14:22.

From: TheOfficeOfJerryHart@gemabank.com
***To:* communications@cadencelifeholdings.com**
Cc: sam.west@gemabank.com
Dear Sir,
Have spoken with Sam. Not a problem. Will see you in Hong Kong.
Kind Regards,
Jerry Hart

"I didn't get this email," he said, handing the phone back to George.

"I know you didn't. But if anyone goes snooping around Gema Bank's IT systems they'll find the email trail. They'll also find a separate thread with your response confirming your visa to travel to China was still good and that you'd be on that flight."

"Cadence Life Holdings? I've never heard of them."

"Frost's been operating through Cadence Life for the last few years. It's registered in Kenya of all places. On the back of your shopping list you'll find the firms he's been cleaning his blood money through."

Sam leant back and lifted his backside from the seat, giving himself just enough room to reproduce the paper from his pocket – this time treating it with more care. He used his lap to smooth out the creases. He counted fifteen companies all of which he recognised as American and European multinationals. Could Frost really be controlling these firms? The suggestion that respected companies like these were used to launder money was absurd.

He opened his window all the way down and the cool morning air rolled off the Thames and swirled around the car. He lit his last cigarette, cupping the flame from the breeze. He tried to digest everything he had just learnt but he was so tired his mind failed him. Eventually he asked: "So there's somebody on that flight to Hong Kong impersonating me?" He looked at George.

She flashed a smile at him, "Yep. And that's your alibi for last night. You couldn't have been at home because you were at Heathrow and then on a flight to Hong Kong."

"So what happens when I don't get off the plane?"

"The police won't know you're in Hong Kong until it's too late." She stopped at another red light and faced Sam. "We'll make sure of that. But when they do, a man travelling on your passport, matching your description will have left the airport for Macau."

Sam inhaled the smoke deep into his lungs and held it there. He finally breathed out gently through his nose and let his head rock back on the head-restraint. He pulled down his sun visor and flipped up the vanity mirror on its back. He examined the swelling on his cheek bone, now extending around his right eye over the lid. The *Mini's* indicator clicked as George turned left into City airport.

The sun had now broken through the grey to reveal another bright morning. She pulled up in the taxi rank outside the small terminal building. A man wearing a fluorescent green vest over his blue uniform, pushing a train of luggage trolleys, stopped next to Sam's open window. Sam raised his left hand, feigning an itch at his hairline, obscuring most of his face.

"Taxis only," said the man now bending down to peer through the window.

"Silly me," said George in a girlie voice – in a moment transformed from government agent to airhead. "I'm just saying goodbye to my boyfriend." She put her hand on Sam's knee and smiled at the man.

"All right, darling." The trolleys rattled into the terminal building as the man left them alone. Sam sat frozen until he was sure he had gone.

"Relax, Sam." She took her hand off his knee and un-did her seat belt, "Just be yourself."

"You mean be Seth *Falcorrs.*" Sam empathised the r – the absence of the s – on the end of the name.

"Touché." George laughed. She leant towards him and opened the glove box again. This time she pulled out a grey mobile phone that looked ten years past its heyday. She switched it on and scrolled through the phone's menu before handing it to him. "This is encrypted. Only use it to contact me when you're sure you're alone, even for text messages. Don't use any other lines, not even if it's for work. My number's in the memory."

"The only thing I need from you are my flight details home." Sam checked the battery level on the phone's black and white, low-resolution screen; noting it was full he switched it off and put it in his hoodie pocket.

"You'll get those from Frost, this is just a normal business trip to meet a client. Keep reminding yourself of that."

"Three days, including today. I want to be back by Friday morning." Sam threw the remains of his cigarette out of the window.

"That's the deal." George removed her glasses and placed them on the dashboard. "Okay, one last time: When you get out of this car you're Seth Falcorrs. Buy everything you need for the trip in Duty Free. Once you're through customs in Inverness you're Sam West again. Remember, Frost can't know that you have any suspicions. One of his people will be at the airport to take you to Aul. When you get there just kiss ass like he's any other client. Collect any information you can. Anything that links Frost or Cadence Life Holdings to a single company on the list is all we need."

A horn blasted behind them. Sam looked out the back window and saw a cabbie gesticulating at them to move. George had already put her glasses back on and started up the engine. Sam picked up the empty holdall between his feet and got out of the car.

"Good luck and don't forget, Aul ain't in the Caribbean – the weather will be real shitty so be sure to pick up a good coat."

Sam nodded and closed his door. The tinted window steadily rose to a close as the *Mini* pulled away. The black cab rolled into the vacated space at the front of the rank – the cabbie glaring at Sam until his vehicle came to a halt. Sam turned away abruptly and walked towards the terminal doors. The empty canvas holdall felt ridiculously light as it swung about on its red and white striped handles. In his other hand he fiddled with the crumpled blue paper; his palms clammed-up with sweat.

04:41

The electric doors to the terminal swept open. More men in florescent green vests came out and walked past him. Sam dropped his head as he crossed the threshold onto the blue linoleum floor. Two policemen dressed in black uniforms carrying rifles stood solemnly next to a pillar six feet away from him. Sam could feel their stares as he passed them. Suddenly everything felt difficult and unnatural. Every move he made became an effort, requiring deliberate thought and attention. Just walk naturally he told himself – you've flown from here a thousand times before. *Walk. Walk. Walk.* But his coordination was shot, his gait uncomfortable. He dragged his steps over the floor, stubbing his toe on nothing in particular, causing himself to stumble forward. He glanced over at the check-in desks and the rows of heavily made-up girls; they all appeared to stare back at him with accusing eyes. He stopped in the middle of the hall and looked for the departures board. It seemed like an age before he spotted it above the escalator at the far end of the hall. Flight SAX231 to Inverness was on time but no departure gate. *Seth Falcorrs. Seth Falcorrs.* He repeated over and over to himself.

Sam walked over to the bank of five self service check-in machines at the foot of the escalator. They were all in use by smartly dressed businessmen with airline regulation, designer hand luggage on wheels; each black case festooned with gold and platinum frequent flier cards. His mouth was dry and his throat sore. He kept swallowing what little saliva his mouth could produce to test the pain in his throat – each time the pain slightly worse than before. He tapped his foot but stopped when the sound caught the attention of the grey-haired businessman in a navy pinstripe suit using the machine nearest him. The nervous energy built inside him. He distracted himself by collapsing the sides of the holdall and wrapping its leather handles around itself, tucking it under his arm like a rugby ball. Finally, the last machine in the line became free. He rushed to it and followed the instructions on the touch screen. He typed F A L C O R R S slowly and definitely. The machine asked for identification – passport or EU driving licence. Sam wiped his brow with the back of his hand. Why did it feel so difficult to do this? He took the pink card from his pocket and placed it on the scanner below the screen. Nothing happened. He looked around at the pillar near the door – the policemen were no longer there. His heart pounded and he tapped haplessly on the screen. A spinning globe icon appeared above the words PLEASE WAIT. Sam sighed and the machine welcomed Seth Falcorrs onto flight SAX231 to Inverness. He rubbed his sweaty hands around the insides of his hoodie pockets while the machine grunted as it printed his boarding pass. Sam checked his watch – 04:59. He looked up at the departures board, still no gate for his flight but he reckoned he had about thirty minutes before boarding.

Travelling up the escalator to customs he got a view of the entire ground floor of the terminal building. He searched for the two policemen but still he could not see them. He ran his hand through his dry, product-less hair. Nothing felt right. He shuffled along the mezzanine level of the first floor towards the first set of security checks. A Sikh man with a burgundy turban and beard in a net sat on a high stool behind a desk.

"Boarding pass, please," said the man. His name badge read *Tara*.

Sam strained a smile and handed over both his boarding pass and the driving licence.

"I don't need that." Tara handed back the licence.

"Sorry."

"It's okay. What happened?"

Sam's heart raced. He stared back at him, "I thought you wanted my identification."

"No, what happened to your eye?" Tara pointed to his own eye to clarify his point.

Shit. Think. Think. Think. "Squash racket. Last time I play that guy."

"Exercise: Damned if you do. Damned if you don't!" Tara chuckled, handing back the boarding pass.

Sam forced a laugh for the twenty or so yards to the next security check but it did nothing to release his tension. He sat down on a steel bench to remove his shoes. He placed them in a grey plastic tray on top of the collapsed holdall. Inside the left shoe he put the mobile phone George had given him and watched the tray glide along the conveyor, into the X-ray machine. Another man waved him into the metal detector. He walked through the machine's empty door frame and an electric alarm bell sounded. Sam froze and looked around, desperate for confirmation that it wasn't him.

"Your belt," said the security man, waving Sam back with a flick of his wrist.

Sam turned back through the metal detector and removed his belt. Immediately his borrowed trousers felt ready to fall around his ankles. He coiled the belt up and put it on the conveyor belt. With his thumb hooked in a belt loop on his waistband, he shuffled awkwardly back through the detector. His belt and tray were waiting for him on the other side. He walked in his socks through Duty Free, to the waiting area where he checked the departure board – still no gate for his flight. The time was now 05:07. He sat down in one of the moulded chairs and put his shoes back on. He re-read the list that George had given him.

The public address system chimed three prescient notes before a woman's voice said, "I'm sorry to announce that flight SAX231 to Inverness is delayed. This is due to inclement weather in Inverness delaying our inbound flight this morning."

Sam made his way to the sparse Duty Free area. There were only three outlets – the expensive jewellers were not an option, instead he made his way to the clothes store. A dumpy, middle-aged shop assistant stopped folding the shirt on the counter in front of her and greeted him in a thick eastern European accent. Sam looked away, raising a hand in acknowledgement. There wasn't much choice in the small store and nothing was to his taste. He picked up the only pair of blue jeans in his size and two pairs of charcoal grey flannel trousers; two formal shirts in white and blue; three pairs of socks; three pairs of boxer shorts, two plain white T-shirts and a black V-necked pullover. He carried everything over his right arm to the counter.

"You want to try on?" asked the shop assistant.

"No, thanks."

She took a lifetime removing the tags, scanning the barcodes and folding the clothes, apparently oblivious to the fact that customers had flights to catch. Sam wanted to say something but held back. She was about to put the clothes into a large carrier bag when Sam stopped her, "I have a bag," he said, placing the unzipped holdall on the counter.

She carefully placed everything inside and totalled up the bill on the till below the counter's glass top.

"Anything else?" she queried.

Sam took out the blue envelope ready to pay when he noticed the security camera above the shop assistant's shoulder, trained directly on him. He ran his hand through his hair, his forearm hiding his face from the camera. "Yes, one sec."

He wandered around the shop until he saw what he was looking for. He tried the black baseball cap on for size, checking himself in the mirror. He'd never worn a cap before. How different he looked. Perfect. Next to the hats were dark-green waxed jackets. Remembering what George had told him about the weather and the delay announcement, he checked the price and found one in his size. He took them over to the counter and said: "And these. I'll wear them now."

The shop assistant removed the tags and scanned them through the till. She frowned as Sam produced a wad of cash from his blue envelope. He put the cap on and pulled the peak low over his eyebrows. Over half the money was gone. He had wanted to buy sunglasses but this was now out of the question. George was wrong that this would be enough for three days. What else was she wrong about?

With the holdall now feeling like proper luggage in one hand, and his jacket slung over his opposite shoulder, Sam went next door to the newsagents. At the back there was a small toiletries section, where he picked up a tooth brush, toothpaste and some disposable razors. At the checkout he added a copy of *The Times*, two bars of dark chocolate and a stubby crossword biro to his purchases. He dropped the chocolate and pen in his coat pocket. When he left the store he checked the departures board: SAX231 was flashing DELAYED with no gate. The time was now 05:32. Sam followed the signs for the toilets. He stood outside the disabled facilities for six minutes, until a mother and her newborn baby left the room wreaking of vomit and shit. He locked the door to the self contained toilet and sink unit. He was sweating all over. Stress, tiredness and hunger mixed into a cocktail of nausea and weakness. He took off Tom's clothes. He had to squat at the half-height mirror to brush his teeth and shave – the blunt, disposable razor and no shaving cream made it the worst shave of his life. His neck burnt through a bright red rash. He splashed cold water on his face and dried himself with rough paper towels. He changed into his new boxer shorts and socks. He took out the flannels and white shirt from the holdall when somebody tried the handle on the toilet door and it rattled in its frame. Sam jumped at the surprise. He listened carefully, motionless. He wondered whether it would look strange to anyone who had noticed he got changed. Was this attracting too much attention? So he put his new clothes back in the holdall and got back into Tom's dowdy chinos and hoodie.

He was barely out of the toilet room when the mother from earlier squeezed passed him carrying her baby tight to her chest. She gave him a dirty look before slamming the door closed. Sam heard the baby scream its lungs out. He went back to the waiting area. SAX231 was now due to board at 06:25. He had nearly thirty minutes to kill. He bought a black Americano and a croissant from the coffee bar and a three quarter bottle of whisky. When he thought nobody was looking he poured a generous double shot into his coffee and placed the bottle in his bag. He sat at his gate, the peak of his cap lowered over his brow, sipping at his drink. He paged through his newspaper but read no more than the headlines. At quarter past six two women in blue uniforms with green tartan trim announced boarding. Sam joined the back of the queue. He counted twelve other passengers. He held his boarding pass and driving licence in one hand. *Seth Falcorrs. Seth Falcorrs.*

The queue inched forward. Sam heard a baby cry again and looked around to see the same mother desperately trying to sooth it, jiggling it in her arms. But it was the two policemen from the pillar downstairs that she was talking to, that captured Sam's attention. They were still clutching their rifles, at least a foot taller than the woman. He turned away, furtively glancing at them from the corner of his eye. The queue moved faster now, only two people ahead of him. He held out his documents, ready to hand them over. The elderly couple in front of him moved on and Sam didn't wait to be asked, thrusting his boarding pass and fake ID over to the *Caledonian Airline* lady with a warm smile. She fed his boarding pass into one end of a machine that looked like a toaster and out it spat his stub from the other. She handed it to him, along with the licence.

"Enjoy your flight, Mr Falcorrs." She pronounced his *name* correctly.

Sam took a final look back at the policemen. They were smiling and laughing with the baby who had been successfully distracted from its crying. Sam didn't turn around again. He made his way quickly down the tunnel and onto the aeroplane.

0b:33

It didn't take long for Sam to find his seat at the back of the small cabin. The blue imitation leather seats were arranged in pairs either side of the brightly lit, narrow aisle. Nobody paid him any attention as he squeezed his way around the other passengers, a mix of elderly holiday makers and tired-looking business men. He put his coat in the overhead locker but before placing his holdall in there too he took out the bottle of whisky and tucked it into the magazine pocket of the seat-back in front of his. He sat down next to the window and fastened his seat belt. An air hostess closed the door at the front of the plane and Sam was relieved that nobody was sitting next to him.

Although he knew it was irrational, Sam was a nervous flier. He'd flown hundreds of times before on business but each time his pre-flight routine was the same. He paid close attention to the listless safety demonstration by the male flight attendant. Then he read both sides of the safety information card, registering his emergency exits and evacuation procedures. Finally, he found the page about the aircraft in the in-flight magazine – this was the first time he'd flown on a *British Aerospace 146*. He memorised its top-speed in knots and the cruising altitude. This peculiar superstition disappointed him but there was always that nagging doubt – that fear – that the one time he overruled it would be the last time he flew.

The Captain's breathy voice was just about audible over the hubbub of the crew and passengers. He apologised for the delay and warned them of storms once they got nearer to Inverness, in about ninety minutes time. Sam eyed the brass-coloured cap of the whisky bottle, poking out of the magazine pocket in front of him. He closed his eyes. The plane taxied around the small airfield before the roar and thrust of the four engines and their steep ascent into the clouds above London. He was asleep until the chime of the fasten seatbelt sign going off woke him. The snapping clatter of the buckles unclipping ricocheted about the cabin but Sam, as always, used the sound as a reminder to check that his seatbelt was still securely fastened. The crew were promptly up serving sandwiches and refreshments from a trolley. They made their way along the aisle from front to back, reaching Sam last. The male flight attendant didn't ask whether he wanted a sandwich, handing Sam the cellophane wrapped roll as he pressed the trolley's brake with his foot. Sam folded down his table and asked for a tomato juice with *Tabasco* and *Worcestershire Sauce*. The air hostess at the other end of the trolley handed him a black coffee. He ate the rubbery cheese roll while he waited for the crew to return to the front of the plane with refills. Then he poured a generous slug of whisky into his tomato juice and downed it in one.

Sam rested his forehead against the *Perspex* window and peered into the grey nothingness of the cloud. In less than an hour he'd be in Inverness where he would be Sam West once more; Sam West the banker on a business trip to assess the viability of converting a stately home on a remote Hebridean island into a hotel. Sam West the fugitive, wanted for murder, forced into a secret mission to expose a global terrorist. He smiled at the absurdity of it all. At how *all* of it was wrong. None of this had anything to do with him. He had no place in any of this, no matter how he looked at it. Yet here he was, dressed in another man's clothes, carrying another man's ID burying himself deeper into the mess. He thought about his father; how he wished he could turn to the seat next to him and tell him everything. He imagined his mother at home watching the television news in horror as she found out her only child was wanted for murder. He knew this was all in his mind but it weighed down on him; this feeling of not wanting to disappoint them never left him.

The plane lurched and the remainder of Sam's coffee tipped onto the tray table and over his lap. He cursed out-loud and used the pathetic doily to blot the brown stains on his chinos. The fasten seatbelt sign chimed back on and the crew came around and cleared up their cups. The plane skipped and bumped. Sam gripped the armrests; the backs of his hands white with strain. The clouds turned charcoal-grey and fat raindrops ran along the windows like slug trails. The Captain returned over the PA system: "A wee spot of turbulence as we begin our decent into Inverness, ladies and gentlemen. Unfortunately the entire north of Scotland is experiencing a depression which has brought with it rather stormy weather. We should be through it shortly."

The cabin crew took their seats at the back of the plane and nattered away to each other, seemingly oblivious to the perpetual jolting and thudding. Sam kept his eyes closed. The bang of the wheels being released from the aircraft's underbelly told him they were landing soon. His breathing was short and tight – his hands still gripping hard.

"Cabin crew doors to manual and cross check," chirped the Captain.

Sam's ears popped and he swallowed hard. The engine sound raised its pitch as the plane slowed and they wobbled down on to the tarmac, bumping three times before the brakes whined, rapidly reducing their speed, forcing Sam forward in his seatbelt. He opened his eyes and looked out of the window. It was pouring with rain. Spray from the tarmac formed a mist around the aircraft, making the fields beyond the runway look like a green smudge across the grey skyline. He took off his cap and ran his hand through his hair. His breathing calmed as the plane made its way to the terminal building.

Sam was out of his seat as soon as the plane came to a halt at their gate. He pulled his coat and bag down from the overhead locker. An air hostess said something about him returning to his seat but she was cut short as the seatbelt sign turned off and the other restless passengers sprang up in unison. Sam was three quarters of the way down the plane before his path was blocked by an old couple in matching blue cagoules and hiking boots. She was carrying an *RSPB Guide to Highland Birds* and he wore a green baseball cap with '*My Kind of Bird Watching*' emblazoned across the front. Sam helped them get their rucksacks down from the overhead lockers. The old lady thanked him with a curious, lingering look at his black eye. This reminded him he had to keep a low profile. The door at the front of the plane opened and the crew smiled as they formed their farewell line. Sam pulled his cap a little lower over his brow and left the plane without making eye-contact with anyone else. It was cold in the tunnel that led from the aircraft to the terminal building. The rain lashed down over the concertina walls. Scotland in the summertime. If this was the welcome visitors bound for Aul were likely to receive then his advice would be forget the hotel, a complete waste of money.

The terminal building was just as compact as London City airport, so Sam was quickly heading towards Border Control. *Seth Falcorrs. The s is silent. Seth Fal-corr. Seth Fal-co-rr.* He repeated silently to himself. It had been so unexpectedly easy back in London but again his heart was beating a little faster. He fingered the forged driving licence in his pocket, not wanting to reveal it until the last moment, as if this somehow mitigated the crime he was committing.

But as he followed the sign around a sharp left turn his fears were allayed. The girl on the immigration desk had little interest in the early morning arrivals. She gave nothing more than a cursory glance at the seasoned business travellers passing her by without breaking their stride, bound for the front of the taxi queue. Sam held out his ID to which she said: "Thanking Yooo".

The baggage hall was empty but the carousel was already moving in anticipation of luggage. Sam followed the suits and their roller-cases towards customs. Just one more control. Again this made him uneasy. He imagined the mirror – which everyone knew was one-way glass – along the length of the Nothing to Declare channel, behind it a couple of officious Customs officers ready to pounce. The golden stars of the European Union flag hung above the entrance way to the aisle. He felt robotic, as once more his thoughts focused on looking and walking naturally to the point it became nearly impossible. He'd made ground on the bald headed man in front who snaked around as he checked a message on his phone. Sam had to stop abruptly to avoid tripping over his Japanese trolley case. He tried to walk around the man but he was blocked as he weaved in front of him once more. Sam stepped back and caught himself staring at the mirrored glass. There, for the last time, Seth Falcorrs staring back at him, tired and afraid. Never a more guilty sight. He rubbed his nose with the back of his right hand in an involuntary motion before dropping his gaze and making his way through the automatic doors into the arrivals hall.

09:40

Private-hire taxi drivers in cheap, loose fitting suits huddled around a steel rail. Sam read the names on the cards they held out in front of their chests: *Mr Lee, Rouse*, *Colquhoun*, *Burton...* But no West. He walked around the rail and amongst the dozen or so people awaiting their arrivals. He tried to remember the instructions Tanya had given him yesterday. One of Frost's staff were meant to meet him at the airport and take him to Aul. That was right. But steadily the crowd dispersed as they found their client or loved one and headed out into the rain. So now what? Sam wandered over to the plastic seats between two car hire kiosks that flanked the wall next to the exit. The rain was lashing down from black clouds that groaned with thunder. He sat down and switched on the phone George had given him. It took over a minute to boot up and another couple to find a network signal. All the while Sam kept a cautious eye on the two policemen that patrolled the concourse. The only number in the phone's Contacts was under the name *G*. Sam was about to hit call when he heard his name called over the airport PA.

"That's Mr West. Could you come to the airport Information Desk at the north side of the Terminal hall, please."

Sam could see the Information Desk from where he was sitting. He stayed where he was for a few minutes, watching, just in case another Mr West approached the desk. He knew there wouldn't be anyone else but a cautiousness pervaded him. He waited until the policemen were heading back up to the other end of the concourse before getting up and walking over to the desk.

"Hi, you have a message for Mr West?" he said to the woman wearing yet more blue and green tartan.

She picked up and read the pink *Post It* note stuck to the telephone on her desk. "Yes. We just got a call saying because of the bad weather there's nobody here to meet you. You will need to make your own way."

"My own way to where?"

The woman looked puzzled "It doesn't say." She held up the note so Sam could read it.

"Did they leave a name or number?"

"No they didn't. If you need to hire a car you can do so..."

"Thanks," Sam interrupted. He turned away. His feet caught on something heavy and solid and before he knew what had happened he had fallen to the floor. He looked up and saw the heavily laden trolley. It wasn't the usual sort of passenger luggage trolley but more the kind pulled by hotel concierge – its brass frame was a good six feet tall and it was full of parcels and cardboard boxes.

"Are you okay, sir?" asked the woman now peering over the desk, down at Sam.

Sam got to his feet. He felt his hot blood flush through his cheeks. "I'm fine." His heart raced again but this time anger replaced the anxiety of fear. "Hey!" he shouted as the trolley moved swiftly along the concourse, amongst the crowds. He couldn't see who was pulling it, his view obscured by its cargo. He picked up his bag and followed, determined to get an apology from the guy pulling it.

The trolley picked up speed until it stopped just in front of the sliding doors to the exit. Sam called out again, "Hey, you!" He closed in on the bags and boxes stacked neatly inside the brass frame. He was now behind the trolley, he stepped out to give the man a piece of his mind until he saw the two policemen stood just the other side, speaking with whoever it was pulling it. Sam pulled back behind the trolley. He stood frozen, conscious that he looked conspicuous and awkward where he was. He took the mobile phone from his pocket and held it to his ear but he focused his hearing on what the policemen were saying. But he couldn't make it out over the din of the arrivals hall. As he made his imaginary phone call he looked at the cargo on the trolley – hessian sacks, bundles of *The Scotsman* newspaper and parcels wrapped in brown paper and string. Sam shuffled a few steps around the trolley and a flash of red caught his eye. One of the parcels at the bottom of the stack had a tear of about three inches along its length, probably caused by his heavy fall. The colour was familiar. Sam wedged his phone between his cheek and shoulder and got down on one knee to retie his shoelace. He took a closer look at the tear in the parcel. The red belonged to a red leather case. A case just like the one his father had left him. He glanced around to check he wasn't being watched before touching it. The smooth calf skin was just the same. The dimensions of the parcel appeared to match too. This must have been his case. Had George found it? No, there wouldn't have been time for that. Perhaps it was Frost himself?

For once something was going his way. A lightness of mood and exhilaration came over him. The trolley moved off. Sam was left on one knee fumbling with his laces as the policemen walked around him, one on either side. He kept his head down. Once they were well past he leapt up and followed the trolley into the pouring rain. A perpetual hiss came up from the tarmac as a stream of taxis rolled through the puddles in the road. Sam remained under the cover of the white steel canopy that hung over the front of the terminal building. He kept a steady ten feet behind the trolley as it weaved in and out of the crowd taking cover from the storm. He still couldn't see who was pulling the trolley. A horn pipped a couple of times. The trolley stopped and so did Sam. A green battered *Land Rover* caked in mud pulled up in the lay-by next to the trolley. Again, Sam used his mobile phone as a prop, holding it to his ear as he watched what would happen next – stepping momentarily into the road to allow the elderly bird watchers from his flight to pass him.

A short man in a worn, grey tweed coat and flat-cap scurried around the *Land Rover*. His bushy white hair looked like a cloud of cotton wool from beneath his hat. His collar was turned up over his face to shield from the rain. He unlocked the double back doors of the vehicle. Sam moved slowly closer, still feigning a phone call. He watched the man in the tweed wave to whoever it was pulling the trolley, before he got down to loading the contents of the trolley into the back of the *Land Rover*. Sam saw his opportunity. "Do you want a hand?" he asked, now stood next to the trolley.

The man in tweed looked up from the bundle of newspapers he was holding. "Aye, thank you young man." His ruddy cheeks glowed against the contrast of the bushy white hair covering his ears.

Sam put his holdall down and pulled up his collar, before picking up one of the sacks and lugging it into the back of the *Land Rover*. He noticed the bag said *Isle of Aul* along its side. It took them a couple of minutes to load everything into the back of the vehicle; Sam having to climb inside at one point, to push the cargo up against the front seats to make enough room. All the time he had half an eye on the briefcase, the last parcel to be loaded into the now fully laden 4x4. Sam watched as the man slid the briefcase on top of the other boxes and parcels until it was snugly positioned, before slamming the double doors closed and taking cover under the canopy. He pulled off his cap and shook his head, like a dog fresh out of a river. "Thank you, again. That was very kind."

"No problem." Sam knew he'd only have one chance. "I see these bags are for Isle of Aul. Are you going that way?"

"Aye," he flicked his eyes at the bruising over Sam's cheek. "And you?"

"I'm trying to get there too. I was hoping for a lift."

The man glanced down at Sam's bag on the footpath and back up at his bruise. "Nobody wants to go to Aul. What's your business there?"

"It's exactly that. I'm going there on business. To Aul House. Do you know it?"

The man's eyebrows rose before he replied: "Aye, I know it alright. I suppose you're here about the sale." He looked Sam up and down again.

Sam figured he was puzzled by his appearance. "That's right. I am here about the sale of Aul House. I've had a terrible journey. First my luggage went missing," He gestured with both his hands at his hotchpotch outfit, "Now my transport to the island has been cancelled – something to do with this wonderful Scottish summer you're having." He rolled his eyes up to the angry sky.

The man scratched the top of his head and pulled his flat-cap firmly over his hair. "And your face. Did that happen on your terrible journey?"

"You could say that. I was working late last night to prepare for this trip. On the way home I was mugged. I should have just given them my wallet." Sam didn't know where these lies were coming from.

The man frowned and looked genuinely concerned, "London, I bet?"

"Yep," Sam smiled, rubbing gently at his cheek, hoping he'd won some sympathy.

"Welcome to Scotland, young laddie." He extended his right hand, "The name's Mackay."

"Seth–," said Sam, immediately realising his mistake he stopped himself.

"Sorry?" Mackay pulled on Sam's hand as he leant in a little closer.

"Sam, I said Sam."

"Okay Sam, climb aboard." And with that Mackay released his firm grip, span around and was quickly through the rain and into the driver's seat. Sam picked up his holdall and got into the passenger side. He looked over his shoulder at all of the things in the back – the briefcase was in touching distance but there was no room for anything else. He kept his now damp holdall on his lap. The diesel engine growled and the windscreen wipers screeched as they competed with the torrent of rain that ran down the steamy windscreen. Mackay opened his window to reduce the condensation but quickly changed his mind as the wind sprayed water into the side of his face. He turned up the blowers and rummaged around beside his seat, producing a grubby chamois leather cloth which he rubbed at the windscreen before tossing it to Sam, to finish the job on his side. But he didn't wait for Sam; pulling away into the short queue of cars leaving the airport.

The radio played nineties pop music that was just about audible over the noisy engine. Mackay sporadically hummed to the tunes as he followed perilously close to a white van in front, along the featureless road out of the airport to the A96. Sam noticed they were following signs for Inverness centre. He wanted to say something but didn't have any words. He glanced at Mackay. Sam guessed he must have been at least sixty five – his reddened cheeks and capillaried nose the result of a life in this harsh climate or a love of booze. Probably both. Sam rested his hand in his jacket pocket, fingers wrapped around his bottle of whisky. The white van pulled off, clearing the road ahead, and the

Land Rover sped up through the deep puddles. Sam closed his eyes.

"What did the police say?" asked Mackay.

Sam opened his eyes and turned sharply in his seat to Mackay, his seatbelt locking with the sudden movement. Was this a trap? "I don't know what you mean. The police?"

"Aye," Mackay pulled one hand off the wheel and pointed at Sam's eye, "do they think they'll catch your mugger?"

"I didn't bother with them. Nobody bothers with the police in London." He thought of George and poor Mrs Price. He realised he'd have to stay more alert and keep a track of all the lies. He had to take control of the conversation and stop the questions. "So, you live on Aul?"

"Born and bred. Be seventy years in December."

"You're a farmer, I take it?" Sam tapped the dashboard.

"Well, a crofter, aye. But this isn't my car. There are no cars on Aul. I only borrow this to collect supplies when I'm on the mainland. And you...You don't strike me as an estate agent."

"I'm a banker. My client has bought Aul House. You say you've heard of the sale?"

"Who hasn't? It's about the only thing that's happened on the island in thirty or so years. What we'd all love to know is who's this client of yours?"

Sam wanted to say 'he's a billionaire suspected of financing global terrorism' just to see Mackay's reaction. "They wish to remain anonymous."

"Why does *Anonymous* send their banker up from London to the house. Is it your great taste in curtains?" He smiled.

Sam wondered how much Mackay really knew. "It's about money. It's *always* about money."

"Money?" Mackay lifted his hands from the steering wheel and shrugged his shoulders, looking and sounding as if he'd never heard the word.

"Sure it is. Money defines us – fearful or greedy. We're either savers or spenders."

"And what are you?"

"I'm looking forward to the rain stopping."

Both men laughed as they slowed down for a roundabout signposted *Culloden*. Mackay took the second exit, and they approached an out-of-town supermarket that marked the outskirts of Inverness. Sam watched locals in anoraks under golf umbrellas scurry from their cars to the sandy-bricked building.

"I'll stop here for fuel. Do you want anything?" asked Mackay. He pulled into the forecourt and stopped beside the first diesel pump.

"I'm good."

Mackay switched off the engine and got out. Sam watched him in the rear-view mirror as he took out his bottle of whisky and swigged it when he was sure nobody was watching. The booze left a hot trail down his throat and the alcohol rushed to his brain. He wanted to take another swig but was conscious Mackay would smell it on his breath. He screwed the lid back on and dropped the bottle back into his jacket pocket.

When Mackay went to the kiosk to pay for the fuel Sam unclipped his seatbelt and leant over the back of his seat. Double checking Mackay wasn't watching he reached with both hands for the brown paper parcel with the flash of red leather peaking through the tear. Pulling it gently towards him he felt a little resistance as it dragged between the boxes either side of it. He tugged at it to set it free but in doing so caught the paper, tearing it further, exposing more of the red within. It was useless, he couldn't move it anymore without tearing the parcel paper from it completely. Sam got up onto his knees, using his extra height to lean over the top of the boxes and look down on the parcel. With the tear now bigger, it was clear to see the briefcase. The stitching matched his father's case exactly. Sam heard something and froze. A pickup truck pulled up next to the pump in front of him, blocking his view of the kiosk and Mackay. He had to be quick. He leant as far forward as he could and reached for the label attached to the parcel. His eyes had to adjust to the dim light in the back before he could read the handwritten label: *Mr John Pinto. Aul House. Isle of Aul*. Sam turned the label over, on the back had been stamped: *Return to, Forster's LLP, Bride Court. London. EC4*. The sound of laughter made Sam jump, spinning around he saw Mackay only a few yards from the *Land Rover* chatting with the driver of the pickup.

Sam dropped back into his seat hoping Mackay hadn't seen him. But his heart was already racing as he processed what he had just read. Forster had sent the briefcase to Aul. To Aul House. He thought back to yesterday afternoon in Forster's dingy office. He remembered how cagey Morris had been about the cupboard. Sam closed his eyes and ran the scene through his mind... the sticky cupboard door... the briefcase Morris pulled out... the sight of something red inside the cupboard before Morris closed the door! There must have been two cases. His father must have left two cases – one for him and one for John Pinto, whoever he was? Sam was certain he'd not heard the name before. But this made no sense. More potential links between his father and Frost, yet more confusion. Sam's breathing quickened and a sickening dread rolled in his stomach. He couldn't make sense of any of it. Was this another part of George's plot or did his father have some connection to Aul?

"Are you okay?" Mackay tapped on his window.

Sam took a deep breath and strained a smile as he wound down his window.

"You look like you've seen a ghost," said Mackay.

"I'm fine. Just tired after the early start."

"Tea or coffee? I got one of each, wasn't sure which you preferred." Mackay held up two steaming white polystyrene cups.

"You life saver. Coffee, thanks."

Mackay passed the cup in his left hand through the open window and walked around the front of the *Land Rover* and got back in. "Good news," he said as he balanced his tea on the dashboard.

"Oh yeah?"

"Aye, I got their last copy of *Cryptic Jumbo*." Mackay pulled what looked like a phone book from inside his tweed jacket. He held it up to show Sam. "This will last me a couple of months, I reckon. I can't get enough of cryptic crossword puzzles. You can'y get them on Aul." He flicked open the book on a random page. "Ah, my favourite: An anagram. Eight across, 'Nice-love aggressively scrambled'." He looked at Sam with expectant eyes.

"Violence."

"Bravo, Sam. You're a man after my own heart." He dropped the book on Sam's lap and started the engine.

But Sam wasn't in the mood for crosswords. He had a puzzle of his own and it span around his mind as they drove into Inverness.

The rain eased off a little but the sun remained lost behind thick grey cloud. Mackay had turned up the radio, filling the uncomfortable silence of the last thirty minutes with *Duran Duran* and *AC/DC*. Sam stared out of the window at nothing in particular as he tried to think it all over. He trawled his memory for John Pinto. Perhaps a colleague, client or friend of his father's? His father had very few friends – and even these were more business associates than friends; drinking buddies who would find him new clients and introduce him to more work. He had no time for friendship, he had no time for anything or anyone outside the narrow confines of his work. It was this single minded selfishness that Sam could now only remember of his father. 'Be great at what you do. Just one thing is all you need and be great at it. Strive for perfection.' That's what he used to say, towering over Sam as he sat at the piano. His father had chosen his work. And he was *great* at what he did. A barrister and QC never out of work and regarded by many as the best in his field. His thoughts meandered into memories of playing the piano with his mother. The hours she'd lovingly spend next to him helping him prepare for his grade exams. The little performances he would give to her and her friends on Wednesday bridge night. Her proud smile... But he was never *great* at the piano. He'd given up trying to be great... Perhaps he'd never tried to be great… Was anything or anyone ever perfect?

"You're quiet, Sam. You'll like Aul if you like the quiet," said Mackay out of nowhere.

"I suppose I am quiet. Tell me a bit about Aul. That's why I'm up here, to find out more about Aul for my client." Sam sat up straight and his worn leather seat creaked.

"It's a magical place. Fresh air. Birds. Sheep. Stunning scenery..." Mackay gazed wistfully into the distance as if searching for the right words.

Sam wasn't interested in Mackay's romantic arcadia, he interrupted: "Who is John Pinto?"

Mackay took his eyes off the road, to look at Sam, "Well you'll find out soon enough. He lives at Aul House."

"He lives there?"

"That's right. Well he lives there until Friday."

Sam was desperately trying to put the pieces of Mackay's answers together, to appear more knowledgeable than he was. "Now I remember reading that in my notes.

Pinto's the vendor. My client bought Aul House from John Pinto and he moves out this Friday. "

"No, no." Mackay shook his head and his big, fuzzy hair appeared to pulsate. "Pinto's the housekeeper. Has been for the last thirty years. Where did you get your information from laddie?"

Sam felt his cheeks flush, "Maybe that punch did more damage than I thought." He forced a short, unconvincing laugh. "Who owned the house before my client? I don't have my notes with me."

"That's a good question. Aul House is the ancestral home of the Laird of Aul, since the seventeenth century. The last Laird..." Mackay trailed off, his gaze again fixed off into the distance.

Sam looked out the windscreen, relieved to see no cars on the road in front of them. "What happened to the last Laird?"

"That's the funny thing. Nobody knows. He was a queer fellow, the Laird. It's been over fifty years since I saw him. It was the War that did it..."

"War?"

"Aye, World War Two. He was never the same after that. Became a recluse, locked up in that big house of his. And then he disappeared..." Mackay rubbed his chin thoughtfully.

"He's probably dead now."

Mackay slowed down and looked hard at Sam – the car still rolling forward as he spoke: "Maybe yes. Maybe no." He returned his eyes to the road and sped on.

"I don't understand. How old is the Laird?"

"He must have been in his late forties when he got back from Singapore. That's where he ended up at the end of the War."

"So he's well over a hundred now. My money's on dead."

"That may be so but don't let too many of the islanders hear you say that. There's many a folk who swear the Laird still roams the island at night."

Sam laughed, "You mean the Laird's ghost haunts the island?"

Mackay smiled. "As crazy as it sounds, many of the locals will not set foot anywhere near Aul House."

Bonkers, thought Sam. "So where does Pinto come into it?"

"As I said, the Laird disappeared. Aul House stood empty for about another twenty years. Then thirty years ago Pinto showed up. Introduced himself as the new housekeeper. He's another chap who keeps himself to himself. Doesn't socialise with the locals if he can help it."

"So, Pinto works for a ghost boss in a haunted house, is that it?"

Mackay shrugged, "Sam, all I know is that serious folk are convinced they see the Laird wandering the island."

"You've seen him too?"

"No."

"Ghost or no ghost. It doesn't explain who Pinto works for."

"You'll find out soon enough for yourself."

11:05

Mackay sped along the A82 between the tall, ancient pines, with their near-orange trunks and deep green needles, flanking either side of the road. A mist rolled and swirled like cigarette smoke over the rippling surface of Loch Ness. Sam sat in silence admiring the view, his mind falling in and out of memories of his parents and childhood. He wondered why his parents had never brought him to the Scottish Highlands as a boy – never too hot and plenty of fishing, just what his father would have wanted for that occasional week he'd force himself away from work, yet close enough to get home should a tasty case come up in London.

The men exchanged the odd word every ten or so minutes. Mackay pointed out landmarks and places he'd visited on his trips to the mainland; Sam feigned interest. This went on for about ninety long minutes until they entered the village of Kyle of Lochalsh and Mackay left the main road and snaked about a series of narrow streets that lead down to the water's edge that spread out before them, managing to shimmer even on the dullest of days. The *Land Rover* stopped and reversed into a parking space parallel to the water. Both men were quickly out and into the blustery coastal air. Sam zipped up his coat and pulled up his collar, grateful that the rain had stopped. He stretched and yawned, enjoying the bracing force of the salty sea air over his face. Arching over the horizon, like a concrete rainbow, stretched a bridge connecting the mainland to a distant island. Sam figured they must have reached the west coast and that must have been Skye Bridge, connecting the mainland to Isle of Skye, his first sighting of the Hebrides. Somewhere beyond lay Aul. He was about to confirm this with Mackay but before he spoke he realised Mackay had disappeared. Sam looked all around him, his ears filled with the squawks of a dozen or so menacing looking seagulls circling over head, but Mackay was nowhere to be seen. He walked around the *Land Rover* searching for the white fluffy cloud of hair. The narrow street was empty. A sudden uneasiness came over him and he was immediately surprised and disappointed in himself for the way he felt. He took off his cap, ran his hand through his hair and leant against the rusty rail that stood between him and the water. He spotted Mackay, striding along a short wharf which lay about ten feet below the level of the road. Moored up against the rickety wooden quayside was a fishing boat that had seen better days. Its scuffed black and blue hull was pockmarked with rust that looked like coffee-rings on a kitchen table. The windows along the tiny off-white cabin were smeared with salty residue. Mackay jumped onto the deck and pulled back a canvas sheet that covered the stern of the dinky vessel. He looked around him and plunged his hand deep in the right pocket of his jacket. He jumped up to his feet, at a speed that defied his age and appearance.

"Here," called Mackay and flicked his hand out of his pocket sending something flying towards Sam.

Sam flinched and took a step back before extending both hands out in front of him; he caught the bunch of keys at face height. "Are you crazy? I could have dropped them in the loch."

Mackay smiled back as if pretending he hadn't heard him. "We need to load her up, there's a storm coming."

Sam looked back across the water. Thick black cloud wrapped itself around the rocky peaks of Skye. He unlocked the back of the *Land Rover* and unloaded the boxes, newspapers and hessian sacks onto the road. He remembered the briefcase and wondered whether now was his chance to take Pinto's parcel. But Mackay appeared at his side and scooped up the briefcase and an armful of other parcels. Sam watched him carefully, half hoping Mackay would notice the large tear in the wrapping paper but he seemed to be in too much of a rush. The two men needed three return journeys each, up and down the concrete steps, to load everything onto the boat before the canvas cover was pulled back over the cargo. Mackay asked for the keys and skipped back up the steps to lock up the *Land Rover*. Sam stood on the boat, swaying gently in time with the current. Again he was disappointed with himself for forgetting there would be a boat ride to get to Aul. Everything was catching him off guard. Nothing felt right. His sense of control ebbed away with every hour that passed. He fingered the bottle of whisky in his pocket, turned away from land and took a large swig. It wasn't long past midday and half of the bottle was gone. He promised himself he'd have no more until it was dark.

Mackay whistled as he untied the mooring ropes and used his heavy, booted foot to push them free from the wharf. Sam noticed *Cryptic Jumbo* rolled up in Mackay's jacket pocket. The boat's diesel engine grunted into action and they chugged out into the loch.

"You'll want this," said Mackay using his right hand to reach for a bright red life jacket while his left remained firmly on the wheel.

Mackay's cheeky smile bewildered Sam, not sure whether he was testing or perhaps even teasing him for being some Big Smoke softie who couldn't handle a fishing boat. Sam took the life jacket and held it by his side. Mackay sighed deeply with satisfaction as he looked out to the distant horizon.

"Looking forward to getting back to Aul, I suppose?" said Sam.

"Aye. It sounds funny but I feel older when I'm away." He looked at Sam, his eyes glossy.

Sam hoped that it was just the salty air stinging Mackay's eyes. "You're right. It does sound funny." Sam laughed. But to Mackay's point, the calming effect of the water was working its magic. The rhythmic hiss of the waves and the steady hum of the engine, played a soothing backing track to their gentle journey out of the loch and into the forever expanse of sea. There was nothing to do except stop, breath the clean air and soak up the spectacular scenery. Sam inhaled deeply until he could taste the bitter-sweet air in the back of his throat. The world felt calm and easy, just as it had done yesterday evening in Frost's Rolls Royce – but how different this was from London. The troubles of last night now felt like a distant memory but there, refusing to be pushed to the back of his mind, was George. Her playful smile. The smell of her perfume. Her birthmark. Her simple, natural beauty. Her cold-hearted efficiency. Sam took out the phone she had given him and switched it on. There was just about enough signal from the mainland to make a call. He found her number and held his thumb over the *call* button. He wanted to hear her again; to hear the relief and satisfaction in her soft American voice when he told her that he was all right and the plan was on track. But he remembered what she'd said about not using the phone unless he was alone. This meant no superfluous communication – *no news is good news*. After all, she didn't care about him; he was likely one of many spooks – professional and amateur – she was running. To her this was work. Business. Was this the same for Tom? What happened to Tom? Could he really have died on Aul? Had George also blackmailed Tom to get him to go after Frost? Were George and Tom lovers? And now, here *he* was, dressed in Tom's clothes; a man wanted for murder; a man on his way to foil a threat to national security. Sam pressed his thumb down onto the *call* button and held the phone to his ear. There was an eternal seeming pause before it rang. He didn't know what he would say when she answered.

"Brace yourself!" cried a voice. Not George's sweet, southern drawl but Mackay's gruff bark, as the boat lurched and lolled over a suddenly angry sea. A rumble of thunder rolled over the now charcoal sky. Water crashed over the starboard side. Mackay pulled down hard on the wheel to the port side as he wrestled to keep control. Sam slipped on the unsteady, wet deck. He landed on his arm, his fall broken by the life jacket he was still holding.

"Hold on. I'd put that jacket on if I were you," called Mackay looking back over his shoulder at Sam before wiping the spray away from his face and returning both his hands to the wheel. He bent his knees slightly to give himself a lower centre of gravity on the treacherous deck.

Sam got to his knees and put the life jacket on. His feet and trousers soaked through. A crash of lightning preceded a cloud-bursting flood of rain. Water was everywhere – above, below and all around. He pulled up the collar on his coat and lowered the peak of his cap over his face. The deck was now covered in an inch of sea and rain. The wind whipped up the waves into a foamy white spray. A haze enveloped them; two men alone and exposed to the ferocious, fickle temperament of nature. The boat rose and fell with the powerful tide. All Sam could do was stagger to his feet and hold onto Mackay for balance. Mackay didn't mind as he hunkered behind the wheel, solid as a rock. Sam's stomach churned and he shivered. He squinted his eyes to look through the misty vapour, turning his face away from the horizontal torrent of rain into which they sailed. There he saw his mobile phone, lying precariously on the canvas cover that protected their cargo. The phone just a foot away from falling into the sea. Sam let go of Mackay and slipped and slid his way along the deck to the stern.

"No. Hold on!" shouted Mackay through the whistling wind.

But Sam crouched down, determined not to lose the phone. Determined not to lose George. Had she answered his call? Was she listening to all of this, worried for his wellbeing? He had to get to the phone. He had to get to George. The boat shifted as if thrown out of the sea, sending them gliding through the air. Sam fell onto his chest, face into the iron deck. The phone slid over the canvas. He jumped up and stretched out both arms. The boat dipped and leapt, sending Sam's feet up and his out-stretched arms down. He caught the phone and pulled it into himself tightly. But his momentum was behind him and he fell forwards, over the stern and towards the wild sea. His cap fell from his head, swallowed into the deep. He closed his eyes and screamed. Resigned to his fate as the world paused and nothing mattered at all. A silence... Until everything went into reverse and he was yanked back into the boat, Mackay's round eyes and crazy white hair filled his vision.

"That was bloody close!" screamed Mackay. He pulled Sam back up the deck, bundled him into the small cabin and slammed the door.

Sam slumped onto a crate that doubled as a seat. Soaked and shivering, he clutched the phone against his pounding heart.

14:55

Sam leant against the rail along the boat's bow. The warm breeze off the land swept over his face, carrying the faintest whiff of what seemed like freshly baked bread. For the last two hours the corrosive, saline sea-air had permeated his being. The sickly taste of salt lingered in his mouth. The steady rhythm of the waves broke time as the boat wound down its engine for the final approach. The wild power of the sea faded into the white, foamy surf that bubbled around the hull. The hissing and crashing of the storm now replaced by the gentle lapping of the tranquil, inky-blue carpet laid before them. The brilliant yellow sun from the west flooded the endless miles of sparkling white sand. Every hue of green, orange and brown ran along the rolling hills beyond.

Mackay appeared by Sam's side. "Well here we are. Aul... Magnificent don't you think?" He breathed deeply and smiled.

Sam turned to Mackay, speaking to him for the first time since he pulled him from the edge, "You saved my life back there. Thank–".

Mackay put his hand on Sam's shoulder and cut him short. "You just be careful, laddie." His strong grip squeezed in a friendly, avuncular way before he returned to the wheel, to guide them safely in.

Sam had to agree. It was magnificent. Serene. Rugged. Untouched. A cormorant flew overhead and landed on the rocky cliffs high above the sands. The engine sound disappeared and they swung up against a wooden jetty.

Mackay had a spring in his step as he was quickly out of the boat. Sam helped him with the mooring ropes before taking his first step onto the Isle of Aul.

A horse drawn cart appeared from the pine trees and clattered down the track towards the jetty. A middle aged woman dressed in a smart matching tweed jacket and long skirt brought the two horses snorting to a halt, just shy of the beach. Next to her sulked a girl of about fourteen or fifteen who looked like her daughter; her tight-fit stonewash jeans and garish pink anorak an apparent rebellion against the embarrassing, arcane mode of transport she was forced to accompany her mother upon.

Sam remembered what Mackay had said about there being no cars on the island. He removed his coat as he finally felt some summer warmth. It was balmy on Aul – about ten degrees warmer than Inverness. The tops of the tall pines that stood between them and the hills beyond swayed in the breeze, but down on the beach they enjoyed the shelter and basked in the glow of the strong sunshine. Mackay waved and called out to the arrival party and they waved back enthusiastically. Sam noticed their suspicious gaze fixed upon him. He waved too and said hi but all he got back was a quick, furtive nod of the head from the girl; her mother just stared back.

Mackay skipped up the jetty to greet them. Sam turned away to face the sea and pulled out his phone. In the tiny screen he caught his reflection, his hair bedraggled after the storm and his eye black and swollen. He ruffled his hair with his fingers but it did nothing to improve the situation. He switched on the phone and to his surprise it picked up reception. He was switching the phone off again when it chirped and an envelope icon appeared on the screen – *1 Unread Message. Sender G.* He felt the buzz of adrenaline shoot through him as he opened the message:

Will be with you Thursday night. Good luck. G x

He read it three times. Each time he pondered the *x*. What did she mean by *x*? Was it a show of affection or just the way she signed off all messages? And why did he need *luck*? He assumed *with you* meant up here in Aul. Why was she coming up to Aul? That wasn't part of the original plan. Was something going wrong back in London or some new intelligence perhaps? He thought about replying but the sound of footsteps on the jetty forced the phone into his trouser pocket and he turned around to see Mackay and the two women next to the boat.

"Sam, this is Joanna and her daughter Isla," said Mackay.

"Hi. How do you do," said Sam.

"How do you do," replied both women in unison, still staring at him.

"Joanna, Isla, allow me to introduce you to Sam West. I picked Sam up in Inverness. He's here about Aul House – he's a banker, you see," said Mackay, looking back at Sam with enquiring eyes as if to check he got all of his facts right.

"What's going to happen to the Laird's house then?" blurted out Isla. She immediately blushed.

"My client hasn't made up their mind. That's why I'm here. What do you think should happen to it?" Sam smiled and walked toward them.

Joanna pulled her daughter's arm as if to pull her away from him, "Aul House is of no interest to us, Mr West." She guided her daughter down into the boat where Mackay had already started unpacking.

It was half past three as the horses plodded inland amongst the trees, following the trail of manure they had left on their outbound journey. Sam walked beside them, his coat over one arm and his holdall over his shoulder, while Mackay sat amongst the sacks and papers in the wagon, behind Joanna and Isla. The mighty beasts huffed and hissed as they pulled their load. The air hung still, yet clean and fresh. He overheard Joanna tell Mackay that the storm earlier had cut the power to the island. Mackay didn't sound the least bit surprised at the news, as if this was a regular occurrence.

As soon as they were out of the woods Sam saw it. There, on the hill in front of them stood Aul House. It was just as it was in the picture. But to see it now was to understand the scale and grandeur of the place. Even from a quarter of a mile away the house looked big and imposing. Leading up to the house snaked a line of evergreen trees. Sam followed the horses for another five or so minutes before Joanna pulled hard on the reins and they dutifully came to a stop.

"That's as far as we go, Mr West," said Joanna.

Mackay was already stood up and sorting through the bags on the wagon. "Sam, if I could ask you to please take a few things up to the house."

"Sure, no problem." Sam put his coat back on to free-up his hands. He went around the back of the wagon where Mackay handed him down a letter and the parcel he recognised as the briefcase.

Mackay frowned at the large tear in the paper. "Oh dear, send my apologies to John. I hope it's not damaged."

"Will do." Sam took the parcel and letter under his left arm. He extended his right hand to shake Mackay's. "Thanks for everything. I don't know what I'd have done without you."

"I'll see you around, Sam."

Both men smiled.

Sam walked around the front and patted one of the horses before saying his goodbyes and thanks to Joanna and Isla.

"Good day, Mr West," said Joanna as she snapped her riding prop and tugged at the reins and with that they were away. Isla looking back over her shoulder, her cheeks still blushed.

Sam watched them trace along the edge of the woodland before disappearing back in amongst the trees. The heathland he stood on was rugged and weather-beaten, only the hardiest of thistles and coarse grasses growing amongst the exposed rocks. An eerie feeling came over him – a sudden awareness of his insignificance and vulnerability. A deep sense of being alone while at the same time a peculiar sensation of being watched.

He looked all around him. Nothing. He concentrated his hearing. At first nothing until he made out the unmistakable sound of running water. Closing his eyes to sharpen his hearing further he located the source under his feet – an underground stream or natural spring running amongst the rocks below. Sam focused on the soothing sound that led him down to the line of trees that marked the way to Aul House.

George's chunky digital watch beeped on the hour, telling Sam it was now four o'clock as the avenue of ancient evergreens stood a few yards ahead of him. This was his last chance and he had to take it. He pushed any fear to the back of his mind and put the briefcase down on the ground. The brown parcel paper around it was two thirds torn along its length. Sam tore it away another couple of inches, allowing him to pull the red leather away from its wrapping. The snap of a branch made him suddenly stop and look about to see who was there but he couldn't see anyone. His mouth was dry and his senses on high alert as he hurriedly examined the case. It was exactly the same as the case his father had given him. Sam got down on one knee and rested the case on his opposite thigh, poised to open it up – his thumbs resting on the golden catches. Then he confirmed this wasn't his case. It wasn't the case his father had given him. Embossed in an elegant, gold script between the catches, underneath the combination lock, was the name: *SETH FALCORRS*.

Sam froze. How could this be? He stood back up and rummaged through his inside pocket to find his fake driving licence. Yes, it matched exactly. What the hell was going on? Did George know about this? Sam got back down to open the case but the sudden electric beep and vibration from his pocket sent him straight back up. He nearly dropped the case in his rush to answer the phone. He knew it would be George.

"Hello, George."

"Sam, is it safe to talk?" Her tone was more business-like than ever.

"Yes."

"Have you reached Aul yet?"

"Yes. I need to tell you–"

"Good. Have you reached Aul House yet?"

"Yes. Well, no not yet."

"Yes or no?"

"I'm nearly there, I'm just about to go in. That's what I need to tell you."

"Sam, there's no time for that. Did you receive my message about Thursday?"

"Yes. What time do you arrive? Where shall I meet you?"

"You don't need that information yet. Just remember your mission. Link Frost to one of those companies on the list I gave you and you're done. I'll see you sometime Thursday to debrief."

"George, did you send me a briefcase? There's a briefcase up here that looks just like the one I had stolen yesterday."

"No, Sam I didn't. I've been unable to track down your case but I haven't given up. Leave that with me."

"Here's the thing. The housekeeper at Aul House is a guy called John Pinto. He's been sent, by my *father's* solicitor, a briefcase matching the one my father gave to me."

"Sam, I don't follow."

"The briefcase I had stolen was left to me by my father, in his will. It's almost identical to the one I'm holding right now, except for one thing."

"Yes, I'm listening."

"It has the name Seth Falcorrs embossed on it."

"Sam, you can't let yourself become distracted from your mission." George's voice had lost its conviction.

"What the fuck is going on, George?"

"Sam, I need time to run some checks. I'm as confused as you."

"Who the fuck is Seth Falcorrs?"

"I need more time." She coughed before continuing, "You need to stay focused and don't blow your cover. You've never heard of Seth Falcorrs, remember. I need to speak to a few people here and understand where that ID came from. Remember you're Sam West, investment banker."

"You don't need to tell me who I am."

"Just don't blow everything because you've been thrown a curve ball." Her voice returned to a controlled, reassuring calm.

Another snapping sound echoed amongst the trees ahead.

"Sam, you ok? Sam..."

A cold chill surrounded him.

"Can't talk now," Sam whispered.

"I'll be in touch." She hung up.

Sam dropped the phone in his pocket and crouched down to pick up the case and his holdall. The brown parcel paper flapping in the gentle breeze that blew across the heathland. All the time, his eyes fixed on the trees.

"What do you want?"

Sam span around and came face-to-face with the twin barrels of a shotgun.

16:11

The man pointing the gun looked deep into Sam's wide eyes. "What do you want?"

Sam took a deep breath before speaking. "I'm looking for Aul House. You must be Mr Pinto."

The man lowered the gun. "And who are you?"

"Sam West. I'm from Gema Bank. I'm here about the sale of Aul House."

"Nobody said anything about a visit from a bank." He raised the twin-barrels up to point at Sam's face and then lowered them gradually down the length of his body to his groin. "You don't look like a banker."

Sam let out a laugh. "I've had one hell of a journey. You have no idea what I've been through to get here. If you stop pointing that at me I'll tell you all about it."

Pinto shrugged, shaking the two dead rabbits tied together by their feet, hung over his left shoulder. "I'm sorry if I've caught you by surprise, Mr West. I'm not used to seeing anyone around here. I was out hunting for dinner. Do you care to join me? It's rabbit stew."

Sam's breathing began to slow down. "I'd like that very much. Thank you."

"Good. Please, walk with me and tell me all about your journey."

Sam gave Pinto an edited and sanitised version of the last thirty six hours. He didn't mention the letter or the briefcase Mackay had entrusted him to deliver. As Sam spoke he turned to Pinto who walked on his right-hand side. It was dark in the shadows of the avenue of trees but every so often the sun would stream through the branches and Sam pieced together a picture of Pinto: He was the same height as him. He had a strong jaw line and broad shoulders. He wore no coat and his shirt sleeves were rolled up above his elbow to reveal muscular forearms. Pinto said nothing as he listened attentively to Sam's account. They left the cover of the trees, over a well manicured lawn and crunched over gravel to the front door. Smoke rose from one of the many chimneys that sprouted from the brown stone house. Pinto unlocked the door and Sam followed him into the dark.

"There's still no power. I'll get the generator going if it's not back on soon," said Pinto. He leant his shotgun down against a rack of antique looking walking sticks next to the door. He picked up a lamp from the sideboard and it squeaked as a pale yellow light lit their way into a spectacular hallway. An ornately carved staircase swept down from the first floor, lined by paintings, stags' heads and shields over whitewashed walls. The house was cold but the air smelled of the earthiness of an open log fire. Sam's eyes adjusted to the light and he saw more. The hallway alone was bigger than his entire mews house in London. Over the many sideboards and tables were glass cases and bell jars, covering tired flowers and plants, all labelled in Latin.

"Excuse the mess," said Pinto, "I'm still packing up and preparing for the party."

"Party?"

"Yes, Thursday night. It's my last night here. It's been thirty years. The trustees of the house are insistent there's a party to say farewell. There's going to be a lot to do to get the place packed up and ready."

"I'm happy to help."

"Don't you have work to do?"

"Yes, but to be honest my client hasn't been all that specific about what they wish me to do. Only that I get a sense for the place and make a few recommendations on what the options for the house may be." Sam didn't know what he was saying.

"*Options*? You mean, turn the place into a hotel or open it up to tourists, like Buckingham Palace in August. Those sorts of options?"

"My client hasn't ruled anything out."

"Where are you staying?"

Sam smiled and shrugged, "I was rather hoping I could stay here. I could help you get the place ready for Thursday night. And to be honest, the locals don't seem the friendliest."

Pinto laughed, his face illuminated in the yellow light like a jack-o-lantern. "That's because they're scared of this place. Do you believe in ghosts, Mr West?"

"Please, call me Sam."

"Sam, can I get you a drink?" Pinto had already placed the lamp on a side table and poured three fingers of whisky from a crystal decanter into two matching glasses.

Sam set down the briefcase and his holdall on the flagstone floor, walked across the hallway and took his glass from Pinto's outstretched hand.

"To new friends," said Pinto.

"To new friends." Sam held Pinto's stare as he drank half the peaty whisky.

"Let me get you something for that eye?" said Pinto with a wince.

"Please, it's no bother. It doesn't hurt."

"It's a constant reminder of your mugging. We can't have that. Follow me." Pinto went around Sam before he could react, and had picked up his holdall and the briefcase.

"I've got them," insisted Sam.

But he was too slow. Pinto had already noticed the torn parcel paper as the briefcase almost slipped from his grasp. "What's happened here?"

Shit, thought Sam. He downed the rest of his whisky and returned his glass a little too heavily to the sideboard, the clatter on the silver tray echoed about the hallway. The alcohol warmed the inside of his mouth. "Oh, I forgot about that. Mackay asked me to give you a couple of things. He said something about the parcel getting torn in transit. He sends his apologies."

Pinto held the case in both hands, as if it were a paperback novel, and examined the half-red leather, half-brown paper exterior. "Did he now?" he said, without looking up. "And was that it?"

"Was what it?" Sam felt his heart racing.

"Was this all that Mackay had for me?"

"No, there was this letter too," he reached inside his pocket, his hands were clammy against the envelope.

Pinto grabbed the letter from him, still without looking up from the briefcase, and wandered into the shadows under the stairs. Sam couldn't quite see what was happening but the sound of keys preceded the opening of a door before Pinto re-emerged without the case or envelope.

Sam kept his fidgety hands deep in his pockets and smiled casually at Pinto, "You said you had something for my eye?"

The lights flickered as the power came back and the hallway lit-up. Pinto looked around the vaulted-ceiling at the dozens of candle shaped electric bulbs that hung from chandeliers above them. "Yes, the light's doing you no favours. Come with me."

Sam followed Pinto through a double-height door, into a cosy drawing room lined with bookshelves. French doors looked out onto the forever expanse of lawns and hills at the back of the house. In the centre of the room a worn sofa and armchair stood around a coffee table. Light flooded in from the windows looking onto the garden, as well as two industrial looking desk lamps on a side table, shining directly into a glass case like the ones that littered the hallway. Pinto waved Sam to the sofa and was, himself, quickly over to the glass case, opening its lid and taking something from inside. He dropped it into a pestle and mortar that stood next to the glass case on the table, and added a drop of something from a canteen.

The clink and scrape of the pestle filled the room, as Pinto turned to face Sam, pounding and grinding with purpose. "You only need a little of this, it's very concentrated." He passed the mortar to Sam.

Sam stood up and peered at the vivid purple paste, no more than half a teaspoon worth clung to the sides of the dish. He sniffed it but it smelt of nothing at all.

Pinto laughed, "Don't snort it!"

Sam's cheeks flushed, "What is it?"

"It's the cure." Pinto sat down in the armchair and swung his boots onto the coffee table.

Sam immediately thought of Jerry in his wood panelled office with his feet on his desk. "What's in it?"

"Does it matter? Give it here." Pinto leaned across the coffee table and took the dish from Sam. "Take a seat."

Sam sat on the edge of the sofa and before he had realised what had happened, Pinto swiped a heavy index finger around his bruise. Sam flinched and a cold, tingling sensation set in as the purple paste dried, tightening and pulling his skin.

"Now, don't touch. Just let it do its thing," said Pinto as he admired his handiwork around Sam's eye.

Sunlight poured into the small drawing room from the windows over Pinto's shoulder. Sam surmised this was Pinto's main room; the cosy proportions and brightness were the perfect antidote to this large, cold, dark house.

Pinto's broad frame filled the armchair, his cropped brown hair the same colour as the shiny leather. His smooth features made him hard to age but Sam remembered what Mackay had said about him being here thirty years – he must have been barely out of his teens when he came to Aul House, he thought.

"It would be good to have someone stay a few days," said Pinto, his boots now back on the coffee table.

Sam sat back into the sofa, springs squeaked through the worn cushion and he shuffled around to get comfortable. The mobile phone in his pocket dug into his side and he thought about his call with George and her reminder to gather evidence on Frost. He had no idea where to begin, so in the absence of any better ideas he said: "Thanks. I'll just need somewhere to sleep. But one of the few instructions my client gave me was to learn about the house – you know, its history... Also, understand what sort of business is going-on, on the island."

"Business?" Pinto's eyes narrowed.

"Understand what's already going on, commerce-wise." Sam felt ridiculous and awkward as he attempted to engineer an opportunity from nothing.

"There's nothing going on around here. As you found out earlier, the locals aren't the friendliest."

"Mackay seems nice enough."

"Is he? I wouldn't know. You can tell from my accent, I'm not from around here."

He sounded very English. "But you've been here for thirty years," said Sam.

"That's right. I've been looking after this place all that time. I'm an Englishman like yourself. I was out of the army and looking for something to do, somewhere quiet where I could indulge my passion."

"What's that?"

"Botany."

That explained the plants, the specimen cases, even the purple paste around his eye.

"The Hebrides hardly strike me as a botanist's paradise."

Pinto stood up, his attention distracted by something above Sam's head. "Things are seldom what they seem, Sam." His eyes followed something around the room. Turning to the window and then to the lamps that radiated brightly onto the glass case. "Here."

Sam got up and joined Pinto. A bumble bee stood on top of the glass case, illuminated by the lamp light.

"What do you see, Sam?"

"A big hairy bee."

"And under the glass, what do you see?"

Sam leant in a bit lower to take a closer look, the heat from the lamps on his face. The bee hovered above the glass, its wings humming gently, directly above an unusual looking purple flower with blue nectar and waxy green leaves. "I see a purple flower." The flower looked exotic. It was no bigger than the palm of his hand; the straggly leaves streaked with purple markings that matched the colour of the flower. The plant appeared to quiver in the light and heat, as if growing before his eyes.

"You see a purple flower while the bee sees an ultra violet light display so fantastic, so enticing that it must get to the flower's nectar. Yet, that wonderful sight is completely invisible to you."

Sam smiled to give Pinto the satisfaction of a point well made. "And what do you see?"

"A pest!" Pinto squeezed the bee between his thumb and index finger.

Sam stepped back and looked at Pinto, their eyes meeting at exactly the same height, just a few inches apart. Pinto smiled, before brushing the bee off the glass with a swipe of his thick fingered hand and lifted the glass lid.

"It's alright," he whispered to the flower, as if consoling a sobbing baby.

Sam could see a small piece of one of the leaves, the size of his pinkie nail, was missing, presumably torn off by Pinto to make the ointment for his eye. It was almost imperceptible but Sam was certain the tendril-like leaves slowly shrivelled around the flower in a protective embrace. He watched it closely as Pinto continued to whisper under his breath. The purple petals a couple of inches long, tapered, like tongues – six in total around a vivid blue stamen in the centre. It was not like any plant he had seen before.

"I thought bees were a gardener's friend?" said Sam.

"I'm not a gardener. I'm a scientist. And there's a time and a place for everything and everyone." Pinto returned the lid gently and turned to Sam with a friendly smile, "It's getting late. Those rabbits won't skin themselves. Let me show you to your room."

They climbed the stairs to the first floor. The landing split off in two directions – east and west; flanked by countless, dark oak doors. White sheets covered what appeared to be paintings, busts and maybe even sculptures dotted along the length of the corridor.

"Your client has bought everything, lock, stock and barrel. All the artwork is theirs. It's worth a fair bit," said Pinto still walking ahead of Sam.

Sam realised he had no idea whether Frost, as a prospective buyer, had ever visited the house or spoken with Pinto before. "Were there many interested buyers for the place?"

Pinto stopped and turned around. "The first I heard of the sale was two weeks ago, the third to be precise."

3 July, that date was forever burnt into Sam's consciousness – the day his father died.

Pinto continued, "The Trust told me I had three weeks to be out. Thirty years' service and now I'm out on my ear."

The Trust presumably managed the house on behalf of the Laird's family. Sam dug a bit deeper. "I wonder what rules The Trust operates under, since the Laird's death. I would have thought the house would have passed to his next of kin."

Pinto turned away and continued his walk along the fusty corridor, they were approaching the end of the east wing. "So you've heard about the Laird then, I suppose it was Mackay?" Pinto stopped beside a door.

Sam put down his holdall on the threadbare Persian-looking rug that covered the wooden floor. "No more ghost stories, please."

Pinto grinned and grabbed the door knob. The door shook violently in its frame. "This was the Laird's room. It's been locked the whole time I've been here. The only room I haven't a key for. I've tried to get in but it's boarded up from the inside, even the windows. If he's still *alive* then this is where you'll find him," he laughed. "And this is you." He turned to face the door on the opposite side of the corridor, turned the handle and went inside. Sam followed.

The room was bright and sparse. Two sash windows overlooked the gardens; Sam recognised the view as the same as the drawing room downstairs. A single bed and bedside table were up against the eastern wall. A sink stood below a mirror which was rendered almost useless by a heavy patina, on the opposite wall.

"It's not much. My room's the last door on the left before the stairs. Bathroom is the room before that, I'll leave you a towel in there. There's plenty of hot water. I'll call you when dinner's ready." Pinto closed the door behind him.

Sam dropped his holdall and jacket on the bed and went over to the sink. The cold tap creaked and spluttered as it coughed up years of trapped air, followed by a stream of murky brown water. Sam looked into the old mirror. He could just about make out his reflection – violet paint below his eye. He washed his face in the icy cold water, rinsing off the ointment. He pulled off Tom's hoodie and used it to dry his face. As he gingerly dabbed his eye he was surprised he felt no pain. He looked again into the mirror, amazed at what he saw. In fact, he was amazed at what he didn't see! He rubbed the misty glass with the back of his hand to be sure but it was still the same: His eye had healed, the bruising that had been there only half an hour ago had disappeared completely. He touched the soft skin around his eye. Nothing. No pain or any hint of the trauma it had endured.

Sam unpacked his holdall, refolded his clothes and arranged them into four equally spaced piles – shirts, trousers, boxer shorts and socks – on the floor at the foot of his bed. He untied his shoelaces, slipped off his leather soled shoes and deliberately positioned these parallel to the pile of two pairs of grey flannel trousers. He took his borrowed chinos off, took his belt from them, and threw them, with the hoodie, his worn boxer shorts and socks, into the holdall and pushed the bag out of sight under the iron bed frame. He coiled the belt as tightly as it would go around its buckle and placed it between the trousers and shirts; finally, adjusting the space between the clothes to re-establish equidistance. He sat on the bed and sniffed the coarse blanket and pillow that were reassuringly odourless, before lying down on his back. The cool air made the hairs on his naked body stand on end and goosebumps mottled his skin. The dimensions and layout of the room reminded him of the room his mother was moved to when her cancer took over. The last three weeks he spent at her bedside. Seeing his father cry for the first time – the only time. Her jaundiced skin around her perpetually optimistic smile.

Every day her hand getting colder, her grip lighter. He closed his eyes and bit down on his bottom lip. He focused on his breathing and refused to cry. His breathing slowed into a gentle, steady flow. A silence and peace fell over him. And for the first time in years he experienced a moment – not more than a second or two – but a moment of nothingness; of just simply being alone with himself, his mind tamed and cleared of fear or distraction.

Something creaked in the hallway, it sounded like an old floorboard. Sam got up and poked his head around the door, keeping his bare body hidden. But in the dimly lit corridor he saw nobody. He looked across the hall at the Laird's old bedroom door and wondered how long it had been locked for and what it was like inside. He imagined it caked in dust, cobwebs and mouse shit. He closed his door and lay on his bed; Pinto, Mrs Price, Mackay, the storm, Jerry, his mother and father, and those ginger-bastard-twin doormen ran wild once more through his mind. But it was George that he focused upon. Her contradictions – her petiteness and her strength. Her backless cocktail dress and her birthmark. Her dancing and her blackmail. She had a hold over him. He convinced himself that she wasn't responsible for Mrs Price's murder. It couldn't have been her idea. She had to be part of a bigger machine. She was only doing her job. She was serving her country, putting the needs of the many – the greater good – ahead of her own. A national interest before a personal selfishness. Service was her reward. Not money as it was his…

He felt buoyed by the thought that in an instant his work had a new meaning. A new perspective. A new purpose. The anger he had towards George for blackmailing him subsided. The sickening relief of his close shave with death on the boat eased. It then occurred to him that his father was somehow implicated in something illegal with Frost, something so terrible he was murdered for it. He pushed the thought away. Instead he fixed upon the real job at hand. He had to find the briefcase that Pinto had locked away downstairs.

19:45

Sam woke with a start, in an instant of panic, before remembering where he was. He'd been asleep almost an hour and a half. The sky was still blue and the sun still strong in the west. He took a hot bath and shaved before his stubble had chance to get too long, saving his neck and face the onslaught of his disposable razor. He changed into his new flannels and shirt. The delightful combination of sleep, clean skin and new clothes made him feel renewed and rejuvenated. He checked his phone for any messages but there were none. Mobile reception in the house was only a single bar and already the battery was a third depleted. He switched the phone off to conserve power and put it back in his jacket pocket.

The smell of home cooked food filled the air along the landing as Sam walked over the creaking floorboards towards the stairs. He counted twelve doors, including that of his own room, coming off the east wing; the landing beyond the stairs, along the west wing, looked about the same length. The mahogany stairs were triple the standard width, decorated with intricately carved flora and fauna in and around the spindles and banisters. Sam was three steps down when he heard the jangle of keys on a keyring coming from the ground floor below. He stopped and leant over the banister to see Pinto going into the room under the stairs, the same room he had locked the briefcase in a couple of hours earlier. Pinto went inside and closed the door behind him. Sam crept as quickly and quietly as he could, sticking to the worn, faded red runner to absorb the sound of his footsteps. The staircase swept back on itself at the half way point, giving him full sight of the door. He was forced to slow himself down to an almost standstill as he made the ten or so paces across the flagstones in the hallway as silently as possible. He put his ear to the solid oak door but couldn't hear anything. Above the door was a wooden box stained the same red-brown as the staircase, the same size and dimensions as a shoebox. Two hinges on one side of the box and a thick flex of wire coming out the opposite side told Sam this must have been the electrical fusebox. He put his hand on the door handle and gingerly turned it a hundred and eighty degrees, feeling the door move away from its frame, ready to pull it open. The element of surprise was everything. He took a deep breath and pulled the door open. "John?" he said in an innocent, inquisitive voice.

Pinto was stood with his back to the door. The room was windowless, lit by a single bulb hanging from the low ceiling, squashed by the staircase above. No more than eight feet long by four feet wide, the pokey room was lined with a matrix of little metal drawers, like miniature filing cabinets. Pinto span around, his face full of surprise. "Yes?" he took a couple of steps towards Sam as he spoke.

Sam glanced around him, and saw the briefcase, liberated from its wrapping paper, lying flat on a desk. He had to take a step back to make way for Pinto as he switched the light off and closed the door behind him.

"Can I help you?" asked Pinto, taking the keys from his pocket and locking the door.

"I was just wondering where you were. I thought I heard somebody in there." Sam nodded his head in the direction of the little room under the stairs.

Pinto smiled, "That's my seed room. Cool, dark and dry."

Sam returned the smile, "Must be pretty valuable seeds if you need to lock them away."

"That's right. They are. Years of work in there." He clenched the bunch of keys in his fist before dropping them in his pocket. "Food's almost ready, but how about a drink first?"

Pinto had set the table in the kitchen with cutlery, wine glasses and a jug of the brown-tinged water, just like the stuff Sam had washed in upstairs. The room was dominated by a black Victorian cast-iron range, set below a huge black canopy up to the chimney. A casserole dish bubbled on one of the hot plates, the steam causing the lid to lift and clatter. Bricks of peat smouldered in the hearth.

Sam sat on a bench at the table as Pinto came in with a couple of drams of whisky.

"Your eye's cleared up nicely," said Pinto. He downed his drink in one.

"I can't believe it worked so well and so fast. What was it?" Sam rubbed around his eye again to make the point it had completely healed.

Pinto turned away and reached up into a cupboard and took out two glasses. He half filled each with the water from the jug. "As I said, it's the cure."

"You mean that purple flower?"

Pinto pushed a glass of the water to Sam. "Maybe it's the flower or maybe it's the water." He gulped down the murky water.

Sam frowned, "You sure that's safe to drink?"

"Of course it is. You're sounding like those idiots from Brussels."

"Brussels?"

"This water is perfectly safe. Folk here have been drinking it for hundreds, maybe thousands of years. There's a natural spring that runs the length of the island that we all tap into."

Sam recalled the sound of running water he had heard coming from underfoot, out on the heathland.

Pinto continued, "It must have been about ten years ago now, we had a delegation from the European Parliament turn up, said they were visiting all the islands, testing the water for purity." Pinto's face came alive, blood coloured his cheeks.

Sam wondered whether he'd been drinking all the time he'd been upstairs.

"They told us our water had to be clear. It couldn't have the trace of mineral deposits that gives it this tinge." Pinto held the jug up to the light.

"Well it's either safe to drink or it's not, surely?" said Sam, dropping his voice a little in an attempt to calm Pinto down.

"Right. It *is* safe. Even the bureaucrats conceded it was safe but it didn't fit their one-size-fits-all view of the world." Pinto returned the jug to the table with a thump, causing the cutlery to jump. "Makes you wonder what we fought the war for."

Sam appeased Pinto by taking a sip of the water. To his surprise it was completely odourless and tasteless, "Seems fine to me."

Pinto smiled. "It's rabbit stew, if you hadn't already guessed. All the vegetables are from the garden." He wrapped a dishcloth around his hands to lift the dish from the range. He served up two generous portions of the stew and cut two thick slices of granary bread. "Now, I have a confession to make." Pinto sat down opposite Sam and tucked himself closer to the table. His expression was serious.

Sam was on edge once more but did his best to remain calm, "What's that, then?"

"It's a little awkward. You see I've done something bad." Pinto scratched the back of his neck. "Can you keep a secret, Sam?" Steam rose up from his plate into his face as he leant in closer.

"Sure."

"I don't know how to say this but…" He rubbed his face. "… I've *stolen* a couple of bottles of your client's wine from the cellar." A huge grin stretched across Pinto's face and he leant back in his supercilious manner.

Sam laughed, "As long as it's good wine, I won't tell. How about that?"

"Deal." Pinto got up and fetched two bottles from the dresser next to the window. They were covered in dust, with red waxed seals over the cork. He placed one bottle on the far end of the table and presented the other to Sam as a sommelier in a French restaurant would, resting the base of the bottle on his forearm and displaying the label, "A *Château Margaux* 1934, sir?"

Sam knew enough about wine to know that *Château Margaux* was one of the most expensive vineyards in France. He couldn't work Pinto out. Was he showing off, trying to impress him? Perhaps he was just lonely in this house in the middle of nowhere.

"Thirty four was the only good year *Margaux* had in the thirties. I'm not much of a wine drinker but I have been looking for an excuse to try this." He made light work of the cork and poured a couple of glasses.

"Cheers!" they said in unison.

The wine was fantastic – ripe with blackcurrant and silky smooth. And so too was the food; the meat, carrots and potatoes were cooked in a rich, herby sauce. Sam complimented the chef and Pinto returned the compliment by topping up Sam's glass.

They ate in silence as the shadows grew longer and blacker across the kitchen as the sun gave up for the day, disappearing beyond the trees and hills. It was Pinto who spoke first, "So, tell me about yourself. Who is the man I'm dining with tonight?"

Sam hated talking about himself. "What do you want to know?"

"What sort of banker are you – what qualifies you to do this? How many big houses have you had to evaluate for your clients? I can't believe this is common for bankers."

It was almost as if Pinto knew this wasn't normal business for Sam. He took another sip of his wine while he considered his answer, "It's very common for a bank to want to thoroughly understand the collateral against its loans."

Pinto nodded, "Do you enjoy your work?"

Again, Sam felt Pinto's questions were rhetorical. "No I don't, to be honest. It's pretty pointless." He felt an unexpected release at saying the words out loud.

"So why do it? Why drag yourself up here for a job you think is pointless?"

"Pointless is the wrong word. I just mean..." Sam's words trailed off as he thought, the booze not helping.

"Yes." Pinto was now leaning forward slightly, in anticipation of Sam's answer.

"I don't know, it's complicated."

"You mean you have grown tired of your job because it lacks meaning for you, Sam. Is that it?"

Sam nodded.

"But you do it because it's easy, because it furnishes a lifestyle you've become accustomed to, even though the job is all consuming and leaves you with little time to have a life. Am I right?"

"That's about it, yes." Sam spread some butter on his bread to avoid eye contact with Pinto.

"Don't beat yourself up, Sam. It took me a while to realise I was wasting my time... living a life without meaning. I spent twenty one years in the army before I woke up and stopped wasting my time. You know, I only joined the army to impress my father." Pinto rubbed his chin.

Sam ran his hand through his hair, he thought of his own father getting Jerry to give him an internship at Gema Bank, the internship then became a graduate job… On the treadmill ever since. "I know that feeling."

Pinto winced, "Fathers," he smiled, "they fuck you up." He opened the second bottle of *Château Margaux* and served up second helpings of the stew. Pinto lit a couple of candles as the sun finally set, leaving the sky utterly black, unpolluted by streetlight. The rustic kitchen glowed in the gentle light and the fire crackled in the range.

Sam felt compelled to say something. "Do you entertain many guests here?" he asked.

"You're my first," said Pinto not looking up from his plate.

"Sounds lonely."

Pinto mopped up the last of the gravy on his plate with his bread. He paused to think about his response before replying. "I was in London briefly before coming here. In London there is everything you could ever want – great food, women, theatres, museums, galleries… you name it, you've got it. But despite that, everyone I met in London, including myself, was filled with a dread of how scarce everything was. We were convinced there wasn't enough to go around. Life was a constant competition – a fight. Survival of the fittest, the wealthiest." He ate his saturated bread.

Sam considered what Pinto had just said, surprised at how thought provoking it was.

Pinto waited until his mouth was empty before continuing, "Don't you think that's funny? Having so much causes you to feel so hungry. Up here it's the opposite. On

Aul you may say there's nothing to do, there's nothing going on. But I tell you, when I'm up here it reminds me just how abundant the world is. A world at peace with itself, where plants, trees and animals get on with their lives. There's more than enough for each of us." Pinto raised his eyebrows as if he'd just had a good idea, "Yes, that's why I've been so happy here. I only hope I can remember that after I've left."

"Why don't you stay on the island then?"

Pinto swigged his wine. "I have plans elsewhere. Plus there is nowhere else to live on Aul. The island's Charter states that a majority of islanders need to support your application to build a new home on the island, and as you may have gathered I'm not the most popular guy on the island." He stood up and cleared the table, gesturing to Sam to remain seated as Sam attempted to help him.

"Why is that?"

"Because I represent *change*. People around here, particularly the ones who've stayed, don't like that."

"I don't follow."

"Oh, you will." Pinto put the plates in the butler's sink and ran the tap over them, "You and your client represent change now." He switched the tap off and dried his hands on a dishcloth. He came back to the table, his cheeks flushed by the alcohol.

"You mean they didn't like you living in Aul House?"

"The Laird was very important to them and the island. His family owned this island for about five hundred years. The story goes that his family helped hide King James I from would-be assassins on this island and in return the King gave them the island to keep. Ever since then they've lived here, as the Lairds of Aul – a title given to them by their many tenant crofters of the time. The last Laird was born in 1900, an only child. He lost his father in the First World War and his mother died shortly afterwards. He was only seventeen when he became Laird but that didn't mean he wasn't ready. From what I've read, he brought the island into the twentieth century with electricity and plumbing. Then the second of the world wars erupted and the Laird, just like his father before him, went off to fight the Hun." Pinto topped up their wine glasses. He held his glass up to the candle light and admired the deep red colour of the wine.

"And what happened to him?"

Pinto looked sternly at Sam, his supercilious expression returned; that glint in his eye, of knowing something Sam didn't, seemed to amuse him. "Let's just say war changed him. Soldiering became his life. He seldom returned to the island again."

"I see. Then he died, without an heir and the house has been held in trust ever since, right?" Sam wanted to prove he was keeping up and secretly enjoyed breaking the raconteur's flow.

Pinto ignored the interruption; recounting the story appeared an almost cathartic experience. "When the Laird returned from war he had become consumed by paranoia and fear of something terrible happening again. In fact, he became convinced Aul would be targeted."

Sam sniggered.

"It's not as fanciful as you think. For centuries Aul was used as a lookout. The remains of the ancient fort still stand on Northern Head at the top of the island."

Sam could see the intensity in Pinto's eyes. "So he left Aul because he didn't feel safe here?"

"No. He dug-in." Pinto stared at Sam. "He took all of the animals and crofts off the land between here and Northern Head, sent half a dozen crofters to the south, and then he laid mines between the house and the fort."

"Mines?"

"Yes, landmines. They're still there." Pinto got up and walked towards the door that led back into the hall but stopped short to reach for a picture frame hanging on the wall. He returned to the table and placed the picture face down on the oak top. He took something from his trouser pocket.

Sam couldn't tell what it was until the click of a switch snapped out a six inch steel blade. The steel caught the flickering candle light as Pinto carefully cut around the brown tape on the back of the picture frame. He lifted out a yellowing piece of paper from beneath the backing card and slid the paper across the table. Sam turned the paper over and saw the date in the corner said 1901, beneath a hand-drawn map of the circular Island. Aul House was just above centre, directly below *Northern Head* at the top. *The Village* and various landmarks were also marked in a neat cartographer's hand.

"All the land between the bottom of the garden, just the other side of the arboretum, up to the beach at Northern Head is covered in landmines. That's one reason why folk don't like visiting the house."

"There goes the hotel," said Sam under his breath.

"The what?" Pinto leant over the table and pulled the map back.

"Nothing." Sam picked up his wine to distract his fidgety hands, his eyes on the blade still in Pinto's hand. "What's the *other* reason they don't come to the house?"

Pinto put the map on the dresser. He used his thigh to return the retractable blade into the handle and placed it on top of the map. He patted his trousers in search of something. "Do you mind if I smoke? I like one after a meal." He found what he was looking for, but only after he'd taken out his bunch of keys and placed them next to the knife. He offered Sam a cigarette from the box.

Sam took one but his eyes and his mind were on the keys on the dresser.

Pinto used the candle from the table to light both their cigarettes, before continuing, "The ghost… It was five years after living as a recluse when the Laird suddenly disappeared. Rumour is he went back into the army. The house was deserted for twenty years. The Laird was gone. Has been gone ever since. But plenty of people claim they see him wandering the island late at night. Some are so convinced they daren't even look at the house for fear of the devil."

"So how did *you* get here?"

"The Laird put the house into a trust before he left, ruling at some point after his death, providing he had no children, the house would be sold and the proceeds be given to the islanders. So, I was hired by The Trust to mind the house these last thirty years. They couldn't get a local to do it, you see."

It was Sam's turn to rub his chin.

"What?" Pinto could see Sam wasn't convinced about something.

"If the locals stand to gain from the sale of the house then why do you say they won't be happy about it? This place will be worth a fair amount with all the land – there's a few thousand pounds per head."

Pinto crouched down to pick up more peat for the fire. "What use is money when there's nothing you want to buy? The folk who cared for money left the island a long time ago."

Sam shook his head and smiled. "And what about governance of the island, how does that work now the Laird has gone?"

"Back to the Charter, Sam. The islanders have been running the island themselves since World War II, since the Laird left to fight. It's simple, when an islander reaches eighteen they get a seat at the Island Council, should they want it; that's where all matters of island government are decided. Your number of years on the island is your number of votes." Pinto shrugged, "It's a system designed to ensure Aul never changes."

"So why don't they vote the new owner of Aul House out, if that's what they want?"

"They can't. The Laird was clear when he drew up the Charter. Aul House was always out of bounds. The house and its owner remain immune."

"Above the law?"

"Above the law."

"And it's housekeeper?"

"Aye." Pinto put on a thick highland accent and grinned. Both men laughed.

23:15

The rain and wind had returned, scratching and rattling the French doors of the small drawing room at the back of the house. Pinto closed the curtains and lit a fire. Sam felt sleepy as he nursed another whisky on the sofa closest to the hearth, the warmth from the flames adding to his drowsiness. Pinto watered his beloved plants around the room, giving extra attention to the purple flower with the miraculous healing properties. Sam remained wary of Pinto; his eccentric obsession with his flowers added to the mystery and intrigue. Both men had had enough to drink, Sam thought now would be a good time to bid good night.

"I should be calling it a night," Sam got up from the sofa, "I've got a big day ahead of me tomorrow."

Pinto continued to tend to one of his plants, his back turned to Sam, "Is that right? What's your plan?"

"I'll start by taking a look around the island, I think. That should keep me busy all morning…"

White light strobed rapidly from behind the curtains, like a gang of paparazzi flashbulbs going off at the window. Before Sam could say anything an almighty crash of thunder roared overhead. The wind and rain picked up. The lights flickered on and off as the house was gripped by a ferocious thunderstorm. Pinto turned around, his intense eyes fixed directly at the light bulb, as if daring the bulb to go off again. Another flash and crash as the rain intensified and the wind howled and whistled louder. Sam remembered the boat earlier and a flutter of anxiety rolled through his stomach.

"Good night," said Sam. He took his glass with him.

"Good night."

Sam was turning the door knob when the lights flickered off and on once more. He heard Pinto mutter something under his breath but he didn't catch what as he left the drawing room and out into the hallway. It was dark and cool, with the sound of the storm now distinctly quieter. Woozy from all the booze, he walked toward the seed room under the stairs, tucked away in the shadows, hidden from the chandelier hanging above the grand staircase. An idea had suddenly consumed him and he didn't hesitate to think anymore. He looked back at the drawing room. The door was still firmly closed. He put his glass down slowly on the step in front of him, careful to place it silently on the runner. Quickly, he went to the room under the stairs. Standing on his tiptoes he reached for the wooden box above the doorframe. He ran his hands around the box's dusty, splintery edges until he found a catch. He fiddled with his index finger until the catch sprang open and the front of the box swung open. The old hinges creaked and Sam froze. His heart was thumping and his palms clammed up. He waited a few seconds before moving again, pulling the door open far enough to be able to see inside. Bingo! It was the fusebox. In the dim light he could just about make out it was an old-fashioned set up of fuses, not the modern trip switches he was used to seeing. There were a dozen fuses and Sam had no idea what was what. He swallowed hard. Stretching as tall as he could he pulled the middle fuse away. He closed his eyes, fearful of an electric shock as the fuse came loose. He opened his eyes again. Nothing had happened. He pushed it back in. This time he tried the first fuse. His shoes scraped over the stone floor as he reached and pulled. *Crack*! His arm was thrown back as a blue spark flew out of the fusebox. The lights went off and Sam was thrown to the ground.

Pinto shouted from the drawing room. Sam couldn't see a thing. It was utterly black. His arm felt numb and pins and needles travelled through his fingers, still gripping the fuse. He got to his feet and groped around for the fusebox. Pinto was still swearing and his voice was getting louder. Sam ran his hand along the row of porcelain components as he felt for the socket to return his fuse back into. The fuse was hot. He found the socket and forced it back in. With his free hand he swung the door closed. It creaked as it went and clattered as the catch locked. Pinto came out of the drawing room. Sam swung around and crept onto the staircase. His shoe kicked the glass of whisky, sending it smashing onto the flagstones at the foot of the stairs.

"Sam?" shouted Pinto. His voice was gruff.

Sam took a deep breath, "What happened? I was on my way upstairs and the lights went off. I dropped my glass. Be careful where you step."

Neither man could see the other in the darkness.

There was a pause before Pinto replied.

Sam could hear him moving through the dark space.

"Is that so?" Pinto's words were slow and drawn out, steeped in suspicion.

"It must have been the lightning." Sam was convinced he sounded guilty.

Pinto's footsteps were getting louder as he moved towards him. Sam stood frozen on the bottom step of the staircase, his hand gripping the banister. Suddenly a heavy hand landed on his shoulder. Sam jumped.

"What's wrong? Not scared of the dark are you?" said Pinto, his warm alcoholic breath in Sam's face.

Sam forced a laugh, "Not with you around."

"Well, I'll need to get the generator going. Will you be alright without me for a few minutes?" His tone was sardonic and he slurred his words. He took his hand off

Sam's shoulder and moved off through the darkness, his boot crunched on the broken glass.

Sam's heart beat faster and his hand squeezed tighter to the rail. He daren't move. Gradually his eyes adjusted to the darkness and the orange glow from the fire in the drawing room was enough to allow him to make out the macabre stags' heads along the walls.

Pinto shuffled around the side tables. Eventually he found the oil lamp he was searching for. Its pale light was enough to light his way to the fusebox. He held the lamp above his head as he inspected the box. Sam held his breath and strained his eyes as he peered at the fuses, hoping for no signs of his involvement.

"It will have to be the generator," Pinto sighed. "It's around the back."

"Why don't you wait until it's light?"

Pinto turned around and held the lamp to Sam's face. Sam squinted as the light dazzled his dilated pupils.

"I have a lot of things to do this evening, Sam."

Sam took a step back, moving up a step on the staircase. "Do you want any help?"

"No, I'll be quicker alone. You take this and I'll see you in the morning." Pinto handed Sam the oil lamp before striding across the hall to the front door.

Sam watched as he put on his coat, pulled up the collar and opened the front door. The wind was wild and the rain sounded like a crowd at a football match as the storm attacked the house from all angles. Pinto slammed the door behind him and the great hall was near-silent once more. Sam couldn't believe his plan had worked. He had no time to waste. He had no idea how long Pinto would be gone for. He was quickly down the stairs and across the hall into the kitchen. The smell of tobacco hung in the air, mixed with the leftover food and peat that smouldered in the range. Thunder rumbled in the distance as the storm moved over the island. The keys were still on the dresser, where Pinto had left them. Sam picked them up. He picked the flick knife up too. It was menacingly cold and heavy. A second of indecision froze him before he reminded himself he was incapable of using it. He put it back down and left the kitchen.

Back in the hallway he double-checked Pinto had not returned before heading to the room under the stairs. There were a couple dozen keys in the bunch and Sam dropped them twice as he nervously tried key after key with his free hand, the other forced to hold the clunky lamp. It must have been the tenth key before he got one to turn in the lock. The door swung open and Sam went in, closing it behind him. The briefcase was directly in front of him. He put the lamp down on the table next to the briefcase. His heart was pounding against his chest. All the time his ears were trained on the hallway for any sound of Pinto.

SETH FALCORRS said the gold letters below the handle. The combination lock was set to 0000. Sam placed his thumbs on the two lock-release switches and pushed. The catches sprung open. The sound echoed around the tiny room. Then silence once more. Only the sound of Sam's breathing. He opened the case. Inside was a navy blue exercise book. It was the sort of book Sam remembered from junior school. He took it out and placed it on the table. He checked the rest of the case but there was nothing more. The case was in every way identical to the one his father had left him. It didn't make sense. He picked the exercise book up and folded it lengthways, shoving it into the waistband of his flannels, hidden beneath his shirt, behind his back. The book felt awkward but it freed his hands to deal with the lamp and keys.

He was on his way out of the room when Pinto came crashing back through the front door, a gust of wind accompanying his return. The front door slammed. Sam pulled back and closed the seed room door, with him still inside. He could hear Pinto moving through the hallway. *Fuck. Fuck. Fuck.*

He crouched down and put the lamp on the floor. Thankfully he had remembered the key for the lock and he locked the door from the inside. The keys jangled as he turned the bunch three hundred and sixty degrees around the lock. On all fours he crawled under the table, beneath the briefcase. He could hear Pinto's heavy footsteps through the hallway. *Shit.* He blew out the lamp and was plunged into total darkness once more. Suddenly the door rattled as Pinto tried the handle. *Fuck. Fuck.* Like a cornered animal Sam made himself as small as possible, his stomach now on the cold, hard floor. Pinto must have been checking the door, reassured it was locked. He obviously didn't trust Sam and there was something in here he was trying to keep to himself. But there was no time to search for anything else. Sam waited until there was no sound of Pinto and got back to his feet. Through the dark he went to the door. He peered through the keyhole. The electricity was back on. He couldn't see Pinto but that didn't mean he wasn't waiting on the other side of the door, just out of sight. Sam stood up. *Think. Think.*

He weighed up his options. Stay or move? He took a deep breath and put the key back in the lock. Everything he did now would be fast and deliberate, if Pinto was waiting for him then he'd fight as ferociously as he could... The key rattled as it turned. In a single move he opened the door and stepped out into the bright hallway. No Pinto. He locked the door. He hurried across the hallway to the kitchen. Pinto was inside, obviously searching for his keys. Sam remembered the flick knife. There was no way he was going in. Back across the hallway he went, to the drawing room. The fire had died down but the lights were back on. Sam dropped the keys next to the glass case with the purple flower, he caught a glimpse of its quivering tendrils drooping around that vivid purple flower. Then he was out and up the stairs, practically running until he was onto the landing, amongst the white sheets covering the artwork along the east wing, looking like pantomime ghosts.

Still wary of Pinto, Sam sat on the floor with his back against his bedroom door – a human barricade. From here he would hear Pinto approaching before it was too late. He pulled the exercise book from his waistband and in his haste his shirt became un-tucked. A rush of the chilly draught that poured in under the door tingled over his spine. But he didn't move. Only his chest rose and fell with the shortness of his breath as he held the blue book in his hands.

He opened it to the first page, the paper was lined and rough, yellowed with age. In the top right-hand corner written in a neat, cursive style was the name *Richard West*. Sam knew the name: His father's late brother, his Uncle Richard who he had never met, who had died a few months after Sam was born. He turned the page. *Notes & Transcripts with Charles Frost* written in the same hand… Sam bit down on his bottom lip, hitched his knees up to his chest for warmth and read…

My name is Charles Frost. Everything I did, I did for my King, my Queen and my country... My story begins with me on my knees... My hands were punctured by thorns. Blistered. Swollen, Bloodied. Slowly I moved – left hand, left leg, right hand, right leg. The weight of my pack slumped over my shoulders. Blood rushed to my head. Sweat and dirt stung my eyes. I could hear the hiss. The river wasn't far... The men were close. Their inane, high-pitched chatter. Gunshots clattered through the trees... Along the slimy, choking jungle floor. I yearned for the river... The tide would set me free. Perhaps a paddy field lay beyond. Shelter and cover.... A dog barked itself into a frenzy. I covered my face. I heard the crack before I felt the pain of the butt of a rifle buried into the side of my face.

I slept for seven days. They removed my handcuffs only to allow me to eat a little rice and fish. I drank coffee and occasionally some whisky. A private helped me down to the latrine once a day but he stood so close it was sometimes impossible to go. When I did, my piss ran red and black. It was backwater fever – this meant the malaria was lifting.

I watched the Japs from my tent. They made hard work of the jungle. They feared its black, cold nights. They dreaded the snakes and giant insects. They regularly got lost. They struggled to hunt the wild boar and monkeys. Their wild, frightened gunfire drained the area of potential food.

I was given time to rest. On the twenty fifth day I could stand without a stick. They had taken my boots. This was good. I needed to thicken my soles before I escaped. Boots would only leave a trail. They allowed me a notebook and pencil. I sat near the fire and wrote. I noted their routine and hierarchy. I drew pictures of the camp. I learnt a little Japanese. My malaria lifted and the headaches and fever subsided.

On the sixty second day we left the camp. We trekked for fifty miles north, following the river. I pretended to be as tired as the scrawny Japs. My hands were cuffed in front of me. A Private kept his rifle trained on me. He didn't mind reminding me of this fact, with the steel barrel hard into my back, when I slipped or moved too quickly. We arrived at a small clearing in the middle of a bitterly cold night. I was told where to pitch my tent. I watched them eat and get drunk around the fire… I wondered whether the Chinese guerrillas had managed to organise themselves enough to provide the distraction I needed to escape. That night I slept well.

It was dawn when the Private kicked me and dragged me out of my sleeping bag. I climbed to my feet. I felt stronger than I had in months. I was pointed towards a small hut. The air was beginning to warm. The sky was all but hidden beyond the dark-green jungle canopy. We entered the hut. In the corner was a bed and table. In the other a Japanese officer sat behind a desk. The Officer ordered my handcuffs be removed and we were left alone.

"Please sit down," said the Officer in confident English.

This was the first English I had heard in over eight months.

"What is your name and rank?" he continued.

Since my capture I had been wondering what to call myself should I have been asked. I had to stall for time as my brain wasn't used to speaking after so long alone in the jungle. "My rank?"

"Come now. Don't play games. We both know you are a soldier in the British Army. Name and rank. As your captor I am entitled to know." The Officer remained impassive.

"My name is Charles Frost," Yes, my brain was back. That name was there all along. I liked it, it was certainly British sounding – English even – and delightfully cold.

"Rank?"

"I'm not a soldier. I work for the British diplomatic corps."

"A spy." He smiled and pressed his palms together, holding his index fingers up to his lips.

"An aid worker," I lied.

"How is your health?"

"Good."

In your notebook you write about an island. I assume this island is Singapore. You were stationed there too?"

"No. I dream of escaping to Singapore." This was a lie. I longed to be back home on Aul – my island.

The Officer laughed. "We have taken Singapore. You will die in this jungle. I will decide when."

"I will not be killed by your men or the jungle."

"My men tell me you have been living in the jungle for a long time. They tell me you have trained and fought with the Chinese resistance. You will tell me everything."

"Your men are mistaken." This was a lie.

"You are mistaken, Mr Frost." He called for the Private.

The Private entered the hut and the Officer's mood changed in an instant. His calm erupted into a puce-faced rage.

The Private raised his rifle. He span to face me. He cocked his weapon. He grinned. He took aim through one eye and emptied the barrel into my right knee.

I passed-out instantly.

I was tied and left to bleed on the mud floor. I tried not to flinch with pain as the Officer collected samples of my blood. He cleaned my wound and bandaged my knee. The Officer and Private lifted me onto the bed and strapped my body down so firmly I could only move my fingers and toes. The bed was dragged into the middle of the room. The Officer slapped me across the face to prevent me from passing out again.

"I will have to operate to remove the bullet from your knee. If I do not your knee will become infected and you will lose your leg. If you lose your leg you will die."

"Do what you like, you bastard." I yelled, as much to purge the pain, as it was anger and contempt for the hideous man.

"I am glad you understand. Do not worry, I am a doctor." He patted me gently on the shoulder in macabre reassurance.

"You're certainly no soldier," I spat.

This angered him and he pulled his pistol from his holster and held it to my head. "I should kill you. But before I do this you will be of some use to us."

I struggled to break free but it was useless. I was bound far too well.

The Officer stroked my shoulder once more. "Despite what you think, you are not my enemy, Mr Frost."

"You don't know what I think."

"My enemy is disease. The mosquito and its malaria is what threatens my men most. My only fear is that my men will be too ill to enjoy winning this war."

"Your men are not soldiers either."

"Careful, Mr Frost." He lowered his hand onto my wounded knee. "I cannot concentrate when I am angry." He re-holstered his gun.

He prepared a syringe and injected my left arm.

The room became a blur, my body limp and numb. But I remained conscious. He began his operation to remove the bullet. He was fast and proficient – obviously well practiced at the procedure. He put the bullet in a small box which he labelled with Japanese characters. He went to his desk and unlocked the drawer. He took out a book and locked the drawer. He sat at his desk and studied the book for some time... Soldiers delivered boxes to the hut. One was full of leaves and flowers. Another contained flasks of water. Three small pestle and mortars were placed on the table next to me. The Officer worked alone, tirelessly, for what felt like the best part of an hour, carefully pounding, crushing and mixing the leaves and flowers into a paste. He consulted his book regularly. He was neat and methodical. He took great pride in his work. From his frequent, bright eyed glances, I could tell he enjoyed me watching his every move.

The Officer gathered up all of his equipment. He washed down the table and his hands. The paste was locked in his drawer. He left the hut and walked around the back. I could see him through the window. He glanced over his shoulder to check he was alone and disappeared into the thick jungle. He was gone two minutes before he returned with a flower that looked like a purple orchid – bright purple petals and wispy green leaves. He carried the plant with peculiar care, sheltering it in his arms, as if holding a newborn baby. Using his knife he took a cutting of one of the leaves. He went to his desk and unlocked the drawer and took out the pestle and mortar. He added the leaf and continued pounding and pressing, adding a little water as he went. He warmed the contents of the mortar over a candle. He took the bullet from its box and using tweezers held it in the flame of the candle, before dropping it into the mortar and smothering it with the purple mixture. He undressed my wound. I knew what was coming next. I closed my eyes and gritted my teeth, determined not to scream as he reinserted the bullet, deep into my knee. A few stitches closed the wound. He cleaned and dressed the knee with new bandages.

I said nothing as he made notes in his book. He moistened a cloth with cool water and wiped away the sweat that covered my face. He returned to his desk and un-locked his drawer once more. This time he took out a gramophone and placed it on his desk. He screwed on the speaker funnel and wound it up, placing the needle carefully onto the record. Beethoven's *Moonlight* sonata filled the small hut. It was a beautiful, welcome distraction from the hell of my situation. The satisfied Officer sat back in his chair and smoked a cigarette.

"Mr Frost, you are brave," he said.

I ignored him. Focussing on the gentle piano and the smell of tobacco smoke.

He continued: "You are enjoying the music, I can tell. I enjoy this music also… I often wonder why I enjoy music so much, why I find it so satisfying… So nourishing. Do you ever wonder about this, Charles?"

I closed my eyes.

"I have studied this point back at home in Japan. Before this war I read the work of many musical scholars. They tell me that what the great composers like Beethoven did so well is to build us up, to bring our senses to a heightened state of attention, to create maximum tension. They take us to that point where we can't take anymore and then…" He paused to soak up some more of the music, as if this was all artfully rehearsed, his speech timed with the music, just as the first movement broke from its theme and the pianist

159

moved up the keyboard into that wonderful climb that illustrated his point. "And then what do they do, Mr Frost? They set us free. They release us from their grip… Resolution. Resolution. Resolution…" Just as the first movement came to an end and the spritely second movement began… "They call this a *cadence*, Mr Frost. And the most satisfying of all is the *perfect cadence*. It is the perfect cadence that tells us we've come to the end. Everything is resolved."

We remained in silence, savouring the music… Until the end of the finale of the third and final movement… Until the perfect cadence.

I was carried to another hut on the eastern side of the camp. The dark, wooden room had one window which had been barricaded with bamboo. A bed and a bucket in the corner. My convalescence was short – my knee had healed within three days, I felt no pain. The Officer came to remove the stitches and examined me thoroughly. He was amazed by my complete recovery.

"You are strong, Mr Frost," said the Officer. "It was a very successful procedure. You have taught me a lot. Thank you for this. Your death will not be in vain."

The Officer left.

I felt strong. Focused. Sharp. I was ready to escape.

With every new day I felt more energy return to my muscles. The scar on my knee had faded away. I was restless in the hut. I demanded to be released back into the camp but I was ignored. My restlessness turned to frustration. Frustration turned to anger. On my twenty third day in the hut I waited for the guard to deliver breakfast. The door was unlocked. The dish was placed on the floor.

Thump! Fractured cheekbone.

Stamp! Broken ribs.

Crush! An inaudible yelp… His final gasp.

I dragged the body into the hut and closed the door. I took the dead man's rifle and fatigue-coat. I laid the body on the bed and covered it with my blanket. All the time I remained calm.

Outside the thick, sweet air of the jungle replaced the stale, rotted stench of the hut. Crouching, I moved swiftly amongst the tall mallows and hibiscus trees. With each quick step I felt the air expand my lungs. My heart pumped with conviction, sending a fierce and chilling blood around my invigorated muscles. A polluting, single minded blood that filled me with a rage like never before. A soldier stood at the latrine. I was instinctive and decisive, leaving the man face down in the mud he had just watered.

It wasn't hard to go unnoticed around the perimeter of the camp, past the short-sighted guards. It wasn't hard to locate the Officer's hut either as I followed the sound of Beethoven. I crouched beneath the window and savoured the music. This time is was *Sonata 21*. My finger was poised on the trigger as I kicked down the door – the whole thing fell off its hinges and slid over the mud floor towards the desk where the Officer sat frozen. He just looked at me and smiled. I cocked my rifle. The Officer's grin broadened and he slowly took another drag on his cigarette.

"This piece, Mr Frost, is my favourite Beethoven piano sonata. In fact it's my favourite piece of music."

I aimed the rifle at his chest. The Officer raised his hands above his head, smoke swirling around his face. He showed no signs of fear. I respected him for this, which is why I must have allowed him to continue.

"Beethoven called this piece '*Waldstein*', dedicated to his patron – Count Ferdinand Ernst Gabriel von Waldstein, to give him his full name. You see, even the most gifted and talented men need a benefactor, somebody to look after them. Somebody who has the resources that will sustain them."

"I don't want your money," I said, striding towards my target, the crosshairs of my sight tracking up between his eyes.

The Officer shrugged and laughed, "I don't insult you with money. I offer you something money cannot buy." His large black eyes glanced down at his desk. There open on his desk was his notebook.

I stepped in closer until my knees touched the desk. The Officer flinched. For the first time I saw his vulnerability, his disappointment. His glance had betrayed him. He was caught in two minds between saving himself and saving the notebook. Whatever was in there was more important than his own life. Then I knew he was a soldier. He was a man capable of putting his country before himself.

The Officer screamed and snatched his notebook off the desk, shouting for help. But I was ready for him. I swung my weapon around and was over that desk, clubbing him with the butt in the side of his head. He fell and I was down on top of him. We mauled on the floor, but I had the advantage throughout, I prized the notebook away from him. The Officer screamed in Japanese, his nose bloodied and hair a mess. I kicked the wind from his solar plexus and this silenced him as I flicked through the book. It was all neat Japanese characters that meant nothing to me. But the detailed, skilled drawings were loud and clear. It was the purple flower he adored so much – the flower he had used on the bullet in my knee. The Officer was writhing and screaming, trying to get up. The *Waldstein* sonata was in its final throws – the grand finale. Crazed cries of panic came from outside as the alarm of my escape was raised. I had to move fast. On the floor next to the desk was a stack of boxes, filled with glass bottles. I kicked them over, glass smashed and liquids ran over the floor. The Officer knew what was coming next.

"Your Waldstein, Mr Frost. I can be your Waldstein," he pleaded.

I took his gold lighter from the desk. The floor and cardboard boxes were ablaze immediately.

The Officer rolled up in a ball as the flames licked up around him. I was out before the smoke could enter my lungs...

I came under fire. I secured the notebook in my pocket and crawled through the long grass away from the camp and toward the cover of the jungle. The gunfire grew louder and closer. I felt no fear. Everything was crystal clear.

I turned around; at the window of the hut stood the Officer, his face black with soot. He was holding his pistol and had it aimed at me. Into the trees I went, immediately cooled by the thick canopy. And there, growing at the foot of an hibiscus, was the purple flower. There were about a dozen of them. I looked back at the window. The Officer just stood there and watched me. He could have fired at any point but he didn't. He knew I had spared his life. I crouched down and used my fingers to dig deep, down into the warm, damp earth. I was quick but careful, going around and beneath the roots. The plant was free, its fine, white roots intact within a fist-full of soil. I looked back at the hut for the final time... The Officer saluted me. I nodded back. That was all that was required.

And I was gone.

Day Three

07:15

Slumped over knees hitched-up to his chest, Sam woke with a stiff neck and aching back. Wedged between his thighs was the exercise book that had kept him up most of the night. He'd read the twenty three pages of hand written notes five times before finally falling asleep. Sam groaned as he got up. Two nights of bad sleep mixed with last night's wine and whisky had left his knees and hips cracking and clicking, his head sore and mouth like cotton wool.

He pulled open the sash window and the room filled with the sound of birdsong. The morning air was chilly but still. Even though the sky was a dull grey the view over the garden and ancient pine forest was breathtaking. Sam splashed cold water on his face at the sink and brushed his teeth. Thankfully he could get away without shaving. All the time his mind worked through the revelations of last night, attempting to make sense of it all. He drank murky water direct from the tap and this immediately subdued his thumping head.

Sam changed into new underwear, his second pair of grey flannels, white shirt, v-neck sweater and coat. It was Wednesday morning. He had two full days before the party tomorrow night, when George would be here. He slipped on his socks and shoes. He put the exercise book and phone in his pocket, rediscovering the bottle of whisky he had left and the chocolate he'd bought at the airport in London. In the other was the phone George had given him. He didn't need to speak to George. He could solve this thing himself, just as he had solved every other problem laid before him. After all, that's what he was good at – solving problems. This was just like finding the right trade at the bank. Gathering all of the information and finding the answer. This was just like the *StarzHotel* deal – about remaining calm and thinking laterally when others lose their heads in fear and panic. He zipped up his coat with a real sense of purpose and went downstairs.

There was no sign of Pinto as Sam made his way across the grand hallway. He walked as heavily as he could across the flagstones to alert Pinto of his presence but Sam was alone. Cardboard boxes secured with brown tape were stacked three high. The bell jars and glass cases of plants that had cluttered two sides of the huge space were gone. Sam went into the drawing room, hoping to get a better look at the purple flower but this room too had been packed up, all that remained were the leather bound books on the bookshelves and the tatty furniture.

In the kitchen the washing up from last night had been done and the pots, pans and crockery all packed away. Sam checked a few cupboards and drawers on the oversized dresser – all bare. He held his hand over the range and felt no heat. Pinto had been busy. All of this cleaning and packing was several hours' work for one man. Pinto could hardly have slept. Hanging on the wall was the map of Aul that Pinto had shown him at dinner. Sam took it off the wall and freed the thin paper from its frame. He folded the map in four and put it in his inside coat pocket. He pulled the nail the frame had been hanging on from the wall and threw it into the dusty darkness behind the dresser. He dropped the empty picture frame in there too. Out of sight, out of mind.

Sam hesitated at the sight of a golf umbrella amongst the collection of walking sticks and riding props in a mahogany rack next to the front door. But he decided against it. It was still dry and he didn't want to be hampered by anything as big as the umbrella.

There was not a single sound in his ears until the crunch-crunch of the gravel beneath his shoes as Sam strode to the village. He felt exhilarated that he was now on the offensive, taking positive steps to solving this problem. But nagging in the back of his mind was the fact he was not sure who he was going to meet or how he was going to solve anything.

As Sam walked he held the exercise book firmly in his pocket. He was certain this was his late Uncle Richard's note book. Sam knew very little about his uncle, but what he did know did chime with what he had read and re-read through the night. He knew Richard had committed suicide just after Sam was born. He was found dead in a hotel room in London. Before that he was a writer who failed to get any of his own work published but had had a degree of success as a ghost writer, writing celebrity 'autobiographies' and pulp fiction. Richard must have been writing on behalf of Charles Frost. As far as he knew, the Frost story was never published. His father had all of Richard's ghost written books in his study. Sam remembered packing them up after his father's death – footballers, comedians and rock stars but no Charles Frost. The hardback copies were dusty, their spines faded and, most surprisingly, un-read. His father had never read them, it was presumably too painful. Richard left no note when he died but his father's personal theory was his brother's perceived sense of failure at never getting his *own* work published had driven him to take his life. Nobody spoke much more about it beyond that.

It was fifteen minutes of walking along a well worn track south before Sam met anyone else. A couple in their fifties riding horses without helmets were heading east. Sam made a point of smiling and waving effusively. "How do you do," he called out.

The couple only nodded and rode off at a canter.

"Great meeting you, enjoy your ride," Sam mumbled under his breath.

Five minutes later the trees thinned out and the track widened into an asphalt path that led down a steep incline into the village. Twenty or so weather beaten pebble dashed bungalows with the odd miserable looking two storey building stood around three sides of a cobbled square. The fourth side was dominated by a church that looked big enough to serve an entire London borough, far too big for this small island community. It wasn't just its size that struck Sam but the uncanny resemblance it bore to Aul House. The brick and the turrets echoed the grand house, so too the shape and style of the window surrounds and lintels. The stained glass sparkled even in the grey light of the morning. Unlike the houses, the stone masonry was immaculate – almost new looking.

Sam slid over the smooth cobblestones. He could feel the hard, round stones pushing into his feet through his leather soles. He headed for the centre of the square where a six foot stone cross stood on a stone platform three steps tall with *Never Forget* carved along the horizontal. He looked around, the place was deserted save for three horses tied up outside one of the larger properties. There were no signs, names or numbers on any of the buildings. All of the windows were veiled by net curtains. It reminded him of a scene from a Spaghetti Western – he was the new kid in town. He was drawn to the horses as the only form of life in this grim place. The front door of the building they were tethered to opened and the sound of music from a transistor radio rattled around the square. Isla, the teenage girl from yesterday's welcome party, stepped out carrying a paper bag. She froze and blushed when she saw Sam.

"Hello again," said Sam.

"Hi." Isla looked down at the ground.

"Bought anything nice?"

"Aye, just breakfast rolls." She raised the bag under her arm a couple of inches, still not managing any eye contact.

Sam stopped to give her plenty of space. "So, I can get some breakfast here, can I?"

"This is Doc Ferguson's place. You can get your morning bread, milk and paper from here." She looked up at Sam. The colour drained a little from her cheeks and her eyes grew a little more inquisitive. She closed the door behind her and went to her horse.

"So you don't live in the village, Isla?"

"No, we live on one of the crofts. Me and mum." She untied her horse and was up in the saddle before she had finished speaking. With a gentle tap of her heel she was on the move.

Sam walked beside her. "I know you're in a rush but I wanted to ask you a couple of questions."

"I know what you're going to ask." Isla looked straight ahead across the square.

"You do?"

"Aye, you want to know about the ghost."

Sam rested his hand on the horse's warm flank, "Sure. But you don't…"

"I've seen it myself… A few times." Her voice cracked as if she were about to cry and her cheeks flushed once more.

Sam shook his head in disbelief. "Seen what exactly?"

Isla pulled at the reins and the horse stopped. She looked down at Sam through small, intense eyes. "The last Laird. He wanders the grounds outside Aul House. He scared the life out of Marmite first time we saw him." She leant down and nuzzled the side of her face into Marmite's mane.

"How do you know it was the Laird? It could have been anyone."

"Everyone knows what the Laird looks like. His portraits are in the church for all to see. It was him, I tell you." She rubbed her eyes with the back of her hand but there were no tears. "I'm not the only one, you know. Many have seen him." The topic of conversation was obviously making her feel uncomfortable. But at the same time she had brought it up.

Sam believed she'd seen someone or something but a ghost was preposterous. "Tell me about John Pinto, the housekeeper at Aul House. What do you know about him?"

Isla patted Marmite and tugged his reins and the clip-clop of hoofs on the cobblestones echoed about the square once more. Sam picked up his pace to remain at their side.

"Mr Pinto keeps himself to himself, all alone in the house. If he's not there he's up on the North Beach, near the spring."

"What's he doing there, do you think?"

"I don't know but whatever it is he doesn't want to be seen."

"How do you mean?"

"If he knows you're there – if he sees or hears you coming – he'll disappear."

"Have you told anyone about this?"

Isla laughed, "Nobody's interested in what I have to say."

"I'm interested in what you have to say, you know that. Could you show me where I can find the spring?" Sam unfolded his map of the island.

Isla glanced down and extended a hand.

A deep voice came from behind them. Sam jumped with surprise and Isla withdrew her hand.

"Is Mr West bothering you, Isla?" said the voice.

Sam turned around. The man was only a few inches from him. Tall and very strong. His bushy black beard covered a stern face. His bloodshot eyes looked through Sam.

"No, Doctor," said Isla. Her voice had lost its spark, subservient once more.

"Very good. Be on yer way then. Don't want ye' mar to have cold rolls."

"No." She looked down at Sam and nodded before trotting away.

"What's on the paper?" said the doctor.

"Just my shopping list." Sam stuffed the map back in his coat pocket. "You know my name, Dr Ferguson. I'm honoured." Sam offered his hand.

The doctor wrung his hand, "And you know mine. You can pick up a few provisions in the pub. We don't have much, mind." He turned and walked back across the square.

Sam followed. Inside the air was heavy with the smell of fried breakfast and tobacco. The cramped entrance way led left through a door marked *Saloon* and to the right through a door marked *Waiting Room*. The doctor went left into the bar. A couple of old men drank tea from chipped cups in the corner. They pulled their flat-caps down further over their wrinkled brows when they saw Sam. The formica tables and chairs looked more in-keeping with a fish and chip shop than a pub. The threadbare carpet exposed a few remaining flecks of brown and orange. The doctor went behind the bar. Sam took a seat on one of the four high-stools, directly opposite.

"Excuse my manner out there, Mr West."

"Sam."

"I'm a friend of the girl's mother. Can't have her talking to strangers." His Scottish accent was heavy.

"I met Joanna yesterday when I arrived. She and Isla helped me to my lodgings at Aul House – I wouldn't say I was a stranger to them."

The doctor picked up a tea towel from behind the bar and began drying pint glasses. "We're all strangers. Not all of us were born on the island like Jo and Isla."

"You from the mainland originally?"

"Aberdeen, aye. And you're a Londoner, I see." He smiled.

The muzak on the radio faded in and out with the patchy reception. One of the men in the corner, behind Sam, had a coughing fit before lighting up a cigarette.

Sam waited for a pause in the coughing before replying. "Sure am. And you're the landlord *and* the doctor, I see."

"That's right. An unusual combo I know but it's how we do things here. We do what it takes to keep things ticking over."

"When does your surgery open?"

"Why, are you feeling unwell, Mr West?"

The men in the back broke into a croaky laugh.

"I'm dying of hunger."

The doctor stepped aside and gestured to the box of bread rolls and pints of milk on the ledge behind him.

"A roll would be great, thanks. And how about a cup of tea, like the guys at the back?"

The doctor placed a plate on the bar and used his hands to choose a roll from the box. He put the bread on the plate and disappeared into a back room. The men in the corner sat in silence reading their newspapers, save the odd smoker's hack. Sam ate the bread; it was still warm, dry, dense and filling. The doctor returned with a steaming mug of tea.

"I assume it was Isla who told you my name?" asked Sam.

"Mackay, if you must know. Told me you're involved with the sale."

Sam was determined not to be ruffled and continued to play as dumb and straight as he could manage. The doctor was just like the cocky hedge fund managers and rival traders he dealt with all the time back in London. Never play their game. "That's right; my client has bought Aul House recently."

"Aye, we'll be at the party tomorrow night. Isn't that right boys." The doctor craned his neck to smile at the two ear wigging patrons. They rustled their newspapers in acknowledgement.

"So, you know John Pinto."

"Everyone knows everyone on the island."

"What do you know about me?"

The doctor shrugged and stroked his beard before pouring himself a pint of water from the sink below the bar. "I know you think we're a strange lot. You think it's strange that a doctor can also be the landlord."

"Not at all. It's comforting to know I can have a skin-full tonight while there's a doctor on hand if I get myself into any trouble."

"But that's it, Mr West. To be honest, if I wasn'ee the landlord I'd be out of work."

"How do you mean?"

"I mean nobody on the island is ever ill! Save for the odd sprained ankle or burnt hand my surgery is the quietest place on Aul."

"Maybe they're all seeing somebody else," Sam smiled.

Ferguson laughed for the first time. His white teeth shone through his jet black beard. "It wasn'ee always like this, mind. I had my usual share of problems." He paused and shook his head. "Including the dreaded cancer."

Sam immediately thought of his mother. His hand involuntarily ran through his hair.

"I'm sorry." The doctor leant in over the bar towards him. His heavy eyelids cloaked his pupils almost completely. "It got my wife, too."

"It got my mother." Sam buried his hands into his coat pockets, suddenly horribly self conscious.

"Perhaps these things happen for a reason. After all, I wouldn'ee be here if she was still alive. No. Margaret would never have liked it here."

The doctor's eyes lost their shine as he stared across the saloon. Sam felt compelled to say something. "So when did it all change? When did this become an island of health freaks?" Sam looked around at the chain-smoking earwigs behind him. His voice was as sardonic as he could make it.

"Last ten years I've seen the improvement or is that decline?"

Sam and the doctor laughed.

"That might explain the ghost of the Laird. Maybe he's too *well* to get into heaven," said Sam, still smiling – his eyes searching for the doctor's reaction.

Newspapers rustled some more behind him. Sam sensed the two men leaning in towards him a bit further. He resisted the urge to spin around on his stool, his gaze still fixed on the doctor.

"As I said, Mr West – you think we're a strange lot."

Sam sighed. "God, not you as well?"

The doctor's smile evaporated. "I'd ask that you don't take the Lord's name in vain. But to answer your question, yes, *me* as well. I've seen the Laird with my own two eyes." The doctor gripped his drink. The murky water swirled around the glass.

"I don't disagree with you…"

"Isn't that comforting," said the doctor before swallowing down the remainder of his water. He took a newspaper from the pile on the end of the bar and rolled it up. "How about something to read? It can get awful lonely around here." The doctor handed the newspaper over. "And, when you meet the Laird we hope you'll be a lot calmer than we were."

The eavesdroppers sniggered behind their papers.

Sam felt his cheeks flush with hot blood. It was time to leave. "Thanks for the breakfast." He left a Scottish five pound note on the bar and slipped off his stool.

The doctor ignored the money as he cleared away Sam's plate and mug. "Sam."

Sam stopped at the door and turned back, "Yes?"

"You're not the only Londoner we've had in here recently."

Sam approached the bar, his heart rate picked up, "Oh, yeah?"

Ferguson's large shoulders leant over the bar, his hairy face only a few inches from Sam's. "Older chap, said his name was James."

The hairs on the back of Sam's neck stood on end, "James who?"

"James West."

Sam squeezed the wooden bar with his free hand, the other wrung the rolled-up newspaper, "When was this?"

"About three weeks ago. I only mention it seeing as you have the same surname as him. Any relation?"

"Describe him to me."

"I'd say he was in his sixties, tall, distinguished looking with pale brown eyes."

"That was my father." Sam let the bar take some of his weight as he leant in further, conscious their conversation was being listened to. "When exactly did you see him and what was he doing here?"

"He only popped in for a drink and asked for directions to Aul House, said he'd arrived that morning and was here to see John Pinto."

"*Pinto*? You sure?"

"Aye." The doctor looked to his right, at a calendar hanging on the wall. "It would have been Monday 27 June when he came in here. Aye, that's right. I remember it as I'd just had a beer delivery and he was my first customer after that." He pointed at the letter D circled on Monday 27 June.

"What time would that have been?"

"Deliveries are at midday, so I'd say about half past twelve he came in. I gave him directions to the house, he finished his whisky and off he went."

"Was he with anyone else?"

"No, alone."

"You didn't see him again?"

"No."

"Nobody else has mentioned him to you before or since?"

"No."

A gust of cold air swept into the bar as the couple Sam had seen riding earlier came into the bar. Ferguson stood upright and welcomed his customers warmly as regulars.

Sam was through the door before it had time to swing shut.

09:37

His early morning optimism had drained away. Sam wandered amongst the jagged rocks and thistles that covered the baron heathland. Out of desperation, more than anything else, he switched on his phone. He watched the screen as it searched for a network connection. The bars in the top left-hand corner established themselves and the phone chimed as an envelope icon appeared on the screen.

In Aul tonight. Travelling with Frost.
See you soon. G x

Another change of plan. What was going on? But Sam smiled. He wanted to see George again. He remembered their night at the club and how easy she had been to talk to. Her great dancing too… but that was before everything else… before all of this… He read the text a couple of times before switching off the phone. Returning the phone to his pocket he felt the map. He got it out and unfolded it. He had to crouch and press it down on one knee to stop it fluttering in the stiff breeze. He worked out he was only a few hundred yards from the area Pinto had pointed-out as the crofter's land. Joanna and Isla must be nearby, and so too Mackay. Sam got back to his feet. The wind picked up pace as its temperature dropped a few degrees, blowing directly across his face. He squinted through stinging eyes, scouring the horizon for signs of a cottage… of life. There was nothing except far off in the distance, what Sam thought looked like a flock of scraggy looking sheep. He cut across the heathland, slowed by the grizzly thistles with giant thorns that grew three foot tall between the rocks. He scuffed his shoes on the hard stone. The idea of farming up here struck Sam as utterly futile and miserable.

Six geese flew over in an elegant V – so low that Sam could hear the whir of their wings through the air. For all of its harshness and inhospitableness, Aul was a natural wonder, almost entirely untouched by man. The dozen or so sheep paid him no attention as they continued to graze on the patchy grass that now covered the earth. It was still moist with dew; Sam's socks soaked up the water through his saturated leather soles. Descending over the brow of a hill, he saw a little white cottage with smoke bellowing from the chimney. More sheep were scattered around the lush, green field that surrounded the property. A light was on inside on the ground floor. The front door reminded Sam of his own, with its peeling green paint.

To Sam's relief it was Mackay's ruddy face that welcomed him in.

"Sam, how lovely to see you."

Sam stepped into the stone floored kitchen. It was delightfully warm. He paused in the doorway to look around the small room. A single door in one corner. An uncarpeted stone staircase ran along the opposite wall to the top floor. Sam was struck by the authenticity and genuine shabbiness of the place. None of the blue painted wooden cupboards matched but together they made for a tight, functional space around an iron range that glowed and crackled in the chimney breast. Pots and pans hung from the ceiling above the only worktop… but not for decorative reasons and certainly not to show-off seldom used top of the range ironmongery, as would all too often be the case in the trendy homes of his colleagues… but only because that was the most practical place for them and, not forgetting, there was nowhere else to store them in his minimal space.

The simplicity impressed Sam. The grazing sheep, the tiny cottage with its ramshackle green door and the genuine, uncomplicated setup triggered a pang inside of him. A pang of something... was it envy or respect?

Mackay's white bushy hair was even messier than yesterday – fluffy and bouncy like a cartoon thought-bubble floating over his head. Sharp white stubble ran around his mouth and jaw. He wore an oversized grey jumper and green tweed trousers. His large feet were bare. His soles were thick-skinned and cracked from years of working on his feet. Sam was waved to one of the armchairs in front of the range, just as the kettle whistled.

"Tea?" said Mackay, already holding two mugs.

"Thanks. I got you the paper." Sam waved the rolled up newspaper as he spoke.

"Very kind. Just pop it on the chair there." Mackay splashed milk into the mugs.

Sam noticed *Cryptic Jumbo* on the armchair opposite. He picked it up and replaced it with the newspaper. He flicked through pages of crossword puzzles – a quarter of them already completed. "This is the *same* copy you bought yesterday in Inverness?"

Mackay laughed, "Aye, it is. I told you, I do like my crosswords! They get progressively harder through the book, so I'll slow a wee bit now." He handed Sam his tea and sat down opposite him, his eyes quizzical. "Thanks for the paper, there will be a couple more in there too."

Sam felt he should say something – explain why he was here. "So, this is you then?"

"Aye, this is me." His eyes darted about the room and he stretched his legs out to the fire, splaying his toes apart.

"You have it *all* here. Everything you need." Sam was immediately surprised he'd verbalised his thoughts.

Mackay ran his hand over his jaw; the bristles on his chin made an audible scratching sound along his rough palms. "Why, thank you. I think that's the nicest thing anyone's said to me in a long time."

Sam forced a laugh. But inside he felt a real affection for the old man. He was the only person he'd met on the island that made him feel welcome. His thoughts flicked back to London, at how easy it was to survive without anyone else, while living amongst millions of strangers. Up here it was the opposite way around. On Aul there were only a handful of people, yet the urge to be connected to others felt stronger.

They exchanged small talk about last night's storm. Mackay explained it was common to have all four seasons in a day, on Aul. Sam learnt talking about the weather was very much an English obsession which Scots, particularly islanders, didn't mind for. This stopped Sam mentioning the incident on the boat on the way over to the island. He wanted to thank Mackay again for saving him from certain drowning but there was something about Mackay's jolly, happy-go-lucky nature which convinced him that Mackay had moved on and yesterday was no longer important.

The tea and the fire had relaxed Sam somewhat. He caught Mackay glancing at the clock on the wall next to the front door. It was half past ten.

"I'm sorry, I've interrupted you." Sam stood up.

Mackay stopped drinking, forcing his words out mid-gulp. "No. Don't be silly. You've not interrupted anything. This is my quiet time. The animals won't need me until the afternoon." He waved Sam back down into his seat. "Ah! What am I saying? It's me who needs the animals, truth be told. Not the other way around... Anyhow, do tell me what you've learnt so far?"

"Learnt?" Sam was wary of Mackay's choice of words.

"Aye, for your client who's bought Aul House. I thought you were on a fact finding trip."

Sam nodded. All the lies and stories were blurring into one. He couldn't remember who or what he was meant to be, to whom anymore! He ran his hand through his hair and his brain spotted an opportunity. "Yes, that's why I'm here. I had a few questions about the sale."

"I see." Mackay pursed his lips as if he knew what was coming next.

"Pinto told me the proceeds of the sale go to the islanders."

"Providing there's no heir." The speed of response told Sam he'd anticipated the question correctly.

"Pinto tells me there is no heir, hence the sale of the house by The Trust."

"Okay."

"So my question is what will you do with the money?"

Mackay bore a befuddled expression as his hand disappeared into the cloud above his head. "I really don't know. The Island Council will deal with that. Why do you ask?"

"It's a significant amount of money. I thought you'd all be interested in what's owing to you."

Mackay shrugged. "I don't need money to be a crofter."

Sam changed tact. "So you're not on the Council, I take it."

"I have my say on matters of interest but the sale of Aul House isn't one of them. I hope your client enjoys the house as much as the Falcorrs' did."

Sam sat up at the mention of that name! "The *who*?" He did his best to hide his surprise but the timbre of his voice was a giveaway.

"The Falcorrs family who used to own Aul House. The Falcorrs' were the Lairds. They were given the island by…"

"King James I," Sam interrupted. "I know, Pinto told me the story last night." But his mind was racing ahead. "What was the last Laird's full name?"

"Seth Falcorrs. All of the family's first born sons took that name. Is everything alright, Sam? You look like you've seen a ghost again!" Mackay forced an unconvincing chuckle as he put his mug on the floor and leant in towards Sam.

Sam was thrown. The fake ID George had given him, with the name *Seth Falcorrs*…

"Sam? Are you okay?"

"Did you say *ghost*?" Sam came out of his temporary trance, latching onto the last word he'd heard Mackay say. "Why is everyone obsessed with ghosts on this island?" It was his frustration and anger talking now. He didn't care for the answer, his mind was still scrambled attempting to make sense of yet another twist.

"As I said yesterday, many people are sure they see Seth Falcorrs around the island." Mackay reached out for Sam's empty mug, "Can I get you another one? Perhaps something stronger?"

Sam remembered the whisky in his pocket. He was tempted but thought against it. He had to remain clear headed. He forced himself to get back on track. "Tell me something. Were you one of the crofters displaced by Falcorrs when he planted his minefield." He handed over his mug.

Mackay was over to the sink in a few paces. "Pinto told you about that too, did he?" He rinsed out the cups, gazing out of the window over the field. "Yes, I was moved here when the Laird came up with his crazy idea. All of us, Joanna too. That was over fifty years ago now." He sighed. "All that wonderful, fertile land wasted."

Sam remained seated but turned to face Mackay. "I had wondered how good this place was for farming, as I walked over the rocks and scrubland out there."

"Up in the north it's very different. It's the spring. Full of minerals and nutrients – the 'good stuff' we call it." He took a glass from the draining board and filled it with water from the running tap. He held the murky water to the window and turned to face Sam. "It's the 'good stuff' that gives it this colour. The land around the spring is *perfect* for farming. Was perfect. Go there now and…" He tailed off and looked out of the window, letting out another wistful sigh.

Sam thought about Isla and Marmite from earlier. She had mentioned Pinto was often up at the spring. *If he knows you're there – if he sees or hears you coming – he'll disappear.* "How far is the spring from the minefield?"

"Not far, just before you get to Northern Head. Between the old fort and the beach."

"Right," Sam pressed a bit deeper. "Pinto told me he was heading up there today. Said he had a lot to do before he left. Any ideas what that might be?"

Mackay dried his hands on a tea towel and came back over to join his guest. He picked the newspaper up off the floor and placed it on his lap before sitting down. He took a pair of reading glasses from a breast pocket hidden beneath his jumper and he scanned the stories on the front page.

"How well do you know Pinto?" asked Sam.

Mackay looked up, the paper now spread open on pages two and three, his nose was scrunched up to hold his glasses in place. "Pinto's a private man. I don't know him that well."

"How private? Have you seen him with anyone recently? I mean somebody from the mainland?"

"No. Who do you mean?"

Sam daren't mention his father. "Never mind. But you do know what Pinto's doing up at the spring, don't you?"

"I have my suspicions."

"Such as?" The heat from the range tingled his cheek.

"Only suspicions, mind. I don't go up to the north if I can help it. Too many memories… But from what I hear, Pinto's growing something up there. No doubt you've learnt he's something of a botanist."

"Yep, the house was full of his plants."

"Right. I've not been in the house for many years but last time I was there it was the same. But there's no excuse for taking that up to the north. The Laird was clear when we were moved south. There was to be nothing farmed or grown by anyone in the north. That applies to the housekeeper of Aul House as well."

"What do you think he's growing?"

"No idea. As I said, I haven't been up there in years."

"Why doesn't anyone stop him?"

Mackay returned to his newspaper, turning the page and scanning the stories. He didn't look up as he spoke, "You won't like the answer, Sam."

Sam coughed, he really needed a cigarette. "Let me guess, everyone's afraid of the ghost!"

"I said you wouldn't like the answer."

Mackay's hair was still wet after being out with his sheep. Sam had prepared poached eggs on toast for lunch and insisted on doing the washing-up as Mackay's attention turned to his other passion – crossword puzzles – now absorbed in *Cryptic Jumbo*. Sam joined him in front of the fire and browsed the newspaper, while rain and wind rattled the window. There was nothing that interested him – most of the stories were about Scots he'd never heard of and mainland political issues that meant nothing to him. On page twelve a headline in the bottom corner caught his eye: *Banker Death. Suspected Suicide*.

The body of a man found on Tuesday under London Bridge is thought to be that of City worker Sam West. While the exact cause of death is still unknown, Metropolitan Police have said they are not treating the death as suspicious. However, in a strange twist, The Met are investigating whether Mr West, 30, a highflying banker at top City firm Gema Bank, had any links to the disappearance of Genevieve Price, Mr West's next door neighbour. Students of Mrs Price's pottery classes, which the sixty eight year old widow gave from her home in Bayswater, raised the alarm of her disappearance on Tuesday morning. Police have appealed for information from the public.

Sam took a deep breath. He felt his body shaking. His palms were clammy and heat from the fire suddenly became too much. He folded the paper and stood up. He went to the sink and poured himself a glass of water which he forced down in one. The water swirled around his churning stomach. He had to talk to George. What was she doing? She had promised him he would be left alone if he cooperated. Her text message this morning was so innocuous. It didn't even hint that things had gone tits-up. There was no suggestion there was a change of plan. As far as she knew he was still gathering evidence against Frost. Mrs Price was murdered but the story was claiming she had disappeared – was George behind this? Sam turned on his phone. The start up sequence took an age and it failed to find any reception.

"That won't work down here, Sam. We're in a bowl."

"Do you have a landline telephone?" Sam leant on the tap. He felt dizzy and his legs were swaying like the grass in the field through the window.

"Sorry, no."

Sam put on his coat.

"You're not leaving in this are you?" Mackay got to his feet.

"Yes, I've just realised I'm late. I had to call the office. Does the name Charles Frost mean anything to you?"

"No, should it?"

Sam was out through the door and into the storm. He ran across the sodden grass and mud, barely able to see through the driving wind and rain. The sheep were bunched together for warmth and protection, lying as low to the ground as they could to avoid the power of the wind. Sam ran and ran, north towards Aul House, ready to confront George when she arrived. Ready to demand his return to the mainland where he would find a police station and tell them everything.

Fuck them all.

He reached the top of the steep bank and got out his phone. He had to unzip his jacket and use it to shield the device from the rain, as he checked whether he'd got any reception. Still nothing. The storm must have been interfering with the signal. He ran on. Not bothering to do up his coat. Around the village and up towards the ancient pines that marked the edge of Aul House's grounds. The rain came down harder. Sam was exhausted. Barely able to breath as he reached the trees, where he stopped and sheltered beneath the branches, trying to catch his breath.

Somebody whistled.

A short, sharp, shrill whistle.

Sam pulled upright and searched around. He saw nobody.

The whistle again.

Sam scanned around him. His heart still pounding against his chest. His lungs empty and tight.

Boom!

Shit.

A gunshot.

Boom! Boom!

Sam dropped to the ground and crawled behind a tree. He lay motionless. Only his eyes moving, searching for the gunman.

16:45

There was movement deeper into the woods. Sam fixed his stare. A man with long crazed hair and beard, carrying a shotgun, coming towards him. The weapon aimed straight at his head. Longer and longer strides through the lashing rain. The wind was blowing across him, sending his blonde shoulder length hair flailing around like a mane. Sam closed his eyes and prepared to die.

"Did George send you?" shouted the voice. The accent certainly wasn't local but in the noise of the storm Sam couldn't place it.

Sam opened his eyes. The barrel of the shotgun inches from his nose. "Yes."

"Then follow me if you want to live. Come on!" yelled the gunman. Then he was off, charging through the woods.

Sam got to his feet. He only watched as the gunman weaved through the trees, as if it were him being chased by the crazed man with a gun. Sam noticed he was barefooted, his feet black with filth.

"Com'on!" yelled the gunman. "Stay here and you will die."

Sam didn't know what else to do except run after him. He followed the man who moved at great pace and ease between the trees and over fallen logs. His clothes were almost threadbare – torn and tattered, black with dirt and grime.

They reached the edge of the woods and the man crouched down before darting through the heather and over the thistles and rocks with no apparent care for the pain he must have felt in his feet. Sam was slipping and sliding, his trousers torn and blood pouring from his knee. But on they went. Aul House was ahead of them. The man was tracking around the perimeter of the formal gardens, obviously staying out of sight of anyone in the house. He only looked over his shoulder occasionally to check Sam was still in-tow. They had been running at full pelt for over ten minutes when they reached a wire fence. Sam realised where they were. The yellow sign with a black skull and cross bones confirmed it: KEEP OUT. DANGER. LANDMINES.

The gunman jumped the fence and ran on as he had before. Sam ran up to the fence and called out, "Stop. Stop. You're fucking crazy!"

The man only waved him over and kept on going, weapon swinging on his shoulder.

Adrenaline and fear overruled Sam's exhaustion. He wiped the rain from his eyes. He shook his head as he placed both his hands on top of a wooden fence post and jumped the top wire. *Just follow him and you'll survive this.* And he ran through his pain to keep pace, hoping he was treading the path his crazy guide was marking for him. The wind was blowing east to west, pushing Sam off his stride. He continued to trip and stumble. Each time wincing at the thought of an explosion blowing him to bits. They climbed a steep hill and from the top they could see the ferocious sea. The North Beach and the ruins of the old fort stood a few hundred yards away. The man kept going, this time east towards some rocks. Sam followed as closely as his body would allow. Finally a fence marking the edge of the minefield was before them. They were both quickly over and stood upon cliffs about one hundred feet above the beach. The man dropped down to his hands and knees and hung off the edge.

"No!" cried Sam.

But it was too late. He was gone.

Sam got down and looked over the edge. Just six feet below was a natural ledge in the rock, protruding twelve inches from the cliff face. The man was shuffling along the ledge with his back to the rock, facing out to the sea that crashed and hissed below. Sam screamed as he lowered himself down. His heels scraped against the rocks as he descended. His hands groped for anything to hold onto. He couldn't look down as he moved sideways to his right, following the madman. And then from nowhere a large, blackened hand appeared and grabbed Sam's right arm, pulling him into the cliff.

Both men sat in the dark. The cacophony of the howling storm and the sea was dwarfed by the two men panting to find their breath. Sounds echoed around them. Sam felt his eyes adjusting to the poor light but not enough to make anything out, beyond the shadows of the madman.

Chink. Chink. Crack. An orange glow enveloped the space as a tiny flame flickered from some kindling piled on the floor.

They were in a cave.

The man blew gently at the flame to coax it into life. It gradually grew as the fire caught. He sat back up and folded his legs, using both hands to tame his hair behind his ears. He extended a hand over the fire to Sam and smiled – his savage face illuminated by the orange glow of the flames. "I'm Tom." His eyes darted around the cave as he spoke – small black beads anticipating imminent attack from the dark, shadowy recesses of the rock. "I know George sent you."

Sam only stared at him. The flames between them grew stronger and taller. The acrid smell of burning wood mixed with the stench of Tom's body odour. Sam shivered as the wind blew in over his shoulders, sticking his sodden clothes against his skin. Smoke wafted over Tom's filthy face and matted hair, but he didn't seem to care, as he sat cross-legged rocking gently back and forth.

"I watched you and the old man arrive yesterday. Is he working for her too?" said Tom. His eyes opened wider, the smoke turning the whites a tinge of pink, making him look even more wild and crazed.

Sam reached inside his pocket. "Do you want a drink?"

Tom flinched and reached for his gun.

"No, it's just whisky." Sam revealed his hand slowly, offering the bottle over the fire; its golden contents swirling around in his shaky hand.

Tom grunted and gazed at the bottle. He shook his head. "No. No time. We don't have time. Where's George?"

Sam took a swig. Short breath and fear caused him to cough as the drink caught in his throat. He felt the immediate rush of alcohol to his brain. "Can I help you, Tom?" He didn't know why he asked that, he just wanted to keep Tom as calm as possible.

Tom rubbed his nose with the backs of his hands, like a squirrel eating a nut. "Your name. What is it?"

"Sam."

"Is that your cover name?"

"No, that's my real name. It's Sam West." Sam thought about *Seth Falcorrs* – that was his cover name. For a split second he considered sharing it with Tom but just as quickly thought against it.

"Why did George send you?" Tom held his hands to the fire.

Sam remembered the article in the newspaper but didn't want to give anything away. "I don't know what you mean?"

Tom grunted and moaned, his rocking grew faster and more pronounced, his eyes blinking rapidly. "No time for lies, Sam. Lies did *this* to me. Did she tell you about me?"

The hairs on the back of Sam's neck began to tingle. "She said you've been missing for a year and a half."

Tom sat up and leant towards the fire. The intensity of his stare grew as his pupils contracted in the yellow light from the flames. "She sent you to find *me*?"

Sam swallowed hard. The taste of the whisky lingered in his mouth. He weighed up his options before responding, glancing at the rifle across Tom's lap. "She sent me to find Charles Frost."

A small smile curled at the edges of Tom's lips. Sam caught a glimpse of his orthodontic-straight teeth.

Tom began to laugh – almost cackling, made all the more macabre by the flickering fire and the echoes of the cave. "She did that to me too. It's all lies. All lies! There is no Charles Frost."

A churning anxiety grew in Sam's stomach. Tom's words confirmed the nagging suspicion that lurked in his own mind. "How did you know George sent me?"

"You were wearing my clothes when you arrived yesterday. Was that her idea? Was she trying to send me a message?"

Sam felt played… "I really don't know what to think anymore." He ran his hands through his hair, his fingers catching in the tangles and knots caused by the rain and wind. "She told me she worked for US Intelligence. She said she needed my help to investigate Charles Frost, who's meant to have just bought Aul House. All I had to do was find information linking Frost to a bunch of companies and I was done. I'm a fucking banker not a spy!"

Tom nodded vigorously. "What did she tell you about *me* – about why I was sent here?"

"She said you were her partner. Said you came up here eighteen months ago to investigate Frost and had gone missing."

"That much is true."

"So what happened?" Sam took another swig of whisky, offering the bottle to Tom but he ignored the gesture.

"There is no Frost. This is all about *Cadence*."

Sam remembered the word... The notebook... The Japanese Officer had said it to Frost in the jungle: '*It is the perfect cadence that tells us we've come to the end*'. "I don't follow."

"You've met John Pinto. I saw you both yesterday. I was watching you in the woods."

"You were watching..." Then it struck him: The vivid image of Tom, this beastly apparition of a man, stalking him through the woods. It was Sam's turn to laugh.

Tom grunted and pulled his rifle to his chest, his expression turned to one of bemusement. "What is it? Pinto is *not* a funny man."

Sam bit down on his bottom lip and shook his head, raising his right palm over the fire to Tom. "No, he's not. I only realised something. Did you know you've been scaring the hell out of the locals? They think you're the ghost of the old Laird!"

Tom lowered his rifle. He looked directly into Sam's eyes. "We'll all be ghosts if we don't stop Pinto. John Pinto has to be stopped."

"I don't follow."

"I came here many months ago. Like you I thought I was investigating a trail that led to Charles Frost. All of the intelligence linked Frost to Aul House. I spent weeks undercover as a fisherman trying to get close to the house. But there was nothing. There's only John Pinto, who claims to be the housekeeper, babysitting the place for the Laird that went missing thirty years ago."

It was all concurring with Sam's take on the story, so he felt obliged to chip in: "Right, the old Laird, Seth Falcorrs."

Tom's eyes grew with surprise, "Yes, that's right. But who was Seth Falcorrs and who is John Pinto? What's the link?" Tom grinned, showing off his immaculately straight teeth.

Sam shrugged his shoulders.

"They're the same person. Don't you see it, Sam?" Tom was up on to his feet. Stepping over the flames, clutching his rifle.

Sam was taken by surprise and lurched back into the rock behind him, thumping his head hard. The terrible smell of months of Tom's sweat in his ragged clothes forced him to turn away as Tom brushed past him before peering out of the cave. "What is it, Tom?"

Tom looked back over his shoulder. "We must be alone for what I'm about to tell you." He searched outside once more, staring down the barrel of his rifle as his head moved three hundred and sixty degrees around the small cave entrance.

"There's no one out there, Tom. Come back inside and tell me what happened. I want to help you."

Tom came back towards the fire and sat down next to him. While grateful for the windbreaker, it also meant Sam was now downwind of the terrible smell. He subtly rested his chin on his hand and used his fingers to cover his nostrils, hoping this only made him look more interested in what his strange host was about to say.

"The Laird, Seth Falcorrs and John Pinto are the *same* person," said Tom. His voice lowered to almost a whisper.

Sam fruitlessly searched his pockets for the fake Seth Falcorrs driving licence. He must have left it at Mackay's cottage. "That's impossible, the Laird would be well over a hundred years old if he were still alive. Pinto is half that!" Sam glanced over Tom's shoulder, wondering how he could make his escape from the madman blocking his way.

"The answer is *Cadence*, Sam. This is all about the flower."

"You mean the purple flower?"

"Very good. I can see why George chose you. You've discovered so much already."

"What's so special about the flower?"

"Pinto calls the flower 'Cadence'. It's more than a flower…" Tom rubbed his face and swept his greasy hair behind his ears, as if readying himself for what he was about to say: "Cadence is an elixir… It brings eternal life." His intense stare softened as if the act of sharing his secret had relieved him of a major burden.

Sam had to cover his mouth to hide his smile. He couldn't risk offending Tom but at the same time things were becoming farcical.

"I know you don't believe me but why do you think I'm up here? Why do you think I've been living like this?" Tom pointed around the cave.

"Why?"

"Because I know too much. Pinto wants me dead."

"Tell me what you know." Sam moved his hand away from his mouth. The growing heat from the fire was now making a real difference.

"It started when I discovered where Pinto grows the Cadence flowers down by the spring. I followed him there about eight months ago. Thousands of the flowers growing around the spring, covering the ground that's meant to be planted with landmines." Tom was forced to stop by his own sudden eruption of laughter. "… What a way to keep people away from his flowers. There are no mines, Sam! Only Cadence."

Sam thought about what Mackay had told him earlier, about his suspicions that Pinto was growing something up near the spring. "I believe you Tom. Go on, what happened when you found the flowers?"

"I watched Pinto. I watched him for weeks, tending to his beloved flowers like a farmer cultivating his crop.

That's when I found this place. I could hide here and wait out of sight and out of the shitty weather."

Shitty weather. That's what George had said. He checked the time on George's digital watch, it was almost six o'clock.

"That's George's watch, isn't it?" Tom's voice broke from its whisper.

"It is. She leant it to me. Just as she leant me your clothes."

"Where is George now?" Tom rested his hands on the rifle across his lap, a gentle reminder that Sam was still his prisoner.

"She'll be here tonight, you can speak to her yourself."

"George is coming here?" Tom was startled by the news. He jumped up into a crouch, his weapon falling on the ground. He ignored it as he used his hands to throw dirt over the fire. The flames receded; dust replacing smoke and the cave was dark once more. Tom stood up and strapped his rifle across his chest. "We don't have time. Follow me." He was quickly away towards the light.

Sam dreaded what was coming next. He got to his feet. The crashing and hissing waves appeared louder and more menacing. He watched Tom slide out onto the cliff-face. But he couldn't move. He looked down at the white foam swirling around the jagged rock below. He looked to his left, where Tom was shuffling confidently along the narrow ledge.

"Come on, Sam. I need to show you."

Sam took another swig of whisky for courage. He winced as he pressed his back firmly against the cliff-face, the backs of his heels scuffing up against the rock. Left foot. Right foot. Along the narrow ledge. He stretched his arms out as wide as he could – his hands feeling for anything to hold onto over the smooth, weather beaten rock.

His pulse raced. The northerly wind blew straight at him, its welcome power pinning him to the cliff.

"Up!" shouted Tom, over the howling wind. He sent down his muddy hand, patting Sam's shoulder.

Sam could only look straight ahead at the horizon. He found Tom's hand with his own. As soon as he felt Tom's grip he reciprocated and in one movement span and pulled with his free hand, sending himself up on top of the cliff. Blood coursed through his body at a thousand miles per hour. Exhilaration replaced his fear.

Tom didn't let go, pulling Sam to his feet and pushing him on ahead. "We must keep going. I must show you."

Back over the rocks and through the heathland. Tom was fast and agile, well adapted to the environment, as he leapt over thistles and rocks. Sam knew they were approaching the spring, as the ground grew more lush with grass it reminded him more of the English countryside. It was just as Mackay had said – perfect farming land.

"Get down." Tom was flat on his stomach in the tall, wet grass.

Sam crouched next to him, only to be yanked further down by Tom, so that both of them now lay side by side.

"Shhhh… He's there." Tom's voice was barely audible.

All Sam could think of was the cold, squelching mud soaking into his trousers and pullover. He slowly adjusted his coat, managing to zip it up under the weight of his body. "Who is it?"

"Pinto. He's down there." Tom pointed in front of them with a nod of this head.

Sam raised his head just above the top of the grass. Thirty or so feet away he saw Pinto, bent over, his back towards them. "What's he doing?"

"He needs to be stopped." Tom got up and looked down the sight of his rifle. His eyes blinking rapidly, his right cheek twitching as he took aim.

"Tom, no! What are you doing?" hissed Sam.

Tom raised his left index finger to his lips, his right still trained on the trigger.

"You're not a murderer. Stop!" Sam saw Tom's finger curl around the trigger. "Fucking hell!" he screamed as he barged into Tom, shoulder first, sending him off balance and down onto the grass. Sam landed on top of him, wrestling the gun away. The stench and grime of Tom's clothes were almost enough to overpower him, but combined with his strength, Tom immediately recovered his balance and forced Sam off and hard into the ground. His knee went deep into Sam's groin forcing whatever resistance he had out of him. Tom pinned Sam to the ground, the rifle across his chest, while he scoured the land for signs of Pinto.

Pinto had obviously heard the commotion behind him and was now running across the field of purple flowers, disappearing behind the distant rocks. Sam gasped for breath. The blow had caused a sharp nausea, deep in the pit of his stomach.

"He got away," grunted Tom, staring down at Sam, with his matted hair hanging like stalactites around his face.

Sam couldn't believe what had just happened. Why had he felt the compulsion to risk his own life for Pinto's? The hopelessness of his situation now meant he had nothing to lose. "Kill me if you want, you crazy bastard!"

Tom scrunched his face up. "I've not finished with you yet." He pulled the rifle off Sam's chest and slung it over his back. He pulled Sam up by his lapels and continued towards the myriad purple flowers. Sam realised it was the same flower that Pinto had used to heal his black eye. The same flower Charles Frost described in the notebook.

"This is Cadence." Tom stood amongst the sea of purple.

They were surrounded by the sweet scent of the flowers. It was suddenly an all familiar smell. In an instant Sam was back in the lift, stood close to George at the safe house.

"Pinto will be back soon. We follow the spring," ordered Tom, running through the Cadence. All the time he held his weapon out in front of him, butt against his shoulder and his finger on the trigger.

Sam held back, his head still filled with the exotic fragrance. Looking down at the ground more closely he could see these were not wild flowers. They had been neatly arranged in rows, like they were a crop. Perhaps fifty to sixty rows, each stretching three hundred to four hundred flowers long – easily the size of a football pitch. It was clear Tom knew where he was going, as he gathered speed. As the flowers thinned out he dropped to his knees. Sam, remained about twelve paces back, as Tom placed his right ear to the grass.

"Come over. Listen," Tom waved his hand in Sam's direction.

Sam could hear the sound of running water without having to lower himself any closer to the ground. "The spring?" he asked.

"Right." Tom pulled at the grass with his bare hands, lifting out handfuls of dirt. His black hands now further caked in wet mud. He looked even more feral as he burrowed away at the soft earth, creating a hole the diameter of a side-plate and several inches deep. "Look."

Sam moved towards Tom slowly. His heart stepped up a gear and his breathing went tight. The pain still in his groin folded around the adrenaline and cortisone that coursed through his stomach. He craved a cigarette.

"You see?" Tom looked up.

Sam could see the steady flow of water running down the hill side. He only nodded back at Tom.

"It's the spring." Tom began filling the hole back in, returning the earth piled up next to it.

Sam thought about the cloudy water he'd been drinking for the last twenty four hours. Pinto's venomous attack on the *EU bureaucrats* who had tried to get it cleaned up. "What are we doing, Tom?" Sam tried to keep his voice as calm and conciliatory as possible.

Tom patted down the grass with both hands and sprang back up. "Now I show you what Pinto is doing. Why he must be stopped." And he was off again, up the steady incline using his hands as well as his feet to scale the increasingly rocky ground.

"Why now, Tom? Why not before? You've been up here for so long."

"Because tomorrow it will be too late. Pinto leaves tomorrow. I've given up trying to gather the evidence against him. No time for that now. He has to die or we die."

Sam looked around for signs of Pinto but there was no one in this wide open blustery wilderness. Only him and crazy Tom – armed and dangerous. He eyed the rifle Tom had slung over his shoulder and considered making a move for it – taking him by surprise would be his only chance to break free. But it was too late. Tom had stopped at what looked like a mound of rocks and boulders dropped onto the hillside. It took Sam twenty or so seconds to catch up, struggling for breath. Tom clambered over the smooth stones and then squeezed between two that wouldn't have looked out of place at Stonehenge, about twelve feet high and a foot apart. Sam went side on, his coat snagging and catching between the stones as he forced himself through the tight space. He lost sight of Tom who was already through. Sam breathed in and pushed his back against the stone, sliding through the final few inches. Stepping free, with his left foot leading, he was pulled down as his weight gave way. His arms flailed around for anything to grip onto, as his back leg followed and was free falling for what felt like an age. He screamed but only the echoes of his voice bounced back before he landed hard on his side.

"You're okay," said Tom, pulling him to his feet.

Sam rubbed his left shoulder that had taken the brunt of his weight. Tom was stood at the foot of an eight foot rope ladder dangling over the lip of the rocky bowl they stood in.

"Watch yourself. You don't want to fall down here." Tom was already around Sam, turning himself around to descend another ladder hanging through a small hole in the middle of the bowl. His head disappeared into the darkness. Sam took a quick look around this circle in the rock, sides smooth from years of wind and rain. He peered into the darkness below. He could see nothing beyond the rusty karabiners attaching the wire ladder around two bolts drilled into the rock.

"Com'on!" came Tom's voice, bouncing around the subterranean darkness.

Sam's palms were sweating and, despite the cold and sodden clothes, he was burning hot. He unzipped his coat and tried in vain to dry his hands on his trousers. The ladder swayed forward and back, side-to-side, as he made his way down into the darkness. His wet, leather soles sliding off the rungs. His shoulder throbbed from his fall. The temperature dropped and the dank air filled with a slight tinge of sulphur. Every sound echoed about the darkness. It was clear he was descending into a large space. Step by step his eyes began to adjust to reveal a vast underground cavern, covered in moss. Below him the water was illuminated by the sky above, revealing a sparkling deep-blue spot beneath the entrance-hole. The rungs went on forever before Tom pulled him and the ladder towards the nearest edge, where he stood on a lip just above the surface of the water. Sam clung around Tom's shoulder, getting a face-full of his greasy hair as he pulled him safely back onto terra firma. Sam took a swig of whisky to replace the taste of months of filth from Tom's hair on his lips.

"How far down are we?" asked Sam.

"The ladder's eighty five feet long and the water is about two hundred feet deep."

"So this is the source of the island's drinking water?" Sam was down on one knee, his hand dipped below the surface of the cold water.

"Yes. It flows up through layers of rock below and then runs down the hill where it's tapped for drinking near Aul House and the village." Tom walked around the narrow lip.

Sam washed his hands and splashed water on his sweaty face. The relief was instant. Opening his eyes, he could see across the underground cave. The space was vast. But more curious was the lip they stood on: It tapered around the perimeter turning into a set of carved steps which Tom was now descending.

"Who made all of this?" Sam called out, gingerly making his way around the water to catch-up with Tom.

"There's so much to learn." Tom continued down the steps, into the shadows.

Someone had gone to a lot of effort to make the place accessible – workable. Sam wondered why. There was a clatter that ricocheted around the rocky walls, followed by a hum as the cavern lit up in a glow of orange electric light. Twelve industrial sized bulbs ran along the walls, blazing from behind thick cloudy glass casements. As the light grew stronger, Sam realised that the space was pentagon shaped, with four out of the five sides dotted with bulbs. The fifth side remained in the shadows. Tom closed the door on the grey wall-mounted box from which ran the wiring that fed the lights. To his right, towering above him, were stacks of wooden crates – four high and twelve along – forty eight in total. Sam knew immediately that Tom had brought him down here to see their contents. His apprehension and fear of Tom was now replaced by anticipation at what was inside.

"Com'on," said Tom.

Sam walked around the water, conscious there were only a few inches of concrete between him and two hundred feet of ice-cold water. Going down the steps, the lip grew wider into a platform six feet wide.

"Help me with this." Tom had squeezed in behind the nearest tower of four crates and was pushing with both hands at the top one. He groaned under the weight of it. Sam was around the other side, arms above his head, hands both sides of the crate, braced to take the weight as Tom sent it his way. Gradually it came, both men huffing in unison. It did Sam's injured shoulder no favours as he staggered back under the weight of the crate, dangerously close to the edge as it came down with a thud. Tom swung his rifle off his shoulder and gripped it like a paddle in a kayak.

Thump! Tom slammed the butt of his rifle in to the top of the wooden crate.

Thump!

Thump!

Sam flinched at the thought of the gun accidentally going off. Tom was oblivious to the danger, going at it like his life depended upon it, his hair flying up with every uplift.

Crack! Snap...

The wood finally gave way. Tom returned his weapon over his shoulder and pulled at the splintery shards with his hands, tossing them onto the ground.

The hairs on the back of Sam's neck stood on end as he got in closer to see inside the hole. "What's inside, Tom?" his mouth was dry. He had to lick his lips as he felt the cold air pulling them tight.

Tom buried his hand inside and pulled it back out, fist closed. He swung his arm out robot style in Sam's direction, fist still gripping tightly to its contents. "See for yourself".

Sam stared at the large muddy fist inches from his chest. With both of his hands cupped as if he was trying to collect running water, he held them out in front of him. Tom splayed open his fingers and a glass vial fell into Sam's palms. It weighed almost nothing and was only three inches long. Inside it a purple liquid – that familiar Cadence-purple. In one end a glass stopper, sealed with a thin line of purple wax. Sam held the vial between his thumb and index finger and raised it up to the light of the nearest bulb. The liquid was viscous and deep in colour. "What is it? I don't understand."

Tom had pulled open a bigger hole in the crate, large enough to see there were hundreds, if not thousands, of the vials inside.

"It's the reason why Pinto is ready to leave the island, Sam. It's the reason he has to be stopped." Tom's blinking had become incessant once more.

Sam stared at the purple liquid in his hand. He sat down on the corner of the crate and closed his eyes. He took a deep breath as he tried to calm himself down. He had to think more clearly. Think laterally. Do what he was good at. "You said Cadence is an elixir. You mean a potion of some sort?"

"Right. That's what you're holding." Tom and his accompanying stench sat down next to Sam. The broken top of the box creaked under their weight.

"And you say that this brings *eternal* life?"

"Right."

"Pinto uses the Cadence flower to make this. Pinto is the last Laird and he is also Captain Charles Frost?"

Tom turned, his shoulder making contact with Sam's. "*Captain*? How did you know?"

Sam realised his mistake. He hadn't mentioned the notebook to Tom. "Yes, I know." He took the notebook from his inside coat pocket. "It's in here."

Tom snatched it away and opened it at the first page. *Notes & Transcripts with Charles Frost.* His eyes appeared to double in size, as he read the name *Richard West* in the top right-hand corner. He laughed that spooky laugh once more. "Sam *West* and Richard *West.* Of course! Was Richard your father?"

Sam had to find out what Tom knew. He had to be forthcoming with answers. "My uncle. Late uncle. Died just after I was born."

Tom looked at Sam. "That's why you're here. That's why Pinto has lured you up here. You're the link to Richard." He pulled a knowing grin.

"*Pinto* has lured me up here. I thought it was George? Tom, I don't understand…."

Tom stood up. His blinking had calmed to a normal rate and his face had lit up like an excited boy who had just discovered all his Christmas presents. "It's the same reason I live like this. I know too much. I have to be killed…"

Sam was sick of the mystery. "Cut the cryptic shit, Tom. Just tell me what's going on. What have I got to do with any of this?"

"The answer's in the book. That's why Pinto wants me dead. That's why Pinto has brought you to the island, to kill you too."

"I've read the book several times, I still don't understand what it has to do with me."

"Not this notebook. I'm talking about the completed biography of *Charles Frost.*"

"You mean my Uncle's book was published?"

"I mean I've read it. Everything is in there."

"Where's the book, Tom?"

Tom laughed. His rapid blinking accompanied his fervour. "That's the funny thing, Sam. Pinto thinks I have it. It's probably why he hasn't killed me yet. But all this time it's been right under his nose."

Sam felt his heart race faster; nervous tension pulled across his neck and shoulders. "Where is it Tom?"

"I put it in such an obvious place, he'd never think to look there!"

"Where is it?" Sam shouted – his echo replaying back to him.

Tom stepped in closer, "The book's on his bookshelf, in the drawing room at Aul House."

"Shit. I was in there last night. You mean the room with the French doors overlooking the garden, right?"

"Yes. It's amongst all the other dusty old books that no one ever reads."

Sam swallowed hard and tried to slow his breathing. He dropped the vial he was still holding into his coat pocket.

"You have to kill Pinto, Sam. Before he kills you." Tom handed Sam his rifle.

Sam took it and hung it over his shoulder. It was much heavier than it looked.

"Everything you need to know is in the book." Tom winked. "Go! Pinto could be back at anytime."

"What are you going to do?"

"I have to destroy this Cadence. Go and be safe."

19:56

Thousands of midges swarmed around Sam's face as he hurried through the rapidly cooling evening air, over rocks and through the fields of thistle and bracken. Thoughts raged as fast as his thumping heart as he tried to process everything he had discovered. But nothing made sense, he only knew he had to get his Uncle Richard's biography of Frost. What was in the book that was worth killing for? Could Tom have been right about Pinto being the one who had lured him up to Aul? It occurred to him he had no idea what the book looked like. How could he have been so careless, to have not asked Tom for a description? Sam recalled the bookshelves in Pinto's drawing room. Leather-bound books covered three of the walls – there were easily five hundred, probably more, hiding the ghost written biography. It was a clever place to hide it but, then again, it was the worst now that Pinto was packing-up to leave. Perhaps he had already found it?

Sam stopped at the fence to the minefield to catch his breath. His shoulder still ached after his fall and his neck cracked with tension that had been building ever since leaving the office back in London on Monday. He was tired, soaked and hungry. He climbed the fence and walked over the lush grass. All the time looking out for Pinto, weary that he had most probably seen him with Tom earlier. His ears were tuned into every sound. Every rustle in the undergrowth and every squawk of a bird in the sky put him on high alert. So much so, that he jumped at the digital chime of his phone. He crouched down on one knee to read the text message.

Arrived at Aul House. Not safe here. Meet me in the village at 9. G x

Sam read it three times. Every time dwelling on the *x*. Was she flirting with him? He got back up and carried on at greater pace. *Not safe*? He considered calling back but his thoughts weren't coherent enough.

It started to rain as Sam hit the steep path that descended into the village. The angry grey skyline was dominated by the spires of St Cecilia's. It was almost rendezvous time with George and excitement and trepidation churned around his stomach. Sam picked up the pace, moving as quickly as his saturated leather soles would allow over the wet cobbles.

The village square was deserted. Sam re-read the text message from George and checked his watch again. But he needn't have bothered as the church bells chimed nine o'clock. He stood in the shadows of the church, scanning the square for George, tossing up whether to play it cool or go on the offensive straight from the off.

The light was fading rapidly as the sun disappeared behind the hidden horizon. Most curtains had already been closed in the windows of the houses around the perimeter of the square. The only sounds from the dozen horses tied up outside the pub and the *tap-tap* of rain on roofs and stone. Sam leant against the stone wall of the church and shifted his weight from foot to foot. His socks were soaked and his fingers already a little numb from the cold; he buried his hands deep into his coat pocket. Fifteen minutes passed and he began to grow impatient. He cursed under his breath.

Beginning to think he had been stood up he decided to go inside the church and see for himself the portraits of the last Laird, Seth Falcorrs, that Isla had told him about this morning. He had a final, unfruitful look around the square for George before tucking the rifle away in the tight gap between the side wall of the church and a free standing bicycle shed. The narrow gap was covered over with cobwebs and only just wide enough to fit the weapon – nobody would have reason to be looking there.

He unzipped his coat and went through the heavy wooden door of the church. The small foyer opened into an impressive space, with vaulted stone roof, painted with vivid fresco artwork that Sam assumed were important scenes from the bible. Black marble against white was used with no regard for cost, to decorate the floor with a series of crosses that stretched the length of the room, up to the altar. Two rows of pews ran with their backs to the wall, down both sides, illuminated by stumpy, glowing lamps every six feet. Sam was immediately taken back to his father's funeral - the smell of incense and candles, the smell of death and misery.

The only two people Sam could see in the church were on the front row of the pew to his right, up near the altar, their heads bowed. Sam recognised them as Isla and her mother Joanna. Thankfully, they hadn't seen him. He stopped and looked around for the paintings of the Laird. There were none in the spaces between the pillars and stained glass windows. No paintings at all. He looked again, now stood in the middle of the aisle in the centre of the church, rotating slowly three hundred and sixty degrees. Still nothing. He continued up the aisle, conscious his footsteps would soon alert attention to his presence. Sure enough, Isla looked up at him. She smiled and waved quickly. Sam returned the greeting and just as promptly returned his sights to the wooden altar, clad in a cream and gold runner with an embroidered cross.

"Can I be of assistance?" The hushed voice came from behind him.

Sam turned around and saw a small round woman in dog collar and black robes peering up at him. "You must be the vicar I've heard so much about," replied Sam in a reverent whisper.

The woman's cheeks flushed, she was probably in her fifties by the looks of her greying permed hair and beige sandals yet clear skinned and almost youthful looking. "Are you here to give thanks to the Lord?"

"Yes and to see the portraits of the last Laird my friend tells me are worth seeing."

The vicar frowned and put her hands behind her back, in a barrel-chested pose of affront. "You can't see them because they are gone."

"Gone?"

"Yes gone. They were taken away about half an hour ago."

"By whom?"

"Somebody from the Aul House Trust. Said they had to go as part of the sale of the house. They took all six paintings away."

"You had no warning that this was going to happen?"

"Certainly not." Her voice peaked in volume and echoed around the church.

Joanna was up and scuttling away down the aisle towards the exit, arm in arm with Isla.

"Very strange," mused Sam.

"Strange, how so?" said the vicar.

"I mean disappointing. I was hoping to see the portraits; I'm very interested in the history of the island."

"Disappointing is the word I would use too."

"Do you know the person who took them away?"

"No. The chap flashed some headed paper from The Aul House Trust and away he went with the paintings. I couldn't stop them as the portraits were only ever on loan." She crossed her arms. "You just don't expect these things to be taken away."

Sam was about to reply when he saw George at the back of the church. She stood hands by her side, wearing a green waxed jacket over a white jumper. Jeans and hiking boots kept her protected against the *shitty weather*. Her face was impassive, yet somehow saying '*Get a move on*'.

The vicar, with her back to George, had not seen or heard her. She continued her rant about the paintings as Sam thanked her and hurried his goodbyes. Looking back down the aisle he was disappointed to see George was gone. He rushed out into the darkness.

"Over here." The familiar voice came from the shadow near the bike shed.

Sam turned and followed the sound. He could only just make George out.

"Sorry I'm late. How are you?" she said, her lazy southern state accent was strangely comforting.

Sam was only a few inches from her when he replied, "I've been better. What kept you?"

"It took me longer than I thought to get away from the house. We only arrived a few hours ago and there's a lot to arrange before the party tomorrow night."

"*We*? Who's we – is Charles Frost with you?"

"No, he's arriving tomorrow for the party. He's making his grand entrance at midnight. You remember, when the gong strikes?"

Sam remembered... The crash of the gong and then being thumped in the face by those ginger thugs. "So who did you come up with?"

"The twins – Frost's body guards, and his chauffeur. Plus a boat load of caterers and party organisers."

Sam felt a surge of aggression. "The twins are at Aul House?"

"Don't get any ideas, Sam."

Sam ignored her, and pressed on. "Have you seen Pinto? Did he say anything about me?"

"Yes, I've just had dinner at the house with him. He's keeping a low profile. Says he's busy packing up the last of his things before leaving the island for good. He seems nice enough."

"He didn't say anything about me?"

"No, should he have? You haven't raised any suspicions have you?"

Sam didn't know where to start. He took a deep breath. "You said in your message it wasn't safe at the house, what did you mean?"

George sniffed, the cold was making her nose run. "Nothing, I just meant we shouldn't be seen together. We both work for Frost – I'm a hostess and you're his banker. There would be no reason why we should be meeting. We're undercover, remember." Her voice dropped to a whisper.

"Can we go somewhere to talk? There's a pub there." Sam pointed across the square. "A lot has happened that I need to tell you about."

"No, we can't be seen together. Tell me, what have you learnt? Have you gathered any intelligence to link Frost with the list of companies on the list I gave you?" Her tone was matter of fact, as cold as the night air.

Sam felt rejected, wishing for a bit more warmth and appreciation for everything he had been through. He wanted to confront her about the newspaper article and tell her to go shove her mission now she had broken her promise – she no longer had any leverage over him. But he held back. He wanted to save this for later. He ran his hands through his hair before replying. "Yes. I have."

George made a tutting sound between her teeth. "You have?" she sounded almost incredulous.

"Yes, I have. You surprised by that?"

"No, not at all. I only thought you would have been more forthcoming. So what have you got?"

"It's not here. We need to go up to the north of the island."

"Where? Why?"

"To the north, up on the cliffs. There's all the evidence you need."

"What's up there, Sam?" She leant in closer.

Sam could feel her minty breath against his nose. He got his first proper look at her porcelain skin and dark red lipstick. He noticed a black snood around her neck and wondered if that was only to protect against the cold, or to cover up her prominent birthmark.

"You mean *who*." Sam smiled.

"Who's up there?"

"Tom. Your old partner is up there and he can't wait to see you."

George stepped back into the shadows, almost falling back against the bike shed. "Are you shitting me? Are you sure it's him?"

Sam enjoyed having the upper hand for once. "I'm certain. He tells me he has all the evidence you need to expose Frost. But he wants to tell you himself. Says he can't trust me. He's been hiding out in the rocks waiting for you to come and rescue him."

"Oh my god. Is he okay?"

Sam smiled. He wanted to tell her that her partner had become a wild lunatic. "He's fine, but he could do with a shower and a good meal."

"This isn't funny, Sam. You have to take me to him, now."

It had all worked so easily. "Sure, follow me."

The instant *high* of feeling in control came crashing back to earth with a bump. George crossed her arms as Sam felt around in the dark recess behind the bike shed, for his rifle. But it was gone.

"Shit!" gasped Sam, now on his knees, double checking the gun hadn't fallen over onto the ground. All he felt was dirt and small stones.

"What is it?" George was down into a crouch to take a better look.

"Look, don't mess around with me, George."

"Huh? What are you talking about?"

"What have you done with my gun?" Sam got back up and wiped his hands on his coat.

"Oh my god, you have a gun?"

"I *had* a gun."

"You're meant to be a banker. Why the hell are you wandering around with a gun, Sam? Where did you get it from?"

"Tom gave it to me. He told me this island isn't safe." Sam started walking towards the path. The wind had swept the fine rain up into a squally mist, it was hard to see a thing.

George was next to him, her elbow occasionally brushed his as they walked into the darkness.

"How do you mean, not safe?" she asked.

"Tom wouldn't say. He'll only talk details to you." Sam was only half concentrating on the answer to George's question. Inside, he was panicked by the thought that somebody had his rifle. Had somebody been following him? Watching him? He looked over his shoulder to check they weren't being followed.

"What is it now?" George looked around too.

"Nothing, I'm just struggling to see." He picked up the pace.

"Maybe this will help." George flicked a switch and a beam of white light shot out in front of them, illuminating the path.

"You've come prepared." Sam was grateful but also aware that if they were being followed the torch made them even more vulnerable – a couple of sitting ducks.

"I'm a professional."

Let's see how professional you are when Pinto comes after us.

Mackay's cottage was about a hundred yards from where they trekked. Sam longed to cut across the field, introduce George to his new friend, and the three of them enjoy a bottle of wine in front of the open fire. Instead, the rain and wind grew stronger – pushing them off balance as they picked their way between the rocks. The wind came from the north, bringing with it the hiss and crash of the sea. Sam felt exposed and vulnerable. Bizarrely this feeling was made worse by having George with him. He couldn't explain it but he felt a strange duty of care towards her. After everything she had put him through he still *cared* for her.

"We should go back," he shouted over the howl of the wind.

"We can't, we've got to get to Tom."

"It's too dangerous. We can try again in the morning."

"I'm not turning back." George made her point by taking bigger strides through the bracken and heather. She was wearing the right clothes and boots for the job at hand, and very fit, powering off ahead.

Sam used the opportunity to check for anyone else following them. But it was useless. It was too dark to see. The clouds had defeated the stars and the moon. Looking back was like staring into a black hole. He turned around and sped up towards the bouncing white beam of light now well ahead of him.

They were soon at the fence marking the perimeter of the minefield. George shone the torch at the sign: KEEP OUT. DANGER. LANDMINES.

"Great, now what?" George was a little breathless as she spoke.

"We go over the top." Sam placed a foot on the horizontal wire.

"You crazy? It's a fucking minefield."

"It's the only way to the cliffs. And it's not a minefield. Somebody just doesn't want us in here."

"Oh yeah? How you so sure?"

"Tom took me through here. In fact, this will be my third time today. This weather's more likely to kill us than any mine." Sam climbed over and extended a hand to George.

She ignored the offer and pulled herself over. "You better be right, Sam."

Sam led the way through the streaky grass. It squeaked under his shoes as the bottom of his trousers soaked up more and more rainwater and mud. George stayed right behind him. He could sense her steps landing exactly where his had landed only moments beforehand. He walked in a straight line, directly north.

"Did you just hear that?" George stopped and clicked off the torch. The wilderness was rendered completely black.

Sam stopped and span around. His senses were on edge, trying to locate whatever – whoever – it was George had heard. "What was it?" he whispered. He reached out a hand that landed on George's shoulder.

She didn't react. Her heavy breathing the only sound he could hear through the wind.

"I don't know. It came from beside us. Somewhere to our right." She was motionless, her voice hushed and flat.

Sam's heart pounded. He looked around in vain. "Let's keep going. Keep the torch off until we're sure it's nothing." He used his hand on George's shoulder to guide her past him and on ahead.

George obliged but just as quickly fell in beside him, linking her arm around his as they walked much more slowly, side-by-side. They said nothing to one another, staring into the blackness. Sam was calmed by the faith George showed in him.

It sounded like a twig snapping beneath a shoe. Sam couldn't be sure whose. It was the last sound he remembered before the blinding blue light and an eardrum pounding boom.

He lay face down.

A horrible quiet.

Where am I? My head. My ears!

Sam struggled to his feet. Dazed and disoriented. Somebody pulled at him. He turned and blinked rapidly. George shone the torch at him. His headache peaked in the bright light.

She's alive! Why can't I hear her?

George pulled him on, his hand in hers. They followed the white spot of light ahead of them as fast as they could.

A shrill ringing pierced the silence and then the sounds started to return. The wind. The heavy breathing. The scuff of boots and shoes. Finally, they came to the fence and over they fell. Up the steep rocky incline and under the shelter of an overhang they sat catching their breath. George flicked the torch off.

"Are you okay?" she asked after several minutes. She turned to face Sam who was wedged up against her, keeping close to benefit from the shelter.

"I think so. Are you? What the fuck just happened?" Sam needed a drink.

"So much for no mines. We should have been killed back there. I thought you'd had your legs blown off when I saw you on the ground."

Sam hitched his knees up to his chest and dropped his head forward. He did his best to force the realisation away. The realisation he'd almost died. Worse, he could have killed George. With both hands in his hair he sighed and breathed deeply, drawing in as much oxygen as he could. *Tom you fucking madman. You fucking maniac.* Sam couldn't believe he'd followed him through this field so obligingly earlier today. He barely trusted a sole in London and, yet, here he was, following lunatics through minefields!

George put a hand on his back. "Sam, it's ok. We're fine now." She rubbed his spine in a small circular motion.

The sensation felt good and Sam never wanted it to stop. Why had he believed a word Tom had said? The man was the real menace on this island. Not the housekeeper and botanist, John Pinto! Sam wanted to come clean to George, tell her exactly what he was thinking.

"We need to keep moving, Sam. It's late and I need to get to Tom. He may have enough to make our move on Frost. We're so close." She stopped rubbing and was up. The torch flicked back on, "Come on. Which way is it from here?"

Sam looked up, "George, there's something I want to tell you about Tom."

"Sure Sam, walk and talk." She pulled him to his feet, her hands soft and gentle.

They carried on, Sam slightly ahead, leading up the steep rock and onto the plateau. They were unmistakably close to the sea. The hiss and roar of the crashing waves against the jagged rock below. They were only a minute from Tom.

"Be careful. One big gust and you're over the edge." Sam had to shout over the noise and bluster.

George shone the torch down at the angry water, a hundred feet or so, below. "Shit, that's a long way. I don't think we can be lucky twice in one night. Where's Tom?"

Sam pointed at the cliff face a few yards ahead of them.

"We have to go down *there*?" There was a sense of resignation in her question.

"We don't have to do anything, George. I think we should wait until the morning. The storm's too bad."

"No. We've come this far." George peered over the edge and shone the torch toward Tom's cave in the cliff face. She used the torch light to trace the path along the ridge six feet below her, back to her own position, then back to the cave. The light shone through a plume of smoke; Tom must have been inside, next to a fire.

"Lower me down, Sam. Give me your hand." She held the torch between her teeth and sat down, dangling her legs over the side.

"No, George. It's too dangerous. I won't help you." Sam was drawn closer to her, compelled to pull her back in-land.

"Tom! It's me George!" She was screaming, waving the torch around in excitement.

Sam looked along the cliff face. Tom's head peered out, staring back at them, illuminated by the torch. His face framed by his filthy, matted, long hair and beard. His expression incredulous as he processed the voice calling his name.

"Tom, I've come back to get you. It's me, *Georgie*."

Tom grew larger as he emerged fully from the rock. He was topless. His back against the rock. Bare chest to the north. Defiant in the face of the wind and the rain that pummelled him. He shuffled toward them. The torch shone against his legs and then his bare feet.

"Be careful!" cried George.

Sam wiped the rain out of his eyes with his sleeve.

"Nooooooo!" The scream was chilling.

Sam winced. He couldn't believe his eyes... Tom flailing with his arms and legs... Down... Down... Gone into the water below.

George screamed. She dropped the torch. "Tom! No..." She broke down.

Sam forced his hands under her armpits and pulled her away from the edge. He picked her up into a fireman's lift. The strength coming from some unknown reserve of energy, over ruling the pain from his injured shoulder. George kicked and punched – screaming and sobbing for Tom. But Sam kept going, squeezing his forearms tighter around her the more she resisted. Eventually she gave up and her deadweight became heavier as fatigue overcame his adrenaline rush.

The old lookout at Northern Head was only a couple of minutes away. The ancient ruins were ordinarily a few old stones but tonight they were shelter. They climbed through a small hole, lined with moss and lichen into a lower level that provided overhead cover.

Once more they were huddled together. Soaked. Frozen. Scared. Shaken.

23:30

The rain had stopped and the wind was now nothing more than a breeze. Such a contrast to earlier but such was Aul.

They shared the last of Sam's whisky. Forced together for warmth; Sam leant against the wall and George with her back against his chest, the smell of her perfume all about him. She pulled his arms around her as she finally stopped crying. She had given him a *warm-pack* which emitted heat when a button in its gel was pressed – its exothermic reaction turning the gel hard as it brought warmth to numb fingers. Sam said very little, only the odd word to encourage George to sleep. It would be light by around five and then they could make their way back.

"Thank you, Sam."

Sam had fallen into a light sleep but didn't mind the interruption. "What for?"

"Thank you for pulling me away from the edge. Thank you for taking me to see Tom." Her voice was calm.

Sam looked up. The clouds had cleared and billions of stars sparkled down at them. The moon glowed like a small sun. It was a miraculous sight. Breathtaking under any other circumstance. "Do you really think that? I can't help thinking if we hadn't come here tonight Tom would still be alive. I wish I hadn't brought you." Perhaps he was too honest?

"No, Tom had been dead for a long time. That wasn't Tom we saw on the cliffs. That was an impostor. A horrible version of Tom… Some product of this horrible place and fucked-up people like Charles Frost."

Sam closed his eyes and swallowed. "George, when will you realise that this thing with Frost is all nonsense?"

George crossed her arms more tightly. "You're referring to the Seth Falcorrs fake ID, I take it?"

That was furthest from Sam's mind but as she had raised it he went with it. "Did you get to the bottom of that?"

"Yep. I hate to admit it but there must be a mole in our operation. My theory is Frost has a person on the inside."

"Any ideas who?"

"Only four people know about our operation. One of them…" she paused, "was Tom. Then there's you and me. That only leaves my commanding officer. I can't raise my suspicions to him, obviously."

"Who is your CO?"

"It's best that I don't tell you anymore. But I've had enough. Tomorrow night we get Frost and we're done. Then we're out of here." George clenched a defiant fist.

Sam could feel her shivering, so he wrapped himself closer around her – the back of her hair and the woollen snood tickled his nose. "Hold on. This has to stop *now*. Tom's dead. My neighbour's dead. We almost died tonight. Enough's enough."

"We're so close. You said Tom had the evidence to nail Frost. Is it in his cave? We can go when it gets light. Do you know what's in there? We can't let all those guys die for nothing."

Sam wasn't sure if she meant this or whether it was another of her games – more emotional blackmail. It was time to play a few more cards. "You have nothing more on me, you know that, don't you? I read the newspaper article about *my death*."

George turned her head, her hair brushing across Sam's face, her cheek and lips only an inch away from his own. Blue light glowed around her silhouette.

"I wondered if you'd seen that. You have to believe that wasn't me. That was the mole. They're working against us. They don't want us to crack this. Don't you see? They have something to hide. There's something worth exposing here. What if there's something in Tom's cave. What if the answer to unlock this is in there, Sam?"

Sam laughed.

"What's so funny?"

"'What if' are the two most dangerous words ever uttered," said Sam through his laughter.

"Sam, you're hysterical. I think you need to sleep." George turned herself around to face him, her back propped up against the inside of his right knee.

"No, I'm not. My therapist, Dr Carter, taught me all about 'what if'. Do you know that? Did your intelligence and background checks tell you that about my *mad* past?"

George ran her tongue along her lips and wiped the excess moisture off with her hand. "No, I didn't know that."

"It's true. I've been going to therapy since my mother died. Every week for ten years. Jesus, that's over five hundred hours talking about my worries, my anxiety, my aversions." Sam stared deep into George's eyes. It felt surprisingly good telling her something she didn't already know.

"No I didn't know about it. Anyway, I'm American, therapy's no big deal."

"I started going because after she died things between my father and me got worse. We stopped talking altogether. I realised it was her that kept us together. I was worried…" Sam couldn't finish his sentence.

"It's alright. Don't worry."

"Worry. Did you know worry is an *aversion*? Worry's an aversion to uncertainty… That's my problem, I find it hard coping with uncertainty. I don't like not knowing. Questions like 'what if this?' and 'what if that?' set me off on a downward spiral of despair. One single innocuous 'what if' can kick start a chain of thoughts that lead me to some very dark places."

"We don't have to talk about this, if you don't want to." Her breath formed minty clouds between them.

"I do want to…" Sam's eyes searched for the words, "*Hypothetical Event Worry* it's called. It's a fictional worry driven by a core value I hold deep inside me… Find your core value and you find why you invent worries in your mind… It took me ten years and thousands in shrink bills to find mine." Sam dropped the *warm-pack* which was now rock hard and out of heat. He ran his hands through his hair.

"You do that a lot. The hands through your hair thing."

"Yep. It's something I learnt in my therapy. I learnt to observe my thoughts and the sensations they cause. Every time I feel they are getting the better of me or a negative sensation is forming, like butterflies in my stomach or muscle tension in my shoulders, I diffuse it by distracting myself with a sensation I enjoy – the feeling of hair running between my fingers.

George took his hand. Her skin was cold. She placed it on her head and gently ran his hand through her silky hair. She leant into him and rested her face on his chest. Her other arm wrapped around his waist.

Sam kept his hand in hers and basked in her intimacy.

They didn't say anything for a few minutes. Sam looked down at George's face. Her eyes closed. He closed his eyes and sighed. "When I discovered my core value it was like staring face to face with my greatest enemy. It was victory and defeat all in one… I literally felt a huge weight lift off my shoulders. I was free… *freer*.

"At the heart of all my uncertainty and all my anxiety was fear… A fear of not being perfect… Perfection was my enemy… It still is my enemy… The idea of not being the best, of underperforming, of letting anyone down… Letting myself down. That's what I fear most. That's what makes me who I am." He opened his eyes. It felt so good opening up and sharing with George, just as good as it did to hold her so closely under the moon and the stars. He looked down at her face, awaiting her response…

But the gentle rise and fall of her chest across his stomach and the peaceful expression across her face told him she was gone. He closed his own eyes and breathed in the fresh sea air. Despite everything that had happened, he felt at peace. Lighter. Happier than he could remember.

Day Four

05:09

Sam watched the sun's orange glow grow in strength across the steel sky. He timed its progress on his watch – the watch George had given him. His left arm was all he could move, as George still slept soundly against his chest, wrapped around him for warmth and still holding his right hand in hers.

Sam was stiff and uncomfortable, the base of his back cramped and in desperate need to stretch. But he didn't mind any of this. Still a serene contentment ran over him. His gaze flicked between the sun spreading across the horizon and George's porcelain skin and slightly blushed cheek – natural beauty all about him.

It was six o'clock when George opened her eyes and sat up right. She stretched both arms out and rubbed her eyes. Turning to face Sam her expression snapped from the hazy befuddlement of early morning, into stern consternation – her eyebrows pinched so hard they almost touched.

"Good morning," Sam smiled.

"We need to go." George was up, dusting herself off.

Sam got to his feet. The stiffness in his limbs meaning he could only move at half the speed George managed. He wanted to say something, ask what last night meant to her, "What's the rush?" was all he could pluck up the courage to say.

George was already climbing over the ancient ruined wall of the old fort. It was the first time Sam had seen her in the light since London. He noted she was wrapped up really warm, even her black socks were insulated. He followed her out as she made her way back along the cliff top. He knew exactly where she was heading as she strode away from him. Sam stopped and looked all around him. To the north the sea was calm – shimmering gently in the early morning sun. To the south the rugged rock and heathland of Aul looked as uninviting as ever. But at least the weather had calmed, the sound of howling gales and crashing waves replaced by birdsong and the squawk of hungry seagulls. Sam took deep breaths of the clean air. A black cormorant flew overhead and landed on the cliff only a few yards from where he was standing. His mind was taken back to when he had first arrived on Aul and a similar thing had happened.

As expected George had returned to the area of last night's incident, holding a tissue in one hand, the other keeping her hair out of her face. Sam approached slowly and placed a hand on her shoulder. She immediately recoiled and flicked him an angry look. Sam pulled his hand away.

"I'm sorry about Tom," said Sam.

Both of them looked down at the rocks and surf below, searching for a body. But of course there was no body. The sea far too powerful to leave anything or anyone at rest.

George dabbed her eyes with the tissue. "Tonight we nail Frost." Her voice was clear and certain. Then she turned and marched off inland.

Sam was relieved she hadn't attempted to get down into Tom's cave but at the same time he felt rejected, jilted after their closeness last night. Had it meant nothing to her? Had she just used him for comfort and warmth? That's all he was to her... a resource... another pawn in her fight to *nail Frost*.

They walked the long way around, following the coast line, avoiding the minefield which had almost killed them only a few hours ago. Sam used the map he'd taken from the kitchen wall at Aul House to navigate along the bridleways and worn paths through the heather and bracken. They said nothing to one another. All the time Sam kept an eye out for Pinto and turned over whether to tell George about the Cadence flower and the purple vials in the underground spa. He held the vial Tom had given him deep in his coat pocket. But there was still something nagging at him, something not clear.

"Have you ever met Charles Frost, George?"

George stopped walking and tucked her hair behind her ears. "No."

"Have you ever seen him, with your own eyes – been in the same room?"

"No."

"But you say you are working for him. Yet you've never met him?"

"Yes."

"This doesn't seem strange to you?"

"No. Plenty of folks work for a boss they've never met. Have you met the Chairman of your bank?"

Sam had to concede he had not. But George's response didn't satisfy him. It felt defensive… evasive. He pressed on: "Have you ever seen a photograph of Frost?"

"No, I have not." George continued walking. She pulled her snood off and unzipped her coat, as the warmth of the now blazing morning sun combined with the heat of walking at speed.

Her biscuit coloured birthmark over her neck caught Sam's attention but he was careful not to stare. "And you don't think it strange that in this day and age nobody's taken a photo of Frost? No CCTV? With all the combined resources of the British and American intelligence forces there's not a single photograph. I don't buy it."

"I know. It's something I've given a lot of thought to, too. It's another reason I'm sure there's a mole in our camp. It's another reason I'm sure someone is fighting against me – and you. I'm sure there are photographs of Frost."

"And you've never challenged your superiors for them. Not even one?"

"It's not how we work. Everything's *need to know*. You are only told something or given a piece of intelligence if it's going to help you achieve your objective. Gossip and interesting information are dangerous. That's how people get caught. That's how people get killed in my line of business."

"What exactly is your line of business?"

"*Need to know*, remember." George carried on down the bridleway.

Sam couldn't believe this was the same person he had opened up to last night. It annoyed him to think he told her about his therapy and his problems. He had told nobody about those things before. He hoped she really had fallen asleep and not just feigned it out of politeness or, even worse, out of awkwardness and pity. His heart raced. He'd had enough of the games.

"I'll tell you something you need to know." Sam grabbed George's shoulder and forced her to stop. They stared at each other. "What if I told you Charles Frost is actually John Pinto. They are the same person. Pinto is behind all of this. He's lured us all here to have us killed."

"I'd say why should I believe that?" She was unfazed by Sam's revelation.

"Because it's what Tom told me. It's why he's been AWOL for eighteen months. It's the reason he was living wild in that cave, in fear of his life, hunted by Pinto."

George nodded her head as she digested the notion. "But what has that to do with you and me? You said he's lured *us* up here."

"I don't know everything but I bet Pinto's your mole."

"I need more than '*I bet*', Sam." George put her hands on her hips.

"How about this?" Sam pulled out the exercise book and the purple vial of Cadence.

George took them. She read the first page and held the vial up to the sunlight. Her eyebrows unfurled and her expression transformed into wide-eyed interest.

Sam talked her through every page of the exercise book and all about the flowers Pinto was growing in the minefield, the underground spa and Tom's insistence that he find the answers he was looking for in the biography back at Aul House.

George listened intently. Finally, she said: "Well done, Sam. Great job."

Sam felt a rush of exhilaration. It was both the recognition and also the fact that George didn't think the story too farfetched or that he was mad to have believed it. But in typical George style she brought him back down to earth: "I only wish you'd told me all of this last night, then Tom may be…" she broke off, unable to end her own sentence.

All Sam could do was walk off over the muddy track, still sodden from last night's rain. "I'm going to find that book and I'm gone from here. I'm not going to hang around to be killed."

George caught up with him. "This is yours." She handed back the exercise book but retained the purple vial. "I'll keep this and get some tests done on it. You don't buy the elixir crap do you? Poor Tom must have been really ill."

"No, of course I don't believe the *elixir crap*. But I do believe that this has something to do with me." He waved the exercise book in George's face. "The answer's in my Uncle Richard's biography of Frost."

"You can't go to the house, Sam. Pinto is there and so are the twins. If Pinto and Frost are the same person then the twins work for him. They'll get you if Pinto doesn't first."

A sudden beating sound split the tension. *Thud, thud, thud*. Getting louder and louder. It was coming from up the track. Sam grabbed George's hand and pulled her into the trees and they crouched amongst the shadows. "Quiet," he whispered.

The horse came galloping past. The rider kicking furiously, forcing it on.

Sam jumped out as the beast charged on, "Isla, hey it's me, Sam!"

Isla heaved at the reins and Marmite shied and snorted as she pulled him around.

Sam ran up the track towards Isla, close enough to see her eyes were swollen with tears.

"Sam, thank god it's you," said Isla. "Come quickly. It's Mackay. Something's happened to Mackay."

07:04

Exhausted, struggling to find his breath, Sam slid down the slope to the croft. George lagged behind, still annoyed with him for allowing anyone to see them together. She refused to hurry. Isla and Marmite were waiting for them outside the croft, having charged on ahead. Isla was banging on the green front door, calling for Mackay.

"Calm down, Isla." Sam was so breathless he could barely get the words out, his chest ached. "Tell me exactly what's going on."

Isla went to the window and up on her tip toes as she peered inside, both hands around her eyes as if she was searching through binoculars. "Look…" Her voice quivered. "I'm sure I can see him, on the floor. I can see the top of his head."

Sam joined her at the window and Isla stepped aside. His heavy breathing misted up the cold glass. He squinted as he looked past the sink and scanned the kitchen floor. "I don't see anything."

"Next to the table, on the left-hand side. His white hair…"

Sam pressed his nose against the glass. He could see something beside the carver chair at the top of the table – something white on the stone floor. "It could be anything… A towel or wool from his workshop?"

"No." Isla was crying. "Something's not right, I tell you."

"Why are you so sure?" Sam continued looking through the glass.

"The sheep are still in the barn. They should be out by now."

Sam stepped across to the front door, trying the knob in vain. "And why are you here so early in the morning? It's only just seven."

"Breakfast rolls." She pointed to the knapsack hanging from Marmite's saddle.

Sam remembered yesterday morning at the doctor's. He suddenly became aware of the bleating sheep in the barn across the field. It didn't feel right. He banged on the door. "Mackay, are you there? Open up!"

George had appeared at the top of the slope, skulking like a grumpy toddler.

"Is that your girlfriend, Sam?" asked Isla through her sobs.

"Absolutely not. Why don't you go around the back and see if you can find a way in through his workshop." He banged on the door again, as Isla disappeared down the side of the cottage. Still nothing. He forced his right shoulder hard into the door. It shook in its old frame. He did it again. Adrenaline and heat grew through his body.

Marmite snorted and pulled against his tethered reins.

"What the hell are you doing?" George screamed over the din.

Sam paid no attention as he forced himself harder and harder against the door. Each blow hurt more and more but this didn't matter.

"Stop! Stop!" George tried to get in the way but Sam couldn't be stopped. He pushed her aside with his left arm.

She stumbled backwards, almost landing against Marmite.

The door gave some more, now an inch ajar, but still held by the lock.

Sam stepped back, pivoted on his right foot, raising his left high from the ground.

"Oh great, now he thinks he's Jackie Chan," snapped George.

Sam uncoiled with tremendous aggression, simultaneously letting out a guttural yell. The sole of his shoe hit the door level with the lock and it continued on, into the house, as the green paint flashed away and the door fell from its hinges – timber and ironmongery crashed and clattered over the stone floor.

George yelled something as she grabbed hold of Sam just as his foot returned to the earth.

They stood side-by-side peering into the dark croft.

There, in front of them, the body of an old man with fluffy white hair, lying on his side on the kitchen floor, his back towards them. Motionless… Lifeless.

Sam ran inside. His knees thudded against the stone floor next to Mackay's head. He turned him over. Mackay's head lolled and made a terrible, hollow crack against the hard surface. His skin was ashen. The horrible grey of death. His once bright blue eyes now matte navy studs.

"No. Mackay! No…" Sam wrapped an arm around him. Tears burst from his eyes.

George pulled at his back, tugging him across the kitchen towards the sink.

Sam tried to push her off, in doing so he noticed his right hand was crimson red, caked in Mackay's blood.

George also saw it and let go.

Sam dropped down, back over the body to see the pool of blood that had collected under Mackay's forehead. He used his left hand to close Mackay's eyes before he slumped back against the leg of the dining table. The tears came harder and faster.

He could hear George speaking to Isla, who had come inside too.

Sam wiped his eyes to see George taking her outside, arm over her shoulder.

"Get a doctor. It will be alright. Ride to the village." Sam heard George tell Isla.

He dropped his head back onto his knees, the sound of his sobs as loud as the thud-thud of Marmite, ridden by Isla, galloping away.

"We need to go," said George, coming back inside. Her curt, bossy voice had returned.

Sam looked up at her standing over him, "What the fuck are you talking about? Go where?"

George crouched down, her eyes level with his. "Get back to our mission. This has nothing to do with us. The last thing we need is to be implicated in any way with this."

Sam looked down at his bloody hands. "What is *this*? Hey? Tell me."

George held her stare deep into Sam's eyes. "This is trouble. It's trouble neither of us needs."

"It's murder," screamed Sam. "It's fucking, murder!" He stood up.

George put a hand down on the floor behind her to maintain balance as Sam stepped past her.

"You call this *trouble*. Can you hear yourself?" Sam spoke through his tears as he walked to the sink. He turned the tap on with his elbow and scrubbed his hands clean. "You're not normal George. You've grown cold. This fucked-up job of yours has made you inhuman." He looked out of the window at the grass. He couldn't bear to see the blood on his hands. "Mackay was my friend. He saved my life. Did you know that? I was trying to call you on the boat on the way over here…" He was too angry to say anymore. He turned the tap off and shook the excess water from his hands.

George was still crouching over Mackay on the far side of the dining table. Sam noticed his forged driving licence on top of Mackay's *Cryptic Jumbo* crossword puzzle book. He must have left the licence here yesterday evening. He picked up the plastic card and looked at his photograph next to the name *Seth Falcorrs*. He shook his head and wiped his eyes on his sleeve, about to toss the licence at the fire when he noticed scribbles over the cover of *Cryptic Jumbo*. He picked it up and stared in silence for some time. "What the… An anagram… He cracked…" A mixture of anger and aggression ran through him "George, look at this."

George stood up, her back turned to Sam, her hair hanging over her eyes.

Sam passed her the book.

She took it without turning to face him, holding the *Cryptic Jumbo* in both hands.

"Charles Frost is an anagram of Seth Falcorrs." Sam coughed as he shouted. "Mackay had worked it out!" He ran his hands through his hair. "It was starring me in the face all along. How could I have been so blind?!"

George put the book on the table, pulled out a dining chair and sat down. She was still turned away from Sam.

"What's up with you? Don't have any answers?" snapped Sam. "Caught by surprise by this one were you? You're not in such a hurry to go now…" Adrenaline pulsated through his entire body, goose bumps tingled down his back.

George leant her elbows against the table and buried her head into her hands. Her shoulders bobbed up and down.

Sam was stunned by the realisation she was crying. Her sudden shift in mood caught him off guard. He put the driving licence in his coat pocket as George's bravado and coldness dissolved in front of him.

"I'm sorry, Sam…" she finally said, head now resting on her forearms against the table. "It wasn't meant to be like this…"

Sam swallowed. His throat hurt from all the shouting.

"I don't know what I've gotten into…" George continued, the timbre of her voice rose higher over a new wave of sobs.

"What about *me*?"

"… Got us both into… They told me this was just a game."

The hairs on the back of Sam's neck prickled at the words. "What?! A *game*?" His heart rate picked up. He gripped the back of the chair in front of him.

George looked up, through bloodshot eyes. "I'm sorry. You have to believe me. I had no idea any of this was going to happen." She tried to look at Mackay down to her left but she seemed unable. "Sit down."

Sam took a deep breath and pulled out the chair he was gripping. It screeched over the stone floor.

George winced at the sound. Tears still rolled down her cheeks.

"Tell me everything. You can start with who you really are." Sam kept his fists clenched on the table in front of him.

"My name is Georgina Norton. I do prefer George. I'm an actress," her accent softened with each word. Gone was the southern drawl.

"Where are you from?"

"New York. Look, please let me finish." She tucked her hair behind her ears and dried her eyes on her sleeve.

Sam turned away.

"I'm just like any dreaming, impoverished actor. Except I'm now over thirty and I have this." She leant her head to one side and pointed to her birthmark. "There's very little work for girls like me."

Sam felt a shred of warmth at her vulnerability but didn't want to let it show, "And what are you, exactly?"

"I'm a damn fine actor that's what I am. You know how good? Good enough for the *New York Times* to describe my performance in *Route 60 Hicks* as 'the most compelling and convincing performance Broadway has seen in years!'"

Sam remembered the girl in the advert on the front of *The Evening Standard* back in London. "You were in *Route 60 Hicks*?"

"I wasn't just in it, I was the lead. Rave reviews, a fifty two week sell-out run on Broadway and now it's going around the world. First stop London."

"But without their star?"

"Right. Replaced by a younger, hotter, defect-free model." George used the back of her hand to gesticulate at her birthmark. She let out a big sigh before continuing, "I knew it was too good to be true. You see, *60 Hicks* was written by a friend of mine from college, so that's how I got the part in the first place. But when the show got so big, even bigger than him and Broadway, that's when the money took over... Just two days before I was due to fly to London for rehearsals they dumped me... Fucking typical..." Her cheeks were red and tears swelled in her eyes. "Then that same day I got a call from my agent about a job in London. They told me it was an executive training course. Some future leaders course that you were on. It was random but the money was over twice what *60 Hicks* were paying and..." She let out a little laugh and sniffed up her tears, "it felt like screw you *60 Hicks* and your sex sells bullshit, I'm going to London anyway!"

"So, this was Gema Bank?" Sam banged the table with his right fist.

"All I was told is this was some extreme management training course. I was to play the part of Agent Hall."

Sam felt lightheaded. He stood up and went to the sink. He picked up a mug from the draining board and filled it with water.

"Could I get one of those, please?" asked George.

Sam gulped down his own, re-filled the mug and handed it to George. He remained standing as George took a sip. "So it was all lies. Everything?"

"Yes." George's eyes were glazed over with tears.

Sam thought back to his meeting with Jerry on Monday. How Jerry had softened him up by talking about his late father first before sending him up here. His mouth was already dry again. His thoughts shifted to the Mayfair club and his first meeting with George. "So all that stuff you told me about your dead father and having to be strong for your mother was all lies too?"

George just nodded.

Tension grew over Sam's shoulders. He sat down again and looked hard at George. "I need to know everything. Who hired you? I want names."

George took another sip of water before answering. She'd finally stopped crying. "The only people I've dealt with were the red headed twins, Clive and Clyde. I can't be sure that's their real names."

"The ginger bastards that hit me, right?"

"Yes. You have to believe me, I didn't know they were going to do that."

"Did you ever deal with Jerry Hart or anyone from Gema Bank?"

George looked perplexed by the name and shook her head. "Only the twins. They pay me in cash and there was no formal contract… Before you say anything, I know that the whole thing sounds dodgy but I wasn't thinking straight after *60 Hicks*. Plus, it was great money."

Sam believed her. "Carry on. What were you told to do by the twins?"

"As I said, they hired me about six weeks ago. My agent got a call, said they wanted me in London that same day. They flew me out first class. That evening I was given the whole story about my billionaire boss Charles Frost and the terrorism plot. My first part was to meet you at the club, get you drunk and slip away when the gong sounded."

"Did you spike my drink that night?"

"No. The barman did."

Sam thumped the table again.

George jumped. "Again, I didn't know. But after I saw the mess you were in I asked him and he told me he was paid to do it by the twins."

"So that whole party at the club in Mayfair was staged?"

"I guess so," George shrugged, "I don't know."

Suddenly a thought hit him. "Hold on. This means Mrs Price isn't dead!"

George smiled. "No, she's not dead. She's fine and her cat. In fact, she let me in to your place to get your Gema Bank ID while you were jogging… I told her I was your girlfriend." She pulled her dimpled grin.

The news that Mrs Price was still alive brought much needed relief. "So the police, the body on the stretcher and the newspaper article…"

"All staged."

"But your driving through London to the safe house? You were so convincing." Sam frowned.

"The twins again – they sent me on a driving course in Northampton. I was taught how to drive at speed, skid pans, handbrake turns and stuff… They even got me a personal trainer to build up my strength and stamina… I was told to get you to that apartment in Isle of Dogs as fast as I could on Monday night."

Sam rubbed his eyes. His head spinning as he tried to make sense of the revelations. He pulled the driving licence from his pocket. "And this fake ID." He tossed it over to George. "It looks so real. How did you get this? It worked through security at City Airport for fuck's sake!"

"All I know is that these guys have a lot of money and resources, Sam." George finished her water and got up.

Sam noticed she avoided looking at Mackay.

"Do you mind if we go outside?" George clearly couldn't bear the sight of the corpse.

"Sit down. We're not going anywhere until you've finished answering my questions."

George nodded with resignation and sat down again.

"So this island and everyone here are actors too?"

"I don't know, Sam. I really don't know… I'm drip fed information. I didn't know I was coming to the island until yesterday."

"But you sent me a text on Tuesday!" Sam patted his sides in search of the clunky old mobile phone George had given him.

"I didn't send those messages… and there's something you need to know about that phone… and the watch I gave you."

Sam pulled up his sleeve on his coat to reveal the chunky digital watch. "Go on, what is it?"

"They are tracking and listening devices. I'm pretty sure that's how they've kept tabs on you since you left London." George curled up her lip and frowned at the watch as if conscious her confession was being listed to.

Sam felt violated. Sickened. He jolted up, sending his chair crashing down onto the floor behind him. He pulled at the watch strap so hard that the clasp sprang open, sending the watch face-first onto the hard stone. He found the grey mobile phone in his coat pocket and smashed that too on the floor, stamping on both of the devices repeatedly until shards of plastic and metal splinters spread out over the floor. He picked up the two shattered carcasses and tossed them onto the smouldering fire, the plastic immediately warping and curling in the heat. He was red faced and breathless, his heart racing. The thought of those ginger bastards – and who else? – listening and tracking him for the last three days revolted and incensed him. He wanted to scream. He looked out through the gaping hole in the wall where the front door had been. Mackay and Isla weren't actors… Surely? He took a deep breath of the fresh sea air and turned back inside.

George was standing again. She'd unzipped her coat. Her white cashmere was too thick for indoors, in front of the fire.

"I see," said Sam. "It's obvious now. The way you're dressed. You knew we were going to spend the night outside didn't you? It was all part of the act… And the minefield, the explosion was all fixed too?"

"Yes. That was horrible. I almost came clean then…"

Sam interrupted. "And the whole thing with Tom! That was all an act… Who the hell is that guy?"

George took a step towards him.

Sam raised his hand. "Who is he really? Because I know what I saw last night. He fell from those rocks."

George stopped. "You saw what you were meant to see. Tom's a Hollywood stuntman. We rehearsed that a few times on the Isle of White… He's fine too. There will have been a boat waiting to pick him up."

Sam rubbed his hands through his hair. Then, when he realised what he was doing he stopped. The action triggered a memory from last night. "Fuck you. Fuck you all…"

"Sam…" George pulled an unconvincing smile.

"No. I told you things last night I thought I would never share. I thought we had almost died. I thought we had just witnessed a man falling to his death… I can't believe you did that to me." He realised he was blushing as his cheeks surged with blood. "Tell me, were you really asleep when I was telling you all that stuff last night?"

George looked to the floor, "No, I wasn't but I pretended to sleep out of respect."

"Respect!" screamed Sam.

247

"Yes, respect." George snapped and screamed back. "I'm human too, you know. You opened up and I respected you for it. It would have been wrong for me to continue the act..."

"Well thank you, George." Sam turned around and stood in the doorway. "And thank you for being such a great listener!"

George appeared next to him. The pair of them looked out across the fields, at the bright blue sky. The cool breeze in their faces. They stood like this in silence.

Finally, Sam asked, "So what's meant to happen next?"

"What do you mean?"

"I mean, according to your script. What happens next?"

George sighed. "There's no script. A lot of it's improvisation... And..." she broke off, unable to finish her sentence.

"What? Tell me. And what?"

George bit down on her lip and shook her head. She pulled something from her pocket – a small black plastic box with an earpiece connected by a thin wire. "I've been using this most of the time we've been together. Getting updates from the twins."

Sam remembered the snood. It wasn't to keep her warm nor to cover up her birthmark. Instead she used it to hide the wire... So the twins had heard everything he said to George last night. He pictured them laughing and mocking him from some dark room. Anger overcame him. He grabbed George by the arms and shook her.

Her eyes were startled and terrified.

"You bitch. You manipulative bitch," Sam screamed at her, their faces almost touching.

"Let go!" She wriggled and tried to pull away.

Sam squeezed tighter. "Can you speak to them through that?"

"No. It's one way. They were listening through your watch. Let me go!"

"What did they tell you last night?"

"Nothing. It was only when you told me about the exercise book and your Uncle Richard this morning that they really had anything to say. Before that everything was going to plan."

Sam let go.

George pushed him in the chest with both hands.

Sam didn't flinch. "And what plan was that?"

George regained her composure, her face flushed red. "The plan was to take you through the minefield and have you believe you were almost blown up. You were to witness Tom's death and spend the night away from Aul House."

"Why?"

"I don't know. As I said, I'm drip fed information. All I know is tonight there's the party at the house that you are to attend. After that I'm done – I'm paid the rest of my money and it's over."

"So that's all this is about to you – money?"

George kicked the doorframe with her boot. "Isn't that all anything is about to *you?* You're the banker!" She crossed her arms and gave him a defiant stare.

Sam attempted to regain control. "So the twins *are* on the island?"

"Yes, it was true what I told you last night. I did come up last night with the twins and the chauffeur – the guy that drove you to the club. He drove us off the boat to Aul House."

"But there are no cars allowed on..." Sam stopped himself and laughed at his own stupidity. "What the fuck am I saying? I'm starting to believe the lies myself now!"

George looked puzzled. "All I know is he drove the twins and me to the house. We unpacked our stuff... Wait... There's a bag for you in the boot of the car."

"For me?"

"Yes, I don't have all the details... but in the bag is a wash kit and a tuxedo for you to wear to the party tonight. At some point beforehand I was meant to give it to you."

"Where's the car now?"

"It's parked outside Aul House. It's a black *Range Rover*."

"What did you do once you got to the house?"

"We unpacked. Had dinner with Pinto and I came here."

"Who had dinner with Pinto?"

"The twins and me."

"So Pinto is another actor, right?"

George shook her head. "I seriously doubt it. I think he's genuinely the housekeeper at Aul House."

Sam laughed.

"What's so funny?"

"You expect me to believe that? After he took part in that farcical scene with Tom out in the so-called minefield. Come on, who is he and what's his *role* in all of this?"

"I'm certain Pinto's not an actor. The way that the twins spoke to him... It's clear he wasn't working for, or with, them. They introduced themselves as representatives of The Trust."

"Who did they introduce you as then?"

"That's the funny thing. They introduced me as the fiancée of the new owner of Aul House. They said I was up here to see what my darling hubby-to-be had just bought. So I played along... A lot of this job has been improvisation."

"You played along, how?"

"Oh, how it was my dream to live on a Scottish island… How he had bought this place as an engagement gift. Pinto seemed really interested. He lapped it all up."

Sam was confused, it was hard to pick fact from fiction. "And who is this fiancé of yours. Who is the new owner of Aul House?"

"Charles Frost," George shrugged.

Sam groaned. "But there's no such person as Charles Frost!"

"I'm not so sure." The voice was deep and gruff.

Sam and George span around in unison.

Both of them stood frozen looking back into the house.

Staring back at them, behind the sight of his shotgun was John Pinto. His weapon raised, inches from George's forehead.

08:00

"That was quite a story. Don't do anything stupid. I don't need to explain why, do I?" Pinto nudged an eyebrow upwards. Mackay's body lay behind his left boot. "Empty out your pockets. Both of you. Slowly. Nothing stupid, remember."

"Oh come on, this is getting ridiculous." Sam stepped toward Pinto putting out a hand to push the barrel of the shotgun away from George's face.

Pinto jabbed the steel shaft hard into his Sam's arm, pushing him back towards the doorway. "This isn't a game, Sam."

Sam realised this was serious. He raised his hands in the air.

George did the same.

"What's this all about?" asked Sam. His legs shook. "There's been a massive mix up."

Pinto was now pointing the gun at him. "Shhhh. Now, do as I said." His voice dropped to barely a whisper. "Empty your pockets onto the floor very slowly. Do it… Now!" He screamed the last order.

George jumped and put down her earpiece and a pair of gloves. From her other pocket she pulled the purple vial Sam had given to her earlier this morning.

Pinto's eyes grew wider. "That belongs to me. Hand it over."

George picked up the vial. Sam watched her hand tremble as she reached out and gave it to Pinto. He snatched it away and dropped it into the chest pocket of his shirt.

"And you? What have you got?"

Sam swallowed hard before answering. "Just these. He reached inside his coat pocket and produced the empty bottle of whisky. Then in one motion snapped his wrist, sending the glass bottle fast at Pinto's face.

Pinto ducked.

The bottled sailed past his left ear and smashed against the back wall.

Pinto leaped out of his crouch towards Sam and buried the barrel of the shotgun hard into his groin.

The wind left Sam and pain burst up through his stomach and down into his legs. The blow was accompanied with such force it sent him off balance, out through the doorway onto the worn grass and mud outside.

Pinto grabbed Sam by his jacket collar and pulled him back inside. Staring at George through steely eyes, he bundled them both six feet back into the kitchen.

"This is no joke. Just look at your old pal here." Pinto, still wringing Sam's collars, forced him to look at Mackay face-to-face, only a few inches apart.

Sam gasped for breath.

"Leave him alone!" screamed George. She dug her nails into Pinto's hand.

In the melee, Pinto let go of Sam sending him down on top of Mackay. Rigormortis had set in, leaving Mackay's body as hard as the floor he lay on.

Sam looked up at Pinto and George fighting above him.

George had locked onto Pinto's right hand. Pinto was trying to pull himself away.

Sam got to his feet. A flailing boot – he wasn't sure whose – cracked him square on the jaw. He fell back down, face first into the pool of Mackay's blood. The warm liquid covered his mouth. He wiped his face on his coat and he tried to get back up.

BOOM!

Sam jumped. He staggered backwards, tripping over Mackay's body and crashed hard into the table. A dining chair fell onto its side.

George screamed. She let go of Pinto.

Smoke wafted out of one of the barrels of the shotgun.

George clutched her left leg as she collapsed.

"What have you done?" screamed Sam getting back to his feet.

Pinto got down on one knee, next to George. He pulled away her hands.

George yelled with pain. Just above her left knee her jeans had turned dark red and black as blood and shot mixed in a horrible mess. Her face had turned an ominous white as she went into shock.

"Get me that tea towel," barked Pinto. He pointed across the kitchen to the sink.

Sam leapt over Mackay's body and did as ordered.

Pinto pulled it off him and tied it tight in a double knot around her thigh.

George winced and went silent. She closed her eyes. Sweat rolled down her forehead as she shook.

Sam held her hand but there was no response. "George, can you hear me? George, it's going to be alright. The doctor is on his way."

Just as he said it the sound of galloping horses could be heard.

"Right. It's time to go," said Pinto. His voice was calm yet firm. He pointed the shotgun at Sam. "Pick her up. Make sure that tourniquet stays where it is. Get her up."

"You evil bastard." Sam didn't care for his own safety anymore.

"Up. Or I'll finish the job." Pinto was still chillingly calm. He took a step to his side to look through the window above the sink. "Yes, it's our friend the landlord doctor. Get her onto your shoulder, we're going through the back."

Sam got his arm under George's back and the other under her buttocks. Still winded from his blow to the groin he struggled to stand with her added weight but from somewhere he found the strength. George sighed as she went up onto his shoulder.

"Through the workshop. Quickly." Pinto forced the barrels into Sam's back pushing him through the workshop and out through the backdoor. The sunshine was bright. Sam could hear the doctor and Isla arrive on two horses, around the front of the cottage.

Pinto closed the workshop door silently. He glared at Sam before peeping a head around the corner of the building.

"Okay. We go. Over to the barn. Not a sound. Don't stop." Pinto pointed to the barn about a hundred yards away. "Go!" He pushed Sam forward.

Sam moved as quickly as he could. Pinto still prodding him hard in the back, checking back over his shoulder at the cottage every few paces.

George made no sound.

Sam wondered if she had fainted… or worse…

They reached the barn. Pinto made light work of the heavy latch, pulled open the large door and pushed Sam inside.

The stench of sheep. Shit. Piss. Animal bedding.

It was revolting.

Stomach churning.

"Put her down over there." Pinto pointed to a stack of hay bales next to the doorway, in a narrow section cordoned off from the sheep.

The sheep shied away to the far corner of the barn. Thirty sets of weary eyes stared back at their uninvited guests.

Pinto stood with his back against the barn doors, a blade of white light shone over his left shoulder, cutting through the darkness.

Sam rested George gently onto the hay bale bed. She remained unconscious, her skin drained of blood and covered in a film of sweat. He took off his coat and folded it in half. Her head felt limp and un-naturally light as he raised it a few inches to slide in the makeshift pillow. He glanced at Pinto and the shotgun still trained at George and him, but Sam felt no fear, his only thoughts were on saving George.

Pinto looked over his shoulder, through the gap, back at the cottage. He studied the scene for a while before turning back to Sam. "It's time you told me the truth."

"I was going to say the same to you."

Pinto smiled. "Don't get smart with me. If you want to save her life do what I tell you."

"Who said I care about her? You heard us back there." Sam pointed through the wall in the direction of the cottage. "I don't give a damn about her." He took half a step towards Pinto.

"Then perhaps we should put her out of her misery now." Pinto aimed the gun at George's head.

Sam's hand sprang out involuntarily, between the shotgun barrels and George. "Do that and you blow your cover." It was Sam's turn to smile although he felt his hand shaking.

"Sit down." Pinto turned ninety degrees, so his shoulder rested against the door, allowing him to see both outside and in.

Sam perched on the end of the bales supporting George.

"We're both victims here. You do realise that, don't you?" Pinto rummaged around in his pocket. He pulled out a soft pack of cigarettes, offering Sam one before lighting them both with his gold lighter.

The nicotine took the edge off Sam's nerves. He took a long drag before asking, "Why did you kill Mackay?"

Pinto looked at the sheep. "I didn't kill him. He was already dead when I arrived at the croft."

"Why should I believe that?"

"Because it's the truth. I was looking for you. I knew you were in danger when *she* turned up last night." He looked at George as he said this. "Like she said to you back in the cottage, she was blabbing on about her fiancé, Charles Frost, over dinner last night at the house. When I heard that I knew something wasn't right. I knew someone was playing games with us. I guessed I might find you here, seeing as you met Mackay on the way to the island. But by the time I arrived last night it was too late. Mackay was dead... Dead because he had worked out the link between Seth Falcorrs and Charles Frost... Dead because he knew too much. Just like you and me."

Sam couldn't believe it. "You'll have to do better than that. Why did you kill Mackay? Why am I here?"

Pinto glanced outside then looked hard at Sam. "It's because of this." He held the purple vial between his thumb and middle finger; smoke from the cigarette hanging from the corner of his mouth wafted around the glass tube. "You know all about this, don't you?"

Sam swallowed hard before taking another drag, he looked away, trying his best to look unfazed. "I don't have a clue what's going on anymore."

"Come on. Start with why you broke into my seed cupboard and stole the notebook."

"Tell me who Charles Frost is and what this has to do with Richard West." Sam stood up as he spoke, he knew he had to remain on the offensive.

Pinto raised his shotgun to point at Sam's chest. "Sit down."

Sam did as ordered and finished his cigarette, stubbing it out on a splintery beam. The smell of tobacco was doing its best to cover the stench of sheep.

"I'm going to put the gun down." Pinto rested the weapon against the door and sat down next to Sam. His landing was heavy. "I can only tell you what I know… Like I say, we're both victims here." He offered Sam another cigarette and passed him the lighter before continuing. "I had never seen that notebook before you brought it up on Tuesday but I recognised the briefcase as Seth Falcorrs'."

"And the name Richard West. Does that mean anything to you?"

Pinto sighed, twin jets of smoke streamed from his nostrils. "Yep, he was Seth's biographer… The sentimental bastard wanted the world to know his story so he found Richard West to pen his memoirs. Like many of Seth's projects it went nowhere… I suppose, Sam *West*, it's Richard *West* that links you to all of this?"

"Richard was my uncle. He died just after I was born. But I had no idea of any of this before getting here."

Pinto nodded to himself. "Is that right?" he asked himself in a hushed, wistful voice, as if piecing the information together for the first time himself.

Sam didn't want to share too much. "So what's the link between you and Falcorrs?"

Pinto rubbed his chin. "I met Falcorrs in Kenya. He was a Special Forces officer. He ran secret missions for the British government, mostly against the rebel forces in Kenya at the time. When we met he was a few years in. He was tired and in a very bad way. He'd seen a lot of bad things. We'd only just met when he launched into his life story about his childhood here on Aul right up to his time as a prisoner of war in Malay at the hands of the Japanese. That's when he told me about the plant – about Cadence." He still held the vial in his right palm, almost mesmerised by the purple liquid swirling around the glass. "I couldn't believe it at first but he convinced me to work with him, to try and understand the plant and its power. That's when it started…" He broke away, absorbed by his own thoughts.

Sam eyed the shotgun only a few feet away. He had to keep Pinto talking. "What started?"

"The start of my life's work… That Japanese officer knew the power of what he had discovered and Seth was beginning to realise it himself. For the next twenty six years Seth and I worked with Cadence, trying to understand its power."

"What power?"

"Its power to heal. Its power to protect." Pinto squeezed the vial tight. "You saw what it did to your eye and that was nothing. A concentration like this," he shook his fist, "can do much more… Much more."

Sam thought of George and turned to see her still looking horribly pale. "Like what?"

"Enough that somebody wants to take it from me and kill me for it."

"Who would do that?"

"Whoever she's working for." Pinto nodded at George.

Sam squeezed his fist tight, his fingernails digging into his palms. "Tell me then, when did you figure all this out?"

Pinto folded his arms and leant back, looking up at the rafters. "Well, let's start with you arriving with Falcorrs' briefcase. I thought nothing of it at first. I thought it had to do with The Trust taking back the house. Then I read the notebook while you were upstairs in the bath. *Richard West's* notebook and *Sam West* upstairs soaking in the bath! It wasn't a coincidence. But it made no sense. If you were looking for answers then why would you do something as stupid as hand me the briefcase and notebook? So, I assumed you weren't the brains behind this." Pinto turned to Sam and shrugged.

Sam stood up. "Looking for answers? Answers to what?"

"You really don't know, do you?" Pinto laughed, a horrible rasping sound mixed with the tar in his lungs.

"Know what?" Sam felt his cheeks burn.

Pinto wiped his grin with the back of his hand, his face red from laughter. "Gosh, you really don't know..." He shook his head in amazement... "Richard West was murdered!"

The news hit Sam hard. He stepped back, his heels hitting the hay bale and he stumbled back down next to George. All the time he kept his eyes on Pinto's but his mind was racing... *Murdered*? It was suicide... Found dead in a London hotel room... That's what his mother and father had always told him... Murder? Could this be true?

"You see, Sam, there's a lot you don't know."

Sam ran his hands through his hair and took a deep breath. He focused on the air leaving his nose as he tried to compose himself. "Who murdered him and why?"

Pinto's grin disappeared and his stare hardened. "Seth Falcorrs, of course. He killed him because he knew too much. Richard knew all about Cadence and the camps. He knew everything so he had to die."

"Can I have another cigarette?"

Pinto obliged and lit it for him.

"What *camps* are you talking about?" asked Sam before taking his first drag.

The question froze Pinto, the dancing orange flame of his lighter the only movement in the room. "Detention Centres, gulags, camps... Call them what you like... They were Falcorrs' reason for being in Africa... It was his and to be fair *Britain's,* best kept secret in Kenya." He lit his own cigarette.

"Go on," Sam ordered, desperate to know more.

"Kenya at the time was in civil war. The *Mau Mau* it was called. Kikuyu tribesmen fighting for the land and rule that was once theirs... Falcorrs and his men tried to stop them the old fashioned way – guns and grenades – but it was much too big for that. That's when the camps were set up... Kikuyu rounded up in their thousands... Women and kids... Grandparents, uncles, cousins... Thrown in the camp without charge... Held prisoner under the burning sun with one meal a day and enough beatings to last a lifetime."

Sam knew very little about the *Mau Mau* but remembered a protest outside the High Court for Justice a couple of years ago. "Still doesn't explain why Falcorrs had to kill Richard."

"It was what went on at the camps that Falcorrs ran, that's what he wanted to keep secret. He wasn't content with imprisoning innocent people and the oppression of the masses. No, Seth took it a step further. He treated his prisoners as guinea pigs."

"Guinea pigs?"

"Yes, human trials for Cadence."

"You mean drug trials?"

"That's exactly what I mean. Except nobody was a volunteer. Nobody was paid. Instead, thousands – and I do mean *thousands* – of men and women were tested."

Sam remembered the notebook and the Japanese officer. "So Falcorrs was just like his captor in the Malayan jungle..."

"He was worse."

"How?"

Pinto held the purple vial up to the light. "Let's just say that hundreds of people have died for this and many, many more made seriously sick."

"And what was your role in all of this? You're a murderer too!" Sam rested his hand on George's boot. She was still horribly still and pale.

Pinto sighed and shook his head, rubbing his stubbly cheeks with both hands. "I was a *prisoner* too…"

"You expect me to believe that?" Sam stubbed out his cigarette on the leather soul of his ruined right shoe.

"I accept that I didn't live like the Kenyan prisoners. But my treatment wasn't far off… I was – I am – a doctor and a botanist. I have a doctorate in botanical medicines, in addition to my medical qualifications. When Falcorrs found this out he knew I was the answer to his prayers. I was the person who could continue where that crazy Jap had left off… Continue that macabre research… Frost kept me prisoner working on batch after batch of Cadence."

"All that madness for a cure for malaria?"

Pinto hacked a cough and spat into the hay. "I wish we'd stopped there. The cure for malaria came early on… It was the cure for everything else…" Suddenly Pinto stopped and got up. He moved quickly to the doors and peered through the gap, his right hand on the shotgun. "The doctor's leaving. Looks like he's told the girl to stay behind."

Poor Isla, thought Sam. "Cure for what?"

Pinto kept his eyes on the cottage. "We soon realised that the subjects tested with Cadence were stronger and healthier than the other prisoners. They weren't suffering from the diarrhoea and dysentery that was common with the others. Those treated with Cadence could even work up to fifty percent longer. It was all great, except for one thing."

"What?"

"Insomnia… They couldn't sleep at all… Do you know what happens to a man who doesn't sleep?" Pinto looked at Sam.

"He stops functioning."

"Right. But a man on Cadence that can't sleep can keep going for about a month. In fact he can do better than a man without Cadence who's getting eight hours every night. But eventually time ran out. Without fail it caught up with them and four, maybe five weeks into the trials it was always the same. The men would go out of their minds. Lunatics. Gibbering wrecks. Even our heaviest sedatives couldn't help them. In the end they either killed themselves or they got themselves in front of a firing squad. It was truly barbaric."

"How long did this go on for?"

"The camps went on for eight years, right up to independence in '63. Just as quickly as they came they were gone. But our work went on well after that. Kenya was different after Kenyatta took over. It was like Italy after Mussolini was toppled, there was a massive vacuum and anyone with a bit of money and ambition put them to good use. Falcorrs went into mining and made a fortune."

"And you?"

"I suppose you'd say I was an employee of his, and yes, before you say it, I know. I could have walked away at any time after the camps. But Falcorrs had changed. Business replaced the fighting and human trials, and *yes*, I admit, I wanted to get Cadence right too…. Too many people had suffered along the way – including myself." Pinto stared at Sam, the haggard frown over his face lifted slightly as if the act of sharing his story was relieving the pain. "We had the money to buy proper equipment and tests were then performed only on rats."

"And was it all worth it?" Sam looked at George, taking small comfort that her chest was rising and falling with her shallow breaths. He had to get her to the doctor.

"We made progress but we didn't get there."

"Get where?" Sam snapped, his voice almost a shout.

Pinto screwed his face up as he checked back through the gap in the doors, back towards the cottage. "Quiet, Sam…" He picked up the shotgun. "We don't have a lot of time. She's going to lose that leg and probably die from her wound if we don't get her sorted out. You don't want that do you?"

Sam stood up, turning away from George, trying his best to look uninterested in her. "Tell me what you were trying to do with Cadence and why my uncle was murdered for it, first."

"We don't have time." Pinto raised the shotgun.

Sam stepped towards him, his heart pounding under his sweat-drenched shirt.

"Falcorrs was convinced he could create the Holy Grail… An elixir… A recipe for eternal life…" Pinto grinned, showing off his brilliant white teeth.

"And let me guess, you didn't achieve it – because it's impossible!" Sam took another step towards Pinto, his eyes now on the twin barrels pointing at his chest.

"Right… We didn't get there *then*… But I have got there since."

Sam stopped.

Pinto flicked his wrist and something shot through the air.

Sam instinctively caught the purple vial in his right hand.

"Give it to her and it will keep her alive long enough to get some more… She's going to need a few if she's going to survive," said Pinto.

"What's the catch?" Sam pulled the stopper out of the vial gently, careful not to spill the contents.

"The catch? The catch is you're going to help me get off this island alive… We're going to leave together tonight."

Sam realised the tables were starting to turn. Pinto needed his help. "This stuff better work. If it doesn't then I'm not helping you with anything."

"Sam, I'm on your side. As I said, this is all about Cadence. Whoever's behind all of this is after the Cadence. It's precisely because it *works* that they're doing all of this to us. Now get her to swallow half of it and then pour the remainder over her wound."

George looked lifeless as Sam lifted her head up slightly and poured a teaspoon's worth of the Cadence between her blue lips. She remained motionless, her skin still ghostly-white. He placed her head back down on his coat, turning his attention to the blood soaked tea towel tied around her leg. "I need your help," he waved Pinto over.

Pinto leant the shotgun against George's hay bale bed and undid the knot in the tourniquet.

Sam winced at the sight of the torn jean and bloodied wounds.

"Sprinkle it as evenly as you can," grunted Pinto, his focus on his patient.

Sam's hand shook as he did his best to apportion the viscous liquid over the holes in George's flesh. The liquid vanished instantly into the dark red punctures.

Pinto examined the wounds, dropping his face to within a few inches of the mess.

Sam saw his chance. He stepped back and around Pinto's hunched frame and scooped up the shotgun. In one motion he cocked the hammer and raised the barrels at his captor.

Pinto was taken by surprise, still holding both ends of the tea towel in his hands.

"Do it back up. Carefully and slowly," ordered Sam, his throat was dry from the cigarettes, but he forced the words out with real conviction.

Pinto crossed one end of the tea towel over the other, then wrapped left over right before pulling the knot tight with an excessively firm tug.

George gasped.

Both men looked at her.

She opened her glossy eyes and blinked repeatedly, sending tears rolling down her cheeks.

"George!" exclaimed Sam.

Her disoriented gaze wandered around the room. "Sam?" her voice was barely audible.

"It's okay. You're going to be fine." Sam moved around the bales so he was level with her head but George had already closed her eyes and fallen back under.

Sam checked her pulse on her neck, there was still a strong, regular flow of blood. Her skin looked a little more normal, as colour had returned to her cheeks and lips.

"She's going to need more if she's to recover," said Pinto.

"Stand up and take your coat off, very slowly."

Pinto did as ordered.

"Now sit on the floor, hands on your lap where I can see them."

Pinto got down on the straw. A few of the sheep scuttled further back into the shadows.

"Sam, I'm trying to help you. I told you we are both victims here."

"Quiet. I'll tell you a few things. Firstly, you will get us off this island and George is coming too."

"She's one of them…" Pinto curled his top lip as he almost spat out his words.

"Quiet! Secondly, you will answer my questions – all of them…"

Pinto rolled his head back and ran his right hand through his hair, letting out a sigh of resignation.

Sam found it curious to see somebody respond to stress in a similar way to himself. He didn't like how vulnerable and helpless it looked. "Put your hands back on your lap."

Pinto complied. "What do you want to know?"

"How did my Uncle Richard get involved with Seth Falcorrs?"

Pinto nodded. "After all the fighting and the camps, Falcorrs became a very, very successful business man. He channelled the ruthlessness he had as a solider into his mining business. We also managed to improve the Cadence too, so that as long as one kept taking it the insomnia was kept at bay. With all the vitality Cadence brought him he was unstoppable. Soon he had several titanium and gemstone mines..."

"How old was Falcorrs then?" interrupted Sam.

Pinto smiled. "Good question. He was in his early fifties when I first met him in 1953, so he'd have been in his sixties by then but, you see, Cadence changed everything. In 1965 he looked not much older than you – in his early thirties. That was the point... He had all the money he ever wanted but he was after the one thing money couldn't buy anyone *else*... Forever youth."

"And what about you – how old are you?"

Pinto's blue eyes fixed on Sam's, "I'm ninety years young this year." His smirk made it clear he enjoyed sharing this unexpected fact about himself.

Sam tried to hide his surprise. Pinto looked barely a day over fifty – his strong frame and agility would have pleased a much younger man. Surely this wasn't real? A potion that brought eternal youth was the stuff of fantasy. He glanced over again at George. She was looking a lot better already. Whatever Cadence was, it did have miraculous healing properties and right now that was all that mattered, he had to get George well again. He looked back at Pinto who was still smiling at him through his lingering stare,

"Let's say I believe your story and you're an octogenarian botanist kept alive by his magic potion…"

"Not just alive but strong and healthy!" Pinto interjected.

Sam wrapped his forefinger around the trigger and took half a step towards him. "Why don't we put your theory to the test."

Pinto's smile disappeared and he leant backward "Don't do anything stupid. I can get us off the island – all *three* of us. I have a boat moored near the fort."

"But your magic potion. Surely it doesn't matter if I shoot you. You're immortal!" Sam's finger pressed against the steel trigger.

"It doesn't work like that," there was panic in Pinto's voice, "Cadence defeats disease and ageing but if you shot me now the blood loss would be too great, I wouldn't survive… If I don't survive, then you'll both die on this island too."

Sam raised the barrels to point between Pinto's eyes. "Let's keep going with your story. So, it's 1965 and Falcorrs has made a fortune mining and he's high on Cadence, looking and feeling half his age. Meanwhile you were his prisoner, forced against your will to perfect his magic potion. Why don't I believe you?"

"Okay, I admit it. After all the fighting and the human trials, things changed. The money started coming in and it meant better equipment, proper labs and growing facilities. We made a few breakthroughs and the real potential of Cadence became clear. You have to remember that I'm a scientist and I was developing something truly amazing… A cure for every known disease. It was also anti-ageing. Not just anti-ageing… but… somehow it turned the clock backwards."

"And you kept this to yourselves? Only you and Falcorrs knew about Cadence?"

"That's right. After the camps all of the human trials were done on Falcorrs personally."

"You weren't taking it yourself?"

"Not then, no. I didn't understand it well enough. Falcorrs was determined to be the only one taking it until he was sure it was ready."

"Ready for what?"

Pinto frowned and shrugged, puffing out his cheeks before he spoke, "Use your imagination. What do you think you could do with something like Cadence?" His eyes locked onto Sam's as if searching for a reaction.

"Tell me, what?"

"I mean, until we could produce Cadence on an industrial scale he wasn't ready to go public. You have to understand, Falcorrs was a very determined man. He had an ego the size of the planet and nothing short of owning the planet was enough. He pumped millions into the project but there was one stumbling block – we couldn't get the plants to grow fast enough. No matter what we did we couldn't propagate on a big enough scale. The Cadence plant took twelve months to flower and no matter what we tried, the plants were hugely susceptible to disease." Pinto laughed, "That was the irony of it all. The oil from the flower could resist any disease known to man but the plant itself was the most delicate thing I had ever known. Back then, only one in ten of our plants were making it to flower. No matter what we tried – hot, cold, damp, dry... Nothing worked."

Sam thought of the thousands of purple flowers growing in the north of the island. "So that's how you ended up here, on Aul, is it?"

Pinto grinned, "Clever lad. That was thirty years ago. Falcorrs came back here – to his *ancestral seat*, as he called it – for the first time since leaving for Africa. I think he was going to sell the place, as Kenya had long since become his home. Also, you have to remember that the rest of the world thought he was dead. He had been presumed dead after being taken prisoner in Malay. The British government had him running completely secret and deniable missions in Kenya. Falcorrs was a ghost. He didn't exist. And then with Cadence he had become a man younger than he was when he left to fight the Germans and Japanese thirty years earlier!"

"Go on. What happened when he got here?"

"I stayed in Kenya. Falcorrs was gone for a month. That was the first time I heard him use the name Charles Frost. As you just discovered, Charles Frost is an anagram of Seth Falcorrs. He must have come back here, to Aul, as Charles Frost, a young man in his early thirties, and nobody recognised him. None of the islanders knew that he was the long lost Laird who had been missing the last thirty years, assumed by all to be dead. But when he got back to Kenya it was all different. You see, he had found the solution to our problem with Cadence! He'd discovered that here on Aul the plant was flourishing! He told me about the land up in the north of the island where after The War he had planted the seeds from that first plant he took from the Malayan jungle. He told me how he pretended to have gone insane and cordoned off the area as a minefield so that nobody would discover the flower, years before. To his surprise, on his return to the island the entire 'minefield' was covered in the wonderful purple flowers!"

"So that's how you got here. You came here as the new housekeeper?"

"Right again. But don't you want to know where Richard West comes into all of his?" His smile widened further.

The pressure in Sam's forefinger grew stronger around the trigger.

Pinto winced, "Easy, Sam. We're getting to the interesting bit now…" Pinto raised his right hand in a gesture of peace.

"Put your hands on your lap and keep talking." Sam's heart beat got faster with each revelation.

"Okay, but take it easy with that thing," Pinto shrugged. "Richard West was a focused young man. He took his research very seriously. He was very thorough. *Too thorough*, that was his problem." Pinto rubbed the bristles on his chin.

"Hands on your lap. How old would you say Richard was when you met him?"

"Must have been mid to late twenties when I met him in '79."

This chimed with what Sam knew. Richard was found dead in a London hotel room in December 1979, aged twenty nine. "Keep going."

"When Falcorrs returned from Aul he had Richard with him. He told me Richard was going to help him write his memoirs."

"This was the first you'd heard of this?"

"Yes. He'd never mentioned the idea before. My guess is after he saw how well the flowers were flourishing up here he thought he'd cracked it – the final hurdle negotiated, but again, Cadence alone wasn't enough for him. He wanted the world to know about the man behind it too." Pinto shook his head. "The man's ego had no bounds."

"So, Richard was a ghost writer for a ghost. Makes sense."

Pinto coughed out a laugh, "I'm sure Richard was paid handsomely. It was also Falcorrs' chance to set the history books straight."

"How so?"

"To get back at the *Ministry of Defence*. He blamed the *MoD* for what he had done and become. He devoted his life to military service – *for King and Country…* It was as if he wanted to distance himself from his military past…" Pinto trailed off, before adding: "… Who could blame him? He had so much blood on his hands."

"*You* can talk." Sam glanced at George.

"That was an accident. Entirely different." Pinto spat into the straw.

"When did Richard arrive in Kenya, what month was it in '79?"

Pinto's head bobbed left and right as he thought about his answer. Finally he replied, "That must have been beginning of March. Yes, it was. Falcorrs left Kenya end of January and returned five weeks later."

That made it nine months before Richard was found dead back in London. The reasons for Richard's death lay in the nine months between March and December, thought Sam. "So what happened next?"

"A few things happened: I packed my things to come here. After Falcorrs told me about how Cadence was flourishing on Aul, it made sense for me to be here. We cooked up this story that I was the newly appointed housekeeper of Aul House. Plan was I'd carry on my research undisturbed at Aul House and Falcorrs would come and join me when his book was done."

"When did you leave Kenya for Aul?"

"I arrived here first week of April. Been here ever since." Pinto gave a wistful shake of his head, staring at the filthy floor.

"And Falcorrs, when did he join you?"

Pinto's eyes flashed up and locked onto Sam's. "I never saw Falcorrs again."

"You said Richard was *too thorough*, what did you mean?"

Pinto still held his intense stare. "It's what got him killed. You see, Falcorrs' plan was to use Richard to tell the world *his* story – his version of history. But he picked the wrong guy for that, in Richard. First Richard started talking to the domestic help and then the miners that worked for Falcorrs, many of whom were Kikuyu, who had direct links to Falcorrs' past... It didn't take long for Richard to pick up on the stories of the detention camps and everything that went on there. My last night in Kenya I overheard a blazing row between Falcorrs and Richard. Richard had threatened to go public with what had happened." Pinto pulled his supercilious smile and there was suddenly a mischievous glint in his eye.

"Are you sure *you* didn't tip Richard off?"

"Maybe." Pinto's smile broadened into a conceited grin.

"Still isn't proof that Richard was murdered by Falcorrs. What aren't you telling me?"

Pinto rolled his eyes. "As I say, I arrived here in April. Falcorrs was good to his word and shipped over all of my research materials and gave me everything I needed to set up here and continue my work. So that's what I did – I immersed myself in my work, without contact from anyone. It was bliss. Even the weather here was a welcome break from the relentless heat. Then, it must have been early December when, out of the blue, I got a call from Falcorrs. He wasn't his usual cool, calm self. No, there was something obviously distressing him. He sounded hoarse and he was on a very short fuse. He told me he was in London. He was *'finishing off some business'* before heading up to meet me here.

"My guess was he was out of Cadence serum too. I'd left everything we had with him in Kenya, which wasn't much more than six months' worth. Remember, he had to stay topped up if he was going to continue to enjoy the benefits. Without it, he was just another old man."

Sam took a deep breath before asking his next question, "What date was that?"

Pinto pursed his lips, appearing to know exactly why Sam had asked. His words came without thought or hesitation: "It was 20 December, 1979."

That was the day Richard was found dead! Sam loosened his grip on the trigger. His legs were shaking and his feet numb from the cold... He desperately wanted to sit down. He took another deep breath. "This proves nothing. How do you know Falcorrs had anything to do with Richard's death?"

"Because it was all over the papers the next day.... If you knew what you were looking for, that is. Richard West was found hanging from his own belt in a London hotel room. The police said it was suicide but I knew this was trademark Falcorrs. We had an unusually high number of 'suicide-by-means-of-own-belt' in the camps... No, that was Falcorrs, alright. No doubt about it... It's clear Richard West knew too much, so he had to be silenced."

Sam felt light headed. His palms were sweating. Hunger and anxiety swirled around his stomach. "And Falcorrs, did he come up here?"

"No, I never saw him again."

"What happened to him?"

Pinto inhaled deeply and, again, looked hard at Sam. "Seth Falcorrs. Charles Frost. Whatever you want to call him, is dead."

"How can you be so sure? You've seen no body."

"It was Cadence. That's what was keeping him alive, and he ran out a long time ago. He couldn't get up here in time."

"It's just a theory. Where's the proof he's dead?"

Pinto spat into the dry straw, he seemed to do this when he got a question he didn't want to answer. "Well, if the fact that Falcorrs would be over a hundred years old now isn't enough reason to be dead then there's also the small matter of Aul House Trust. Like I told you at dinner, I've been here thirty years. A few months after Richard's death I got a letter from The Trust saying Falcorrs had passed away and the house would stay in trust. I was allowed to stay until the house was sold."

"There was no funeral for Falcorrs?"

"Not that I'm aware of. He had no friends and I wasn't interested in going." Pinto closed his eyes and leant back against the splintery, wooden beams.

Sam checked on George. There was little change but her breathing seemed more natural. His brain was doing overtime, processing all of the new information. He wasn't sure whether he could trust Pinto. Suddenly the notebook and briefcase sparked a thought. "The Trust, I suppose they have solicitors?"

Pinto looked up, apparently curious of Sam's question or perhaps the tone of voice in which it was asked, "Yes, why?"

Sam raised the gun just enough to remind Pinto who was in charge, "What are they called?"

Pinto hitched a knee up near his chin and leant back as he thought about his answer, "Morris Forster, of Bride Court, London."

He knew it! His father's solicitor and good friend. Sam bit down on his bottom lip as he wondered what it all meant. What did this have to do with his father? What was his father trying to tell him?

"You know that name, don't you Sam?" Pinto's voice suggested the question was rhetorical.

There was no point trying to hide the fact, he had to open up a little in order to piece things together. "So what if I do?"

275

"Then maybe there's a clue with Morris Forster that can help us work out who's behind all of this. Who's doing this to us?"

Sam took a step toward Pinto. "Forster is my late father's solicitor too."

Pinto eye's narrowed and Sam noticed his Adam's Apple roll as he swallowed hard, "You mean Richard West's brother is dead?"

Sam watched Pinto closely, "That's right, James West. He died on 2 July."

"Right… The day I was informed about the sale of Aul House…" Pinto glazed over, deep in thought. "Do you believe in coincidences, Sam?"

"No."

Pinto smiled, "Me neither. What did James die from?"

Sam didn't like where this was going but he felt drawn into the chain of thought, "Heart attack."

"Are you sure? Where was he found?" Pinto leant forward.

"At home."

"Was he alone when he died? Did James live with anyone else?"

"He was alone."

The glint returned to Pinto's eyes. "Don't you see? Whoever is behind this is also behind James's death. And now they want to kill you and me." Pinto burst out in hysterical laughter. The sheep closest to him shuffled backwards, intimidated by the wicked sound.

"What's so funny?"

"Don't you see?" Pinto leapt to his feet.

Sam wrapped his finger around the trigger and screamed, "Sit the fuck down!"

Pinto raised his hands above his head, his face was bright with his apparent epiphany. "Sam, can't you see what this is all about. Don't you want me to tell you what's going on?"

"Sit the fuck down!" Sam's heart was pounding, he knew he didn't have the resolve to shoot but he had to maintain control of the situation. "Down!" he repeated, with even more force.

Pinto took a half step towards him, there wasn't a shred of fear in his demeanour. "Let me tell you Sam, as you obviously haven't worked it out yourself..."

"No, you tell me why my father was up here on Aul exactly a week before he died, looking for you?" Sam raised the barrels to Pinto's face. "You didn't know I knew about that, did you?"

Pinto shook his head, "I don't know what you're talking about, Sam."

"Bullshit!"

"What makes you think he was up here, on Aul?"

"Dr Ferguson told me."

Pinto continued shaking his head, "It's not true. The truth is Ferguson's behind all of this. He's lured you up here with George's help to avenge your uncle and now your father's death. You kill me and you've done exactly what he wants."

"What do you mean? My father had a history of heart trouble. It was a heart attack." The shotgun was visibly swaying in Sam's hands.

"You don't believe that any more than I do." Pinto's voice had softened into a reassuring, nurturing whisper, his extended right hand tracing the sway of the shotgun's barrel. "You know you don't want to shoot anyone, Sam... We're in this together... If we work together we can both get off the island alive, George too."

Sam blinked rapidly and looked at George. As he did he felt the shotgun pull as Pinto yanked it cleanly away from him. It all happened so fast, yet there was relief at no longer being responsible for the weapon and the next move. His mind was drowning in the maelstrom of thoughts and fears all of this information had yielded.

Pinto was quickly over to the barn door, peering through the crack towards the cottage, gun over his shoulder. "Right on cue: Ferguson's returned…" He spoke with his back turned to Sam, obviously no longer fearing Sam's ability to resist.

Sam sat next to George, glad to take the weight off his wobbly legs. He could see back at Mackay's croft, through a crack in the barn door. "You're going to have to convince me Dr Ferguson is behind all of this."

"He's the only newcomer to the island since I arrived. In fact, he arrived soon after Richard was murdered. He's also a doctor, so he'd know how to kill a man and make it look like a heart attack."

Sam puffed out his cheeks, pausing his breathing as he considered Pinto's theory – there was a possibility this was true, Ferguson had told him yesterday that he was from Aberdeen, having come here after his wife had died of cancer. Had his Uncle Richard confided about Cadence to Ferguson? Did Ferguson then come here looking for Cadence to cure his dying wife? Was that just another lie?

Pinto placed a gentle hand on Sam's shoulder. "And now Ferguson's here, at the scene of the next death. What a coincidence… What's the betting Mackay died of a heart attack? You know I didn't kill Mackay, don't you?"

Before Sam could reply he saw the giant bearded figure of Ferguson appear from the dark void at the front of the cottage, where there was once a front door. He was striding with great purpose directly towards the barn, his oversized paces making short work of the muddy grass that lay between them. Sam stepped back, his breathing short and shallow, once more, his bewildered, vacant expression handed further control back to Pinto.

"He's going to kill us if he finds us. We have to move," said Pinto as he slung the shotgun over his shoulder and was over to George, scooping her up into his arms. She didn't stir, lying limp in his tight grip. "I'll take her. I can get her some more Cadence. Meet me at eleven tonight, at the underground spa. I'll have a boat ready to leave the island." Pinto scurried into the flock of sheep at the back of the barn. The animals parted, and like a sheepdog he coaxed them towards Sam who stood frozen at the double barn doors.

"A boat at the spa – how?"

"You'll see. Don't forget your coat, you'll need it."

A cacophony of bleating sheep flooded Sam's ears. He looked back through the crack. Ferguson was only six feet away from the door, his face twisted with anger, weapon poised to kill. "Shit!" Sam weaved between the sheep as they rushed past him.

Suddenly light flooded into the barn as Ferguson swung the doors wide open.

"Out here!" hissed Pinto, as he shifted side-on through a single door in the shadows at the back of the barn.

Sam ran towards him, his path now free from the escaping sheep. Peering over his shoulder at the brilliant white light, he saw the sheep bursting out onto the grass – their fast moving wool looked like the white, foamy surf of the waves last night at the cliffs.

Ferguson made a moaning sound as he was sent off balance and down onto the grass, by the sheep around his long legs.

This was enough to give Sam time to leave through the back.

Pinto had already reached the brow of the hill, almost disappearing over the top. His pace and strength like no other man Sam had met. "We have to split up. Remember tonight!" He nodded Sam away in the opposite direction and then he was gone with George.

Sam ran and ran, slipping and sliding up the slope.

"STOP!" came Ferguson's cry.

Sam just kept moving, forcing himself forward and away…

BOOM!

… Fuck! More gunfire…

Sam collapsed and rolled over the brow of the hill and tumbled down the other side. He jumped to his feet and ran.

He ran.

He ran until he could run no more.

14:00

The bells of St Cecilia's clock tower echoed around the deserted village square. Time had almost ground to a halt. Somehow it was only two o'clock in the afternoon. Sam lay chest down in the dirt, hidden deep in the swathe of gorse that covered the high-ground around the cobbled square. Shivering, starving, burning from thirst and fear, his bloodshot eyes were fixed on Ferguson's pub-cum-surgery, which lay about two hundred yards from his vantage point.

The village was its typical lifeless self, made worse by the fact that Ferguson's place remained closed. Hopeful punters had started to arrive at around eleven but gone away disappointed. Word must have gotten around this tight-knit community about the tragedy at Mackay's croft, perhaps that's where everyone had disappeared to? Sam imagined Ferguson taking control of the crime scene, manipulating the islanders into believing his version of events – a version that put Sam firmly in the firing line of blame. Little did they know that their friendly island doctor and landlord was in fact the murderer. Poor Mackay. Sam sighed and closed his heavy eyes but all he saw was the haunting image of Mackay's cracked skull on the kitchen floor.

For the last five hours he'd barely moved a muscle, paralysed by fear and deep in thought. Questions span around his head, mixing with one another. Where were Pinto and George? There was no chance Pinto would have gone back to Aul House, that would be too dangerous. Particularly if Clive and Clyde were there. No, Pinto was heading north when he saw him last, he most likely went to his stash of Cadence in the underground spa near the ruin. Sam wondered whether he should double-back and attempt to make his way up there as well. But it was too risky, it meant going past Mackay's croft, coming face-to-face with Ferguson.

Something moved in the square, causing a glimmer of light to catch his eye. Sam dropped back down onto his chest behind the gorse, peering through the branches. The pub door had been opened from the inside. Sam scanned the square for any signs of life. Just then, somebody stepped out from the unlit pub hallway, immediately followed by another. Sam recognised them, their matching stocky build and burnt-orange hair – the twins, Clive and Clyde. A zip of adrenaline pulled tight in his chest as Sam remembered the punch one of them gave him. He watched as longhaired Clyde locked the pub door behind them, checking the key had done its job by firmly wringing the knob. Side-by-side they waddled across the square, collars turned up on their expensive black woollen overcoats.

So Ferguson and the twins were in this together.

Sam remained still, only his eyes moving as he watched Clive and Clyde disappear beyond St. Cecilia's. Then he was up, doing his best to ignore the ache in his stiff legs as he slipped down the muddy bank, onto the cobbles, running across the square towards the church. The sound of his shoes on the stones echoed about the cottages and shops, his breath heavy, forming clouds before his face. He stopped at the church, back against the rough masonry, his head peering around the corner. He could see them about a hundred yards ahead, moving at speed along the path to Aul House. Clyde turned around, his pony tail swishing across his brother's neck. Sam jerked back behind the wall, his chest falling and rising, gasping for air. He took a deep breath and held it, tuning his ears for the sound of the two thugs charging back towards him. But there was only the unnatural silence. Once again he dropped to his knees, peeping around the corner, just able to see them, now twice the distance away.

Amongst the trees Sam moved, stopping periodically, keeping his distance, studying the twins. It was clear that they knew where they were going, not once stopping or hesitating as they moved quickly along the network of paths. The silhouette of Aul House was stamped onto the horizon, as they made the ascent up the hill amongst the avenue of pines.

As the forest thinned-out and dirt track gave way to gravel a whole new scene revealed itself. The natural world replaced by the driveway, teeming with life. Thirty or so people wearing white coats, carrying tables, chairs and boxes, were busy about their work, crunching over the white gravel. They paid Clive and Clyde no attention as the twins vanished amongst them.

Sam hung back at the edge of the forest, watching and learning. Eight carts, each hitched to two horses, were stationed along the western side of the driveway. More white coated men and women unloaded their cargo before disappearing into the house. This wasn't a removal team but more like an arrival party. But why? Surely the party tonight would no longer be happening? Pinto was gone and would surely not be returning to the house. Ferguson and the twins knew their fucked-up plan was unravelling. Sam rubbed his stubbly cheeks, about to run his fingers through his hair when he remembered George – he remembered last night at the old fort and then he remembered the sight of her bleeding and pale in the barn. Cold and fear infused to a rage that now bubbled inside of him. He zipped up his coat and buried his filthy hands in his pockets. He inhaled deeply through his nose and strode out confidently from the trees and onto the dusty white stones.

Head bowed and ears focused on the crunch, crunch of the many shoes on the driveway, Sam stepped around a mound of horse shit and behind the nearest of the carts. Hanging over the side of the cart was a white coat. He could just about get it on over his own coat, doing up the two buttons for further cover. He picked up a cardboard box that chinked with the distinctive sound of glassware as he walked through the crowd and through the open front door into the grand entrance hall of Aul House.

Nobody paid Sam any attention as they hustled in and out of the house around him. Sam stood still, soaking up the transformation of the space since yesterday morning. All signs of Pinto were gone. The walls were bare – the stags' heads and pictures all taken down. Sam looked around for Clive and Clyde. He put the box down on the floor at the foot of the stairs, noticing the frayed red runner had been replaced by a new, thick piled deep red carpet, fastened down with ornate brass rails. After checking nobody was watching him he tried the handle on the small door under the stairs. The handle turned and the door opened but inside was bare, all signs of the old seed room removed.

Most of the white coats were now moving between the front door and a room off to the eastern side of the house. Sam cut across them, to Pinto's drawing room. Again, checking as casually as he could that nobody was watching him, he leant on the handle and pushed the door ajar, squeezing through the narrow gap before closing it behind him.

Golden sunshine flooded into the room through the French doors. The smell of tobacco infused with the sweet smell of Cadence took him straight back to the evening he and Pinto spent in here. Unlike the hallway, the room looked just like it had before he left yesterday morning – the tatty old sofa and armchair in an *L* around the fireplace, with the other three walls flanked by floor-to-ceiling bookshelves. But gone were all signs of the Cadence flower, Pinto would have made sure of that. Turning around to leave, something caught Sam's eye. Those words: *Perfect Cadence*. Running down the spine of *every* book that stood on the bookshelf to the left of the door – the spines were all the same distinctive vivid purple of the Cadence flower, with the words written in golden letters: *Perfect Cadence*, *Perfect Cadence*, *Perfect Cadence*... Over and over… About fifty books per shelf, across nine shelves from floor to ceiling.

'*I put it in such an obvious place, he'd never think to look there!*' That's what Tom had said last night... '*The book's on his bookshelf, in the drawing room at Aul House.*'

Sam was certain the books hadn't been here the night he spent with Pinto, nor yesterday morning before he left for the village. Sam pulled out a copy. It was hardbound and about an inch thick. His heart pounded against his ribs as he turned to the first page…But it was blank... So too the next... and the next... Thumbing through to the back cover it was the same... Every page blank! He dropped the book on the floor and picked another one from the shelf and again the same – all blank.

"Quite the reader!" came the exclamation from across the room.

Sam jumped and dropped the book on his foot. Spinning around he saw Clive and Clyde stood at the open doors onto the garden.

"We were wondering when we'd find you," said Clive. "Come here!"

Sam wasn't sure who said what, as he grabbed another book from the shelf and sent it flying across the room. The twins raised their arms in front of their faces as they moved towards him, ducking behind the sofa as Sam sent a volley of books spinning towards them. He noticed blank pages in all of them as they landed splayed open over the floor, sofa and armchair. He moved to his right, in front of the fireplace, trying to get to the open French doors. Clive and Clyde smiled from behind the sofa, one moving to his left the other to his right as they homed in on their prey.

"No getting away now," said Clyde pouncing forward with his pudgy hands outstretched.

Sam swung a punch but missed.

Clive came in from the left, grabbing a handful of Sam's white coat at his shoulder.

Sam dipped, sent off balance from his air punch, down onto the sofa in front of him. An elbow or knee landed onto his back between his shoulder blades, the pain searing up and down his spine. He screamed but the sound was muffled by his face buried deep into the sofa. A sharp tug at his hair yanked him up onto his feet. He gasped for air... And then *pow*! The air left him as Clyde pummelled him in the stomach with his fist. Sam thought he'd been sick, lurching forward, his hair breaking free of Clive's hold, bent over double... In one motion he went forward, getting his foot onto the sofa and up over the back, aided by the springs in the cushion. He felt himself spin around as Clive was left tugging at the overall he shed like an old skin.

"Come here!" The twins screamed and snorted as they scrambled over the sofa themselves. Mouths foaming with saliva... Clyde's hair had come free of its pony tail, now covering his face.

Sam slipped on the books that littered the floor but was back up to fling open the door with such force that it swung wide open allowing him out before it bounced back in its frame. He grabbed the handle as a fat hand wrapped its bulbous fingers around the door, pulling it open. Sam groaned as he pulled with all his weight and strength. The door slammed closed with four lifeless fingers still pointing at him. The scream from inside the drawing room was guttural and filled with anguish.

There was a commotion behind Sam as the staff in white coats stopped and gasped at the scene taking place in the hall. Sam tugged at the handle several times, pulling with anger and revenge, watching the fingers turn white as the cries inside the drawing room grew louder. Somebody put a hand on his back but Sam was away and through the crowd and up the stairs. At the first floor he turned right, running along the long oak panelled hallway. He tried every door – each locked, even the bathroom and the bedroom he had spent the night in.

The sound of Clive and Clyde heading up the stairs came bouncing along the hallway, one still whimpering from the pain of their broken fingers. Sam tried the door to his old bedroom again, fruitlessly barging against the solid oak with his shoulder. He was trapped at the end of the hallway, there was nowhere else to go. He went to the window and looked out, there was no way he could jump without killing himself.

"Where are ya?!" Came the cry over the thud of heavy boots on the stairs.

Sam looked to his left, at the door opposite his bedroom – The Laird's old room.

'The only room I haven't a key for,' is what Pinto had said.

Sam closed his eyes and tried the handle. His hand rolled ninety degrees and the door gave way. He opened his eyes wide as he plunged into the darkness. His heart felt like it stopped as the door slammed closed and the rattle of a key in the lock told him he was trapped in the blackness and nothingness.

"Please, take a seat, Sam." The voice came from the darkness.

Sam pressed his back against the door, searching for the man who had spoken. He struggled to slow his breathing down, the taste of the cold, dusty air clinging to the inside of his mouth.

There was a scraping sound to his right, then a faint orange glow just above floor-level – a snap and crackle as the flames grew, dancing higher and higher in the grate. The fire lit up the hearth to reveal the tall, thin frame of the man staring back through brilliant blue eyes.

Sam immediately recognised him. "It's you from the car on Monday night." His words came slowly as he tried to make sense of what he was seeing and saying. "You drove me to the club in Mayfair."

The man closed his eyes and dipped his head in a deferential bow. His cadaverous features accentuated by the orange, flickering light from the fire. The sharp bones across his brow, cheeks and jaw cast deep shadows in the recesses of his pale skin and around those deeply set blue eyes.

"Please, sit down." The man sat down in one of the two high-backed, leather armchairs in front of the fireplace.

Sam remained locked onto the brilliant blue eyes as the creaks and groans from the floor boards beneath his footsteps echoed about the room; the cold replaced by the warmth of the fire with each step, dust-filled air replaced by the scent and acrid taste of the smoke from the burning logs. He sat down, only a few inches from the man in the black suit, white shirt and black tie.

"You're Charles Frost," said Sam. He was deliberate, forcing conviction in his voice.

"I am," Frost nodded.

"You're also Seth Falcorrs." This time there was less conviction in Sam's voice, almost a question, disbelief.

"Yes, Laird of Aul, but nobody has called me Falcorrs or Laird for a very long time. It's been Charles Frost since The War."

"Why are you doing this to me?"

Frost leant forward in his chair, his stare piercing. "I want to make you an offer."

"What offer?" Sam glanced away into the darkness behind Frost's chair, in an attempt to look apathetic but inside his heart was pounding, questions spinning around his head.

"I'd like to offer you a job."

Sam forced out an insincere laugh, "You mean like the bullshit job as your banker to buy this house? Or is this the job as the spy to foil international terrorism? Which one is it?"

The corners of Frost's mouth twitched as a smile came as quickly as it went. "I'm talking about a very real job. A new start for you. An end to the irrelevance of Gema Bank. A chance for you to do something that really matters." Frost leant further towards Sam, the reflection of the flames glistening in his eyes. "I'm talking about an end to your loneliness."

Sam ran his hand through his hair, wincing with pain as his fingers tugged at the windswept knots.

"That's what you want, isn't it Sam – an end to your loneliness? You see, it takes one to know one. It doesn't matter what you have earned or what you have achieved, if you have nobody to share it with it's pointless. I'm offering you an end to that."

Sam's fight was sapped by Frost's words. "Tell me about this job."

"I represent an organisation that has a very simple objective: To ensure the continued success of the human race. You see, we believe that without our work, humans will continue to do just that – *race,* compete with one another and fight each other and this planet into oblivion, instead of living in harmony with the true abundance of nature. Our species faces many challenges – climate change, drought, famine, drug resistant bacteria, cancer, malaria, the list goes on – none of which will be solved by governments and big business alone.

"The reason for this is simple, Sam. You see, our lives are too short. If you're lucky you get eighty or ninety years, just long enough to encourage you to have a good crack at your own life but with no genuine interest in anyone beyond yourself and…" Frost's words trailed off and he gazed into the fire, "… and your children, if you're lucky enough to have them. Survival of the fittest, capitalism, we give it many names… *There's no such thing as society. There are individual men and women and there are families. And no government can do anything except through people, and people must look after themselves first."*

Sam recognised the Margret Thatcher quote.

Frost continued, "So that's where we come in, we preserve a longer term view. We've been doing so for many centuries."

"What are you, *The Masons* or *Illuminati*?" Sam scoffed.

Frost smiled and shrugged, "We're known by many names but we prefer to leave names to others – to those on the outside – it helps with our anonymity. Our work is best done in secret, behind the scenes. Nature has chosen us–"

"Chosen you, how?" Sam interrupted.

Frost nodded and sat back in his chair, crossing his right leg over his left knee. "*Mother Nature* finds us. She seeks out a few of us who can break the cycle of life and death – or at least get a significant reprieve from it – and devote ourselves to the preservation of our planet and our species."

"You mean the purple flower? Cadence, you call it."

Frost rubbed his chin and smiled, showing off his unnaturally straight, polished teeth. "Pinto calls it that, I understand, but again, I prefer to give it no name. Out of respect, I suppose. When the flower finds you, you have no choice but to change. When it found me in the Malayan jungle I was changed forever. I was no longer Seth Falcorrs or Laird of Aul, I became Charles Frost."

"Do you really expect me to believe any of this? I know about the illegal camps in Kenya, the human trials and the murders!" Sam shuffled forward in his chair ready to stand.

Frost shook his head. "No, you know only what you've been told by John Pinto. I admit I was involved with those camps, it was the last shameful act of a soldier who knew no better. I make no excuses for my conduct. I never have and I never will deny it. But the human trials were performed by Dr Pinto, as camp doctor, without my knowledge." A hint of colour formed in Frost's hollow cheeks, those blue eyes shrunken by his anger.

"Why should I believe you?"

"*Mother Nature* finds you. Pinto is trying to find her but she can't be found. He's spent the last thirty years in this house, and almost the same again in Kenya before that, trying to unlock the secrets of the flower but he'll never succeed. He's blinded by his greed and selfishness. He's just like that Japanese Officer in the Malayan jungle who imprisoned and tortured me." Frost put his hand inside his jacket pocket and produced a leather-bound book. "This is the Japanese Officer's notebook I took when I escaped with the flower. The answers are all in here but, just like Pinto, he couldn't see beyond his own ego." He returned the book to his pocket.

"This is your house, though. Why have you allowed Pinto to stay here?" Sam had so many questions to ask but he forced himself to slow down and be methodical and structured in his enquiries.

"Now we're getting to the heart of things. Perhaps a drink?" Frost was up quickly, his tall frame towering over Sam. He walked around the back of his chair and prepared two drinks from a table hidden in the darkness. He returned with two generously poured crystal glasses.

Sam downed half and savoured the heat of the whisky trickling down his throat to his empty stomach.

Frost stood next to the fireplace. He placed his un-drunk glass on the marble mantelpiece and carefully laid two more logs into the heart of the blaze, his hands seemingly impervious to the heat. "Soon after my escape from the Japanese the Americans dropped the atomic bombs on Hiroshima and Nagasaki and war was over. I came back here, to Aul, with the flower and notebook. I was feeling fitter and stronger than I had in my life, despite spending the previous two years living in the jungle off little more than insects and rainwater. All that time I had been missing in action, presumed dead by the *Ministry of Defence* and both they and I quickly realised that I was more useful dead than alive, so to speak."

"You mean deniable, dirty work." Sam finished his whisky with his second gulp, the alcohol streaming through his blood to his brain.

"Yes, that's when I changed my name to Charles Frost, an anagram of Seth Falcorrs – the name given to all first born Falcorrs sons. Seth Falcorrs was dead and Charles Frost was born." He turned to Sam and smiled, the fire crackling and roaring as it consumed the new fuel. "Just as Sam West is dead."

One of Sam's questions had been answered but he pressed on. "So it was you that planted the newspaper article about my death. How? Where did you get the body from?"

Frost laughed, "To quote the great writer, and fellow Scot, John Buchan, *'You can always get a body in London if you know where to go for it'.* As for the article itself, let's just say I have very influential friends in the press. Look at it this way, you're in good company, many of our members have stepped out of the public eye by staging their deaths, some – including a couple of American Presidents – have done it through very public assassinations." Frost dismissed his last sentence with a nonchalant flick of his wrist and a broad smile, a glint in his eye. "I see you need another drink, please have mine." He offered Sam his glass from the mantelpiece.

"Are you trying to tell me…" Sam was stuck processing the implications of what he had just heard, taking the glass from Frost's outstretched hand.

"Am I telling you to get drunk? Oh no, there will be plenty of time for that later, but too much to do before then. You'll certainly need your wits about you." Frost sat down again and continued before Sam could speak, "I knew that flower was special so I cordoned off the most fertile land on the island, up near the old fort, north of Aul House, where the mineral-rich spring feeds the soil directly. I sent the tenant crofters down to the south. They thought I had gone mad, so I played up to it and put word out that I had laid landmines in the area to protect the house. Then I planted the seeds from the back of this book." Frost patted the book resting against his chest. "Within a few months the land was awash with the purple flowers, acres and acres of them. But I didn't need them. I was feeling stronger and even looking younger every day and I had to leave Aul, after all, Seth Falcorrs, Laird of Aul was meant to be dead but here I was, a middle aged man who looked and felt like a twenty year old! I put this house in trust and disappeared.

"I took the *MoD* up on their offer and went to East Africa, Uganda, initially, to protect British interests on the railway extensions. That's what took me into Kenya and the *Mau Mau* uprising." Frost shook his head, his pupils shrunk into a pinpoint focus, encircled by those bright, unnatural blue irises, "To think we fought the Nazis to defeat fascism and there we were less than ten years later doing the same to the Kikuyu. Don't you see, Sam? This is why governments and their armies can't be left un-checked. This is why our work is so important."

"What exactly was your role in the camps and where does Pinto fit into all of this?" Sam had nearly finished his second glass of whisky, his hand was shaking as the alcohol raced through his tired, hungry body.

"Remember, I no longer operated as a bonafide British soldier. I was more of a gun-for-hire, doing the dirty work the British could never be officially associated with. My men and I captured Kikuyu and brought them to the camps. Sometimes we captured whole villages and effectively built camps around them to keep them detained. What went on in the camps was none of my business, my job was to capture and hand over to those that ran the camps."

"You mean you turned a blind eye."

"Yes, I did." Frost closed his eyes and bowed his head in that deferential manner as before.

"And Pinto, where does he come into this? You said he was a camp doctor." Sam poured the dregs of the last of his whisky onto his tongue, he felt dizzy leaning down to place the empty glass on the floor next to his chair.

Frost squeezed the arms of his chair, the backs of his hands turning white under the pressure of his grip. His expression was pained, making him look like a condemned man awaiting his final moment in the electric chair. "Pinto comes into this because, like you, I couldn't cope with my loneliness. I met Cecilia in the Rift Valley in Kenya, she was the daughter of a Dutch couple who put my men and I up for a few nights. She was only twenty five, I was almost twice her age but, remember, I looked and felt just as young as her. We fell in love immediately and wanted to be married. But I couldn't marry her unless I told her the truth about me and the flower, about who I once was and who I had become." Frost smiled, "She didn't mind my age and we were soon married. We were together for two years, although I didn't get to see as much of her as I would have liked with the *Kenyan Emergency* growing ever more serious. But I still remember the day she told me..." Frost trailed away.

"Told you what?" asked Sam.

Frost looked hard at Sam, "She told me she was pregnant." A huge smile spread across his face, eyes glistening with joy. "The next eight months were the happiest of my life. Then the day came. The midwife and doctor arrived at the farmhouse early in the morning and just before sunset I was a father, staring into my daughter's blue eyes – blue just like her father's eyes – looking back at me for the first time." Suddenly a darkness struck Frost's face, "As I held our daughter, Cecilia began to violently fit; both the doctor and midwife had to pin her to the bed for her own safety. Then, just as suddenly, she fell into a deep coma. The doctors later confirmed it was pressure on her brain, caused by a tumour, exacerbated by the labour. It wasn't fair, here was I, stronger and healthier than before, thanks to the flower, holding the daughter she had spent the last nine months carrying for us, while she suffered, having never even held her own daughter." Frost wiped a tear from his eye with a handkerchief.

"That's when I went to Pinto, as the only doctor I thought I could trust. I told him all about the flower and what it had done for me. I was so desperate for help. I begged him to use the flower on Cecilia, to help her get better again." Frost's voice broke as the emotion overcame him, he bit down on the knuckle of his forefinger before continuing, "But it was too late. Nothing we tried with the flower worked and she passed away two months later. She never met our beautiful daughter."

"I'm very sorry," said Sam. "Another drink?"

Frost wiped away another tear, "Yes, please, allow me." Again he was quickly around to the table behind his chair. He spoke as he prepared drinks, "That's when Pinto took the flower and my secrets back to the camps and used the prisoners as lab rats. I had no idea. Although Pinto kept in contact with me, obviously keen to understand more about the transformation that had happened to me since discovering the flower. I had no idea about what was going on in the camps. I was a widower and a father. I devoted my life to my daughter." Frost returned with two more drinks, this time downing his in one.

Sam attempted to do the same but the whisky caught in his throat and he was force to stop and cough.

"You've had enough," said Frost and snatched the glass back from Sam.

Sam didn't argue; the alcohol and the fire were having a powerful soporific affect, his eyes heavy. He stood up to combat the tiredness, his head feeling light as the blood drained to his heavy legs and feet. "So how did Pinto end up here at Aul House?"

Frost stepped closer to Sam, several inches taller than him, his eyes glossy and puffy from the tears. "Keep your friends close and your enemies even closer, that's the old adage isn't it, Sam." Frost revealed those bright white teeth through a thin smile. "Pinto's searching for the flower and its secrets but he fails to realise he'll never find it as the flower hasn't chosen him."

"But I've seen what he's doing at the spa, he's made crates of serum from the flower. He's certain he's going to be rich. He has George, you know she's dying, don't you?"

"I know, Sam. I know. But what he's done is temporary, impermanent, a sticking plaster that treats the symptoms but not the cure. There are plenty who'll pay handsomely for what Pinto has, you'll meet many of them tonight. But what Pinto doesn't understand is that nature decides who gets cured and *Mother Nature* has chosen you, Sam. You are ready to take this job." Frost put a heavy hand on Sam's shoulder, "You've proved why *Mother Nature* chose you. You've been up against so much since James died, this week in particular, yet you've faced it all with such bravery and unrelenting resolve. I'm truly sorry if I put you through too much but I only wanted to give you a taste of what I went through as a soldier before I realised I had been chosen. It's amazing what such extreme circumstances can push you to do, wouldn't you agree? You really learn what you're capable of, who you really are. There's no way to discover this unless you're working for something bigger than you, for something and someone that matters."

Sam pushed Frost's hand away and stepped towards the fire. "What do you know about my father's death? Why was your name written on a piece of paper he was holding when he died? Why was he up here on Aul two weeks before he died? Did you kill him and my Uncle Richard?" Sam slurred his words. He steadied himself on the mantelpiece. "And Mackay, you killed him too!"

"I didn't kill James or Richard or dear Mackay. I've known poor Mackay since he was a boy, I was also good friends with his parents, believe me when I tell you that I'm feeling more pain than you about Mackay. You will find your answers tonight, Sam. You can ask Pinto all of your excellent questions yourself. Then we can see about the new start for you, your new job."

The room felt like it was moving, Sam needed both hands on the mantelpiece to stop himself from falling into the fire. The heat was overwhelming. "Why me? What has this to do with me?"

"It's as I told you, you've been chosen, Sam. All that I ask is that you don't give up now. Find the answers to your questions. You're so close now."

Suddenly there was a banging and rattling sound. Somebody was trying to get in to the room. "He's in here!" shouted Clive and Clyde.

Sam turned and charged past Frost, through the darkness, back at the door he'd entered the room by.

"Sam, I think you've had too much to drink. What are you doing? Where are you going?" said Frost.

"What is Cadence? Will it really save George?" demanded Sam.

"Not what, but *who* is Cadence? That's the question you should be asking, Sam" said Frost.

The door shook even harder as Clive and Clyde barged at it; the crack of splitting wood warning of imminent danger.

The lights came on.

Sam winced as his pupils contracted.

The door burst open. The twins bundled in. Sam looked back at the fireplace but Frost had disappeared. Vanished.

Sam scrambled backwards, over a fully dressed four poster bed caked in decades of dust that puffed up around him.

The twins coughed and spluttered as they dived onto the bed but Sam was already off the other side and around the carved wooden posts and out of the room. Adrenaline cut through the blur of whisky in his brain.

Back down the hallway and down the stairs he went, the twins grunting and snorting as they followed. The entrance hall was clear as he ran towards the open front door.

"Step outside and we'll kill you!" cried one of the twins.

Sam was pulled back by a tug at his collar. Reaching to his right he grabbed one of the carved walking sticks in the umbrella rack next to the front door. In one movement he sent the butt backwards and into Clive's midriff then in reverse, the tip of the stick back over his shoulder and into the side of Clive's face. The hand around his collar set him free as Clive fell to the floor. Sam turned around to see Clyde pull up next to his felled brother, his left hand above his head in a sign of surrender, while his right was limp across his chest in shades of bruised blue and purple. Sam raised the walking stick, poised to bring it down hard onto Clyde's face.

Clyde instantly curled up in anticipation of the blow.

Sam dropped the stick and ran for the bright light outside.

Once more there was no life outside. The commotion of earlier was gone. No horses. No carts. No boxes or white coats. Now only a black *Range Rover* parked on the driveway, the driver's door wide open.

Sam jumped inside and closed the door, just as the twins appeared from the house. He hit the ignition button. The engine started and Sam shifted it to *Drive* and floored the accelerator. Wheels span on the gravel before the car sped across the driveway and over the lawn. In the rear-view mirror Sam could see the twins watching him. Then at ear-bursting volume the sound of piano music filled the car. It was so loud Sam couldn't think. So loud it took a moment to recognise the piece. But when he did, he knew it was another trap. Beethoven's *Waldstein*. The final part of the rondo, thumping chords charging up and down the keyboard. He tried the volume on the radio but it didn't work. The sound continued to blast out. He screamed out of frustration and slammed his foot onto the brake but nothing happened. The car sped on. The steering went loose as the wheel took on a life of its own. He bumped and lurched as the car bounced down the hill towards the forest. He tried the door but it was locked. He pulled on his seatbelt. The last few bars of the rondo… The grand finale…

…And then the tree.

22:00

First came colour – reds, browns, purples and blues. Then sound and smell – the crackling and smoky scent of fire. Sam sat up, then dropped his head between his knees allowing the blood to regulate, stemming the dizziness.

He was in a room with white washed stone walls. The gentle light from the open fire that burnt over logs at a hearty rate. A lamp on the table did the rest, through a pale grey shade.

He was on a single bed against the wall in the corner of the room. He got up. He was wearing new shoes. Black leather shoes. Expensive, handmade shoes that fit perfectly. A full length mirror next to the bed showed him the rest… He stared at the black dinner suit, white shirt with winged collar and hand-tied bowtie. Once more, the fit perfect in every dimension.

His hair was styled just how he liked it. He rubbed the back of his hand across his stubble-free cheek. When did this happen? How did this happen?

He looked at his wrist. Reunited with his *Patek Philippe* watch he had given to George in London. Where had the last seven hours gone? The last thing Sam remembered was the car and the music. The drinks Frost had given him had obviously been laced with some kind of sedative. He cursed himself for falling into yet another trap.

There was a single door from the room. He opened it. Cold air flooded in, blowing through his hair, pulling the skin tight on his face. The sun had just set. Final streaks of red and grey light fading away on the horizon. Sam stepped outside onto the short, rough grass. He could just about see the stone walls of the bothy he was in. The descending darkness prevented him from seeing much more. He went back inside and closed the door.

Draped over the end of the iron framed bed was a black woollen, full length overcoat. Sam didn't need to try it on to know it was another perfect fit... It was the table that caught his attention now. He raised the silver dome to reveal a fillet steak with dauphinoise potatoes and spinach. Next to the plate was a green salad. The food was still warm. He began to salivate at the sight and smell. Before he knew what he was doing he was eating as fast as he could. The food was exquisite. Never had a meal tasted so good. He thought better of the large glass of red wine but gulped two glasses of the cloudy Aul water in quick succession.

The effects of the food were instant and gratifying. Life returned to his muscles and his mind...

I'm still alive.

They could have killed me but instead they've clothed and fed me... Why?

– *'Not what, but who is Cadence? That's the question you should be asking, Sam.'*

Who is Cadence?

Could Seth Falcorrs/Charles Frost really be alive?

What was the job offer?

Have I just seen a ghost? How did he vanish like that?

George! Where's George?

– *'Meet me at eleven tonight, at the underground spa. I'll have a boat ready to leave the island.'*

It was now ten minutes to eleven. Sam slipped on the overcoat, did up two of the buttons and went out into the darkness. The cold forced his hands into his coat pockets but his right hand wasn't welcome. He pulled out the pistol slowly and carefully, his hand now shaking ever so slightly.

He gripped the handle firmly, his finger resting on the trigger.

Remembering where the last remnants of light had been on the horizon he tried to orient himself but just has he thought he'd located west his attention was caught by a soaring orange flame rising up into the night sky, followed by an ear-shaking boom. The distress flare had gone off only a few hundred yards ahead. He ran in its direction, pistol out in front of him. There was no fear now, only determination to find answers and George.

It didn't take long for Sam to realise where he was. The monolithic rocks were familiar. He moved sideways through the narrow gap between the stones, just as he had done yesterday but this time careful on his way down the first ladder. Then, taking only small steps he found the hole.

He had to return the pistol to his coat pocket and undid his buttons to negotiate the second ladder. His shoes slipped on the steel rungs as he descended into the cavern. He swung off the ladder onto the narrow lip around the underground reservoir, landing with little sound.

Sam was quickly around the edge, pistol out in front of him once more. He found the crates he was expecting. Inside, those purple vials, thousands and thousands of them piled high. It was eleven o'clock precisely, Sam crouched behind the crate Tom had smashed open last night, his finger poised on the trigger.

The rumble came from the darkness. Then a blue-white light illuminated the water. The grunt of a small engine. Sam got lower, peeping around the side of the crate. The small boat came to a halt, yards from where Sam was hidden. The engine settled to a low hum.

Pinto jumped off and flicked a switch on the wall and the light above his head glowed.

Sam sprang up. "Turn around." He pointed the gun at Pinto.

Pinto took his hand off the light switch and did as ordered. He was still wearing the same clothes as earlier, face thick with stubble and eyes tucked behind dark bags. "You're a bit overdressed, don't you think?" He kept his hands out beside him, fingers splayed.

"Where's George?"

"I'm here, Sam." The voice was weak. It came from the boat.

Sam saw her face peering out from beneath a blanket. She was propped up against luggage at the back of the vessel. "George?"

"Yes. I'm fine, just tired." The colour had returned to her skin but her hair was a mess and her eyes dim.

"What has he done to you?" Sam stared again at Pinto.

"Nothing, it's Okay. He's given me that purple medicine. My leg feels much better."

"I've removed as much of the shot as I could. She's had plenty of Cadence. She's going to be fine," said Pinto. "Now we need to get going. Do you mind putting that down, we've had enough accidents for one day." He took a step towards Sam.

Sam jabbed the pistol at him. "We're not going anywhere until you answer a few more questions."

"We don't have time."

"*Who* is Cadence?" Sam shouted. The word 'Cadence' echoed around the cavern.

"I don't know, Sam. Who is Cadence?"

"Don't bullshit me, Pinto."

"I'm not. You know what Cadence is, it's *this*." He pointed to the purple vials exposed through the broken lid of the crate. "It's what's saved her life. Let me tell you why we're here, if you haven't already worked it out. This is the source of the island's drinking water. You can reach it from above, just as you've done, but you can also travel along the network of underground tunnels which lead to the river.

304

The Laird connected them together as part of his island defences... You see, I've been adding Cadence to the water for years. The natural mineral deposits in the water made it ideal for concealing the taste and colour." That supercilious expression returned to his face.

"What?" Sam was taken by surprise.

"That's right. You must have noticed yourself just how healthy everyone is on Aul. They all have me to thank. And now, I've perfected the formula it's time to get rich. You and me, Sam. We'll have it all – health and wealth."

"Why did you kill Mackay?" Sam took a large stride towards Pinto.

Pinto raised his hands above his head shuffling backward, his eyes bulging with alarm.

"Me? We've been through this. It wasn't me! It was Ferguson."

"Lies! Tell me why you killed Mackay!" Sam shouted, now only a couple of feet from Pinto.

The two men stared into each other's eyes.

"I think you should answer the question, John." The voice came from behind Sam.

Pinto looked shaken by what he saw over Sam's shoulder. "It's you..." His voice trembled. "You're alive... But how?" There was terror in Pinto's strained face.

"Hello, John. It does appear that way, doesn't it?" Charles Frost stepped out of the darkness and stood next to the boat, holding a glowing oil lamp, those unmistakable bright blue eyes in that cadaverous face. He had changed into a black dinner suit and coat that both matched Sam's. Next to Frost was Ferguson, also dressed the same way.

"So Ferguson was your eyes and ears. He's been watching me all this time," said Pinto, shaking his head in apparent disbelief.

"That's right – what better way to know a community than as its doctor and only publican – but I've been back to the island many times over the last thirty years," said Frost.

"So you're the ghost they're all afraid off! Bloody hell, they weren't all crazy," Pinto laughed but it did nothing to disguise his unease.

"You're the only madman on this island, John," said Frost.

Ferguson's long legs made light work of the step down onto the boat, where he picked up the shotgun Pinto had leaning against the boat's wheel and dropped it into the water. He then went over to George, looked at her injured leg and nodded back at Frost.

"I'm very sorry Miss Norton," said Frost.

Ferguson adjusted the blanket covering George's legs and carefully propped her up to make her more comfortable.

"You were never meant to be hurt but I commend you for your bravery. I hope you can forgive me for what has happened to you. But it's Sam you really must thank, he's selflessly looked out for you. Now Dr Ferguson will see that you make a full recovery and find you a change of clothes. And, as promised, you'll get the salve you need to remove your birthmark once and for all." There was concern in Frost's tone.

George was too tired and weak to respond.

Ferguson began loading the crates onto the boat.

"Stop!" shouted Pinto.

Sam raised the gun to Pinto's face. Ferguson continued heaving the crates onto the boat, even he found the weight of them a strain.

"You can leave the open crate for John," said Frost to Ferguson, pointing at the crate with the smashed lid. "The rest you can take."

"So that's it, is it? You've come to steal my hard work." Pinto spat his words out, terror now mixed with a red-faced rage.

"It's not for me, John," said Frost as he walked over to the open crate, placing his lamp down on top and examining one of the purple vials. "There's a party tonight. It's a shame you're going to miss it. You'll miss the delight on every guest's face as they receive some of these." He held the vial up to the light. "This little formula of yours is going to pay off a few debts I've accumulated over the years, as well as buy me *a lot* of favours. The great and the good of politics and business will all be here. Imagine what you can achieve with them in your pocket. Just imagine what they'll do in return for some of these." He opened up the vial and sniffed it, frowning at the scent.

"It's nonsense, Sam. Don't believe a word," said Pinto, forcing a smile at Sam, beads of sweat running along his brow. "He's taking it for himself, he needs the Cadence to keep him alive."

"You just don't understand, do you John? Once was enough for me, that's all I needed. It's all I'll ever need. Your formula is impressive, I'll be the first to admit you look good for your age. Ninety next month, if I'm not mistaken. Many happy returns. But I'm afraid to say, I'm not sure how many more birthdays you'll see, your formula is merely delaying the inevitable, it's cosmetic. You'll never find what I have, it can't be found, it can't be synthesised." Frost tossed the vial into the water.

The boat's engine started.

"You don't know what you're talking about," yelled Pinto. "That formula can cure terminal illness, even paralysis!"

"I'm well aware of what it can and can't do, John. Dr Ferguson has been in here many times over the years to take samples of your formula. He has a team of scientists working in the United States who understand what you have better than you! You've achieved something quite remarkable but not perfect." Frost remained impassive.

"My formula is perfect!" Pinto screamed.

"Nothing is perfect. Prepare the vials for our guests, Dr Ferguson," said Frost. "Don't worry Miss Norton, Dr Ferguson is the best physician money can buy."

Ferguson steered the boat back towards the tunnel. George rested her head back onto Pinto's luggage.

"George!" shouted Sam, then he lurched forward as Pinto shoved him in the back, forcing him down onto the rocks.

Pinto jumped for the boat as it passed.

Sam stuck out a leg, catching Pinto on his left shin, the tangle of limbs sending Pinto off balance and down onto the concrete platform beside the water's edge. Sam was straight up, pointing the gun at Pinto who lay pained on his side.

"Now, I think you should answer Sam's questions," ordered Frost. His voice loud and every bit the army officer. "Let's start with why you killed Mackay?"

Pinto continued to shake his head, as if in a trance, watching the boat disappear and with it any resistance left in him. "That nosey old fool. I went over to his place looking for you, Sam. He said you had not long gone but then he started asking all these questions about Seth Falcorrs and Charles Frost. He had your driving licence with the name Seth Falcorrs and the newspaper article about you being found dead in London. He accused me of being behind it. Then he wanted to know about the flowers… He was putting it all together…"

"So you shot him?" said Sam.

Pinto nodded, "He knew about the briefcase too."

"What about the briefcase?" asked Sam.

"When you turned up with the briefcase, I knew who you were and I *thought* I knew why you were here. But I was wrong; you had no idea did you? I was convinced of this when you pulled that little stunt with the electrics after dinner, just so you could take a look inside the briefcase. That's when I knew we had to get out of here. Remember, it was Mackay who gave you the briefcase to give to me, that was no coincidence."

"What the fuck is going on?" shouted Sam, his eyes flitting between Pinto down on the ground and Frost a few feet to his right, lit-up by the lamp he left on top of the remaining crate.

"Wrong again, John. It was me who planted the briefcase," said Frost, before turning to Sam. "You remember the clumsy luggage porter who tripped you up in Inverness Airport? That was me. I knew I could connect you and Mackay as he did his provisions run to the mainland, as well as get you the briefcase, but it was never my intention for Mackay to get hurt. It was a mistake to have involved him. I will see to it that he gets a proper funeral at St Cecilia's. As you've probably already worked out, I had St Cecilia's built after my own dear Cecilia passed away, she's buried there too. I will have Mackay laid to rest next to her tomb, he was like family to me."

"Shut up, both of you!" Sam took a step back and shifted a few paces to his left, the pistol now trained on both Pinto and Frost. "There were two briefcases. I saw both of them in Forster's office. Then I was mugged outside St Paul's for mine. Why?"

Frost raised both of his hands and stared deeply at Sam. "It's time for the truth, John. All of it."

Pinto laughed, "The truth! You faked your death and changed your name and you're asking *me* for the truth?" He climbed to his feet, his hands also raised above his head.

"Very well, I'll get us started. Do you mind if I lower my hands, Sam? I promise you I'm unarmed," said Frost.

Sam nodded. "Place them palms-down on top of the crate. You too Pinto."

Both men moved slowly around the crate until they faced each other, hands flat on the splintered wood of the broken lid. Sam stood between them, weapon poised.

Frost turned to Sam, "Earlier today I told you that you've been chosen. The reason I know this to be true is because I myself have been chosen, and when you're chosen it doesn't mean taking oil from a flower for the rest of your life, it means every cell in your body is different, it's in your blood."

"I don't understand," said Sam, his outstretched arm aching from the weight of the gun.

"I'm telling you that you and I share the same blood." Frost smiled, his blue eyes welling with tears. "I'm your grandfather, Sam."

Sam lowered the gun. His body felt as if it had shutdown as he tried to adsorb Frost's words. His breath squeezed his chest tight.

"My daughter, Cadence, is your mother." Frost took his hands off the crate, raising them out in front of him, as if ready to embrace Sam.

Sam stumbled back into the rock wall, raising the pistol at Frost. "Get back! What are you talking about?" he screamed. He looked at Pinto who still had his hands down on the crate but now his head and shoulders were slumped down in front of him.

Frost didn't move, still smiling at Sam, arms out in front of him. "Tell him, John."

"It's true," said Pinto, his voice barely audible, head still bowed.

"I promised you an end to your loneliness, Sam. Here it is–" said Frost.

"What do you know about me and my loneliness?" shouted Sam, taking a pace towards Frost, the pistol only inches from his chest.

"As a child you lived alone in that big house in London. You played the piano so you could spend as much time with your mother as possible. When she died you were devastated but you thought it would bring you and your father together but it didn't, did it? Instead, he became colder and more distant, didn't he? So you took the job at the bank that he wanted you to take – did he get it for you, Sam? I thought as much. And since then you've put every piece of yourself into that job you detest, just to get his attention, to get his love."

"Shut up!" yelled Sam.

Frost continued, "All those visits to your therapist, Dr Carter, trying to find an answer. I know about it all because I've been watching, quietly from the shadows. And now I've come into the light because it's time you knew the truth. The truth that James West, the man you thought was your father, who you thought rejected you and didn't love you, was a great man. He was not cold. He was not heartless. He was a man who, thirty years ago, found himself holding a baby boy in his arms, given to him by his brother, Richard. The woman you called mother, Mary West, treated you as her own, but you were not hers, you are Cadence's son."

Sam's arms and legs shook, straining to breathe through the tension in his chest. "This isn't true," was all he could force out. He pulled his coat off, the release of heat from his body was almost overwhelming.

"It's true," said Pinto, almost down on one knee, the crate keeping him from falling forward.

"Glad you've found your voice, John. Do you want to continue?" said Frost, his voice steeped in disdain.

Pinto just stared at the purple vials in the top of the crate which were now at his eye level as he slumped even lower.

"Very well, allow me." Frost picked up the oil lamp, his pallid skin looked ghostly in its light. "After Cecilia died I devoted my life to my daughter, Cadence, and my work. I went into platinum mines. Business was very good and I soon became very rich. All the while I was growing stronger and cheating the onset of old age. In fact, when Cadence turned twenty one, I looked more like an older brother than her father.

"For the first few years Pinto would be a regular visitor to the mines but soon the visits stopped. They had to stop, didn't they John, because you were also turning back the clock and you had a plan of your own, didn't you!" Frost shone the lamp in Pinto's face.

Pinto cowered, covering his eyes from the glare of the lamp, reduced to a pathetic mess.

"Say something, man!" roared Frost.

"None of this would have happened if you let me understand the flower. You let me in when you thought I could save Cecilia then you just threw me away," stammered Pinto.

"Get away from him," said Sam, pointing Frost away from Pinto with a wave of the pistol.

Frost stepped to his left and looked at Sam. "I was approaching seventy and Cadence was twenty one. I had raised her as well I knew how and she was soon to be a qualified school teacher. Naturally, there were always questions about my appearance. Cecilia and I had agreed that we would not tell our daughter the truth about my age and the flower, until she was an adult. Cadence had always believed that I was half my age, she the product of a teenage, shotgun wedding. But the time had come to tell her the truth and to prepare for the public demise of Charles Frost, time for me to retreat into the shadows.

"That's when I found Richard West. You see, my story needed telling properly, from start to finish. I wanted Cadence to know exactly who Seth Falcorrs and the Laird were and how and why I had become Charles Frost. I couldn't think of a better way to do this than write my biography. Richard was an exceptional ghost writer. We worked together for six months. He researched everything so thoroughly, each date, time and place. I told him absolutely everything, including about Pinto and the camps. It also explained why I had to leave and retreat to the shadows.

"We finished the book in March. I bought Richard a red briefcase as a thank you present. Then I went to Cadence's school, where she was teaching, to give her a copy of the book I called '*Perfect Cadence*'. I still remember the children flooding out for the last day of term before the spring break and that's when I also saw a young looking man, smartly dressed, carrying a bunch of flowers."

"You should have killed me then!" screamed Pinto.

Frost ignored him, "That was the first time I'd seen John in almost a decade and now he looked half his age. Another teacher told me he was Cadence's boyfriend and had been for over a year."

"We were in love!" Pinto pulled himself up and charged at Frost.

Frost stepped aside, grabbing Pinto by the wrists, sending him into the rock.

Pinto groaned and gasped.

"Nonsense! You only went after her because of me. I wouldn't give you what was important to you, so you took what was important to me." Frost adjusted his bowtie before continuing, "I was naturally outraged at this so I confronted the pair of them. In my rage I gave Cadence my biography and told her where she could find Richard if she didn't believe me. I told her who Pinto really was and about the camps." Frost paused, then he perched on the edge of the crate and shook his head, "It was all wrong. It wasn't meant to be like that. I didn't speak to her again until…" He broke down.

"Until what?" ordered Sam, the thud of his heart almost audible over Frost sobbing.

Frost looked at Sam and sniffed back the tears, "Until I found her in a London hotel room, dying next to Richard West's body."

The three men were silent. The only sound now was the trickle of water echoing around the cavern. The air was cold but sweat covered Sam's face and hands. He was desperate to remove his bowtie but couldn't risk taking his eyes, or the gun, off Pinto and Frost.

"Who killed Richard West?" asked Sam.

"John Pinto," said Frost. He stood up, composing himself once more.

Sam and Frost faced Pinto, who remained with his back against the rock like a cornered animal.

"If you knew it was me then why did you leave Aul House to me in your will?" said Pinto, to Frost.

"So you did kill Richard?" said Sam.

"Yes, I did. He took Cadence back to London with him in April 1979. It took me eight months to track them down. Richard had told her everything about the camps and the flower. She studied the biography. She didn't want to have anything to do with me anymore. Killing him was too easy. Made it look like suicide with his own belt."

"You sick bastard! Sam pulled the hammer back on the pistol and pointed it at Pinto's forehead. "Why did you kill him?"

"He wouldn't give me his research notes, the evidence he had about me and the camps. It was that bloody red briefcase that I wanted and he wouldn't tell me where it was." Pinto showed no remorse.

Sam took a step towards Pinto and whipped the butt of the pistol across his face.

Pinto doubled up, clutching his face.

"Why did you kill Cadence, you said you loved her?" shouted Sam.

Pinto didn't move or respond.

Sam swung his knee into Pinto's groin, "Answer me!" he screamed.

Pinto staggered back against the rock and sucked in the damp air, before finally finding a gap in his pain, "Because she was hiding something from me too."

"What was it? Tell me!" Sam raised the butt of the pistol again.

Frost's strong, cold hand wrapped around the gun and Sam's own hand, suspending it above Sam's head. "Sam, I promised you an end to your loneliness. I promised you a second chance but think very carefully about what you do next." Those bright blue eyes shone brighter than ever before as he gently released Sam's hand. "Answer him, John."

Pinto looked up at Sam, "It was my temper, I couldn't control myself. I loved her so much, you must believe me. She was hiding our baby. She was hiding you."

Sam couldn't believe what he was hearing. The ground started to move. The sounds about the room swirled and buffeted in his ears. He swung the gun around as he tried to make sense of it all.

"Tell him everything! I followed you to London back in '79, don't think I don't know the truth!" ordered Frost.

Pinto's nose was running, his face red and puffy from tears. Still he only looked at Sam, "She told me I would never be able to see you because you had been adopted by Richard's brother and sister in-law, James and Mary West. Every day I wish I hadn't killed her. Everything I've done with the flower is for her, that's why I named the flower Cadence."

"Sam, you can't kill your father, no matter what he has done," said Frost.

"Shut up! What the fuck did you set all of this up for then? This is what you wanted. You want me to revenge your daughter's death," tears blurred Sam's vision.

Frost smiled, "She's not dead, Sam. That's what this is all about. Cadence is still alive."

"What? It's not true," said Pinto, his voice hoarse, almost gone, his eyes lifeless in defeat.

"She is," said Frost. "That's how the flower works, that's how *Mother Nature* chooses you, Sam. It's in the blood. From me to Cadence, from Cadence to you. Like Cadence, you don't need the flower, the flower is you. In time you will learn how to use your gift."

"Where is she now?" demanded Sam.

"Cadence and I haven't spoken since I picked her up off that hotel room floor on 20 December 1979. She told me she didn't want anything to do with me ever again. She blamed me for losing you. She also made me promise to leave Pinto alone, no more killing she demanded. So I made Pinto a trustee of the house in my will. I knew he would take it, as he knew the flower was thriving here. It was the best place for him to hide, or so he thought. It was the best place for me to keep an eye on him, keep him under control.

"It pained Cadence so much to put you up for adoption but she wanted you to be safe, away from Pinto, with a couple who always wanted children of their own. That's where Richard West helped her. He knew his brother and sister-in-law desperately wanted children but couldn't have any of their own. Richard also gave his brother his red leather briefcase with all of his notes and a copy of my biography. You see, James West, the man you believed to

316

be your father, knew the truth all along but he kept it from you because he loved you. He loved you deeply, Sam." Frost smiled warmly, life coming to those gaunt cheeks.

Sam moved backwards, towards the edge of the concrete lip they were standing on. He went down onto his knees and splashed the ice-cold spa water onto his face with his free hand, the other still pointing the pistol at the other two men. The relief was instant. He took several large gulps before standing to face Pinto and Frost again.

"Why was my father up here a few weeks ago?" asked Sam.

"He came to see me. He told me he was dying of cancer. He wanted to see if I was real, see if the information his brother had given him really was true," said Pinto.

"What did you tell him?"

"I told him he had the wrong person and he should go back to London."

"Bullshit!" yelled Sam. "You knew he had the briefcase and the information about you in the camps. You killed him too didn't you." Suddenly there was clarity, Sam charged over to Pinto. "He was going to tell me the truth. That's why he invited me over to his house for dinner. But you got there first didn't you? You wanted the briefcase. But you couldn't have the briefcase because my father had left it with his solicitor, Morris Forster. He left it to me in his will. So you killed him, to set his will into motion. Then once I got the briefcase you had me mugged for it, was that you outside St Paul's?"

"Does it matter?" Pinto stared at the water, "You're right, it was me, I killed him." Pinto laughed, "I could've saved him from his cancer with a few vials of the serum but he didn't want it. Stubborn fool. So I injected him with concentrate… Immediate cardiac arrest." He laughed even louder as a mania possessed him, "He was holding a letter from ten years ago, from Frost – condolences for his wife's death. She died of cancer too. I could have saved her as well if he'd come to me sooner. I wonder if he would have been willing to make the trade to save her life? What do you think, Sam?"

"Shut up, you sick bastard." Sam took a deep breath and switched to Frost, "It was you who planted the other briefcase with Forster. You got Forster to switch cases. How?"

Frost shrugged, "Forster should have died long ago from his emphysema. I simply offered him a reprieve, for a little favour in return. But don't you see, Sam? James West was willing to die for you, to make sure you knew the truth. That's why we're here now, so you know the truth." Frost began swinging the lamp in front of his face, the light swirled around the cavern, shadows rising and falling in macabre shapes over the rocks and across their faces.

"Sam, don't listen to him," pleaded Pinto, "Let's start again. I'm sorry for everything. It's my temper, I can change. I've got the formula right now. I'm your father. Put the gun down, please."

Sam ran his hand through his hair. "You're not my father. My father is dead!" he closed his eyes and pulled the trigger.

He pulled again and yelled…

… and again… He yelled…

… But no bang. No recoil from the weapon…

Sam opened his eyes, sweat running down his face… Pinto still stood before him, wincing through his fear.

"It was never loaded, Sam. I couldn't let you do it," said Frost. He swung the oil lamp high above his head and suddenly smashed it down onto the crate, sending shards of glass everywhere as the blaze erupted.

"NO!" bellowed Pinto, leaping into the flames to save his Cadence.

Frost stood sill, just inches from the inferno. "He said, his father is dead."

Pinto looked through the fire at Frost. The words he had just heard must have registered deeply and he let out a harrowing, horrible moaning roar as the flames engulfed him.

Frost straightened his bowtie and stepped back into the darkness.

Sam staggered around the crate looking back at Pinto flailing around in a ball of flames, screaming in agony.

Through the darkness Sam went, smoke chasing him and the sound of Frost's fast footsteps ahead. A doorway in the rock led into a tunnel. Still the sound of fast footsteps ahead, up and up and up he went along the steep incline, following the sound until the boom and eruption back in the cavern below. The ground shook. Then a blaze of electric light and Sam slowed to catch his breath. No more sound of footsteps. He went into the light. He was back in the Laird's bedroom, having entered through the fireplace – a passageway connecting the Laird's bedroom with the underground spa.

The room was spectacular. It had undergone a total deep clean since this afternoon. The four-poster bed resplendent in red and gold. Oriental silk wallpaper with birds of paradise and orchids. Portraits of the Falcorrs family on every wall – nearest a portrait of a tall, blonde man with a thin face wearing a kilt. His brilliant blue eyes staring back. The plaque on the frame read:

Seth Falcorrs, Laird of Aul

Next to the bed was a mahogany table. Upon it a red leather briefcase. Sam opened it. Inside a dozen or so vials of the Cadence serum. Next to them a pile of passports – British, American, Swiss, German, French, Australian and more. Each one with Sam's photograph in – the same one lifted from his Gema Bank security pass – all with the name *Charles Frost*. Inside an envelope were bank books to numbered accounts in Switzerland, Luxembourg and The Caymans – all in the name *Charles Frost*. More envelopes stuffed full of high denomination currency – Sterling, US Dollars, Euros, Swiss Francs.

Under the money were two more books. The Japanese Officer's notebook, described so vividly in Richard's notes, its pages covered in *Kanji*, Latin and intricate drawings of plants. Inside the back cover a pressed Cadence flower and small envelope of its minuscule seeds. But it was the purple hardback with the gold leaf typeface that caught Sam's attention – *Perfect Cadence: The Authorised Biography of Charles Frost by Richard West*. Inside the front cover was a handwritten message:

Dear Sam,
Loneliness is my punishment, not yours.
Your life has just begun...
Love,
Seth / Grandpa.

Sam read the message over and over before he noticed the two first class flight tickets to Mombasa, Kenya, poking out from the middle of the book.

A sound came from the hallway outside. Sam closed the briefcase and went over to the door. He opened it, just as George was stepping out from the room opposite. She looked beautiful in the full-length black dress, as she had done the night they first met.

"Are you okay?" was all Sam could find.

George smiled, opened her clutch bag and took out a handkerchief. She wiped Sam's brow and mouth and then kissed him.

"Thank you," she whispered into his ear as she took his hand in hers. "Are you okay?"

Sam squeezed gently, "I feel much better already."

He kissed her again.

The crash of a gong came from downstairs. Then a repetitive, rhythmical clapping of many hands, slowly built in speed and intensity.

It was precisely midnight.

Hand in hand they walked down the hallway towards the clapping.

"Hey, not so fast, my knee's still stiff and I'm wearing *really* expensive stilettos."

Sam looked at George and noticed her birthmark. "You know you can sort that out now?" he said, gently shaking the briefcase, causing the glass vials of Cadence to chink inside.

George beamed, dimples in both cheeks. "I know…But I wouldn't have met you without this." She stroked the side of her face with the back of her hand. "You don't mind if I keep it, at least for now?" She squeezed his hand tighter.

"Don't change a thing." He kissed the pigmented skin on her neck.

Down the grand staircase they went together, the noise growing louder and louder, the energy now palpable. They turned the bend on the stairs and the rhythmic clapping broke into an eruption of cheers and applause. The entrance hall was full of wide-eyed, expectant people whistling and clapping, all dressed in dinner suits and cocktail dresses, just like Monday night in Mayfair. A band struck-up some swinging jazz and some began to dance.

Sam noticed the front door at the far side of the hall open. It was Frost with Clive and Clyde. Clive had a swollen black eye and Clyde had his right hand in a sling, they both nodded at Sam as they left. Frost stopped on the threshold and looked back up at Sam. He pointed to his breast pocket on his jacket and smiled, before waving and closing the front door behind him.

Sam checked his breast pocket and found a white card inside. The handwritten note said:

Congratulations, you're hired. Smile, you start tonight.

Sam and George stepped off the last step in unison. As they landed, scores of hands thrust in their direction.

"Good evening, Mr Frost."

"Good evening, Mr Frost."

"How do you do, Mr Frost."

Morris Forster and Mrs Price were applauding from near the kitchen. Sam waved and tried to get over to them but couldn't make it through the crowd.

More hands to shake… A bracing, square-jawed man in a white tuxedo, with a neatly clipped beard and blonde shoulder length hair, grinned through his bright white teeth. "How do you do, Mr Frost."

"Tom! Is that you…?" But before Sam knew what was what he was pushed through the crowd, greeted by more and more…

"Nice to meet you, Mr Frost."

"How do you do, Mr Frost."

"It's an honour, Mr Frost."

Then, just as they reached the front door, Sam saw Jerry Hart standing next to his wife, Janie, in her wheelchair, smiling in her own way.

Sam opened his briefcase. "These are for Janie." He handed half a dozen vials of the Cadence serum to Jerry.

Jerry stared deep into his eyes and smiled, "Thank you, Mr Frost. Thank you!"

Coda

◆

Orange dust covered everything in the back of the 4x4. They had travelled for thirteen hours by road, with the last hour through the bush – the twisted baobab trees offering little shade from the blazing sun.

The travellers were weary but that didn't stop them from staying alert, on the lookout for the village that was meant to be nearby. He checked the map again and she reassured him that this would be the one. No more dead ends. This would be the one.

He loved her optimism.

She loved his big heart.

At first it was just another skinny cow – a grazing rack of ribs, but then there were goats and huts and soon tarmac replaced the orange clay and the village announced itself.

He stood up in the back of the 4x4. She held his hand, remembering what happened the last time he did this.

Their driver, Nderi, said something before he slowed right down and stopped.

The hand-painted sign said *SCHOOL*.

Children streamed out of the single storey building that reminded him of an English Scout hut.

They jumped down from the vehicle, little expectant faces all around them.

"You remembered the candy, right?" she asked and laughed.

But he wasn't listening… He had found her…

…The teacher on the veranda with the perfect blue eyes… Perfect Cadence.

Acknowledgements

Thanks to Joanna and the Hackney gang for giving me the writing bug and to Andrea at *Literary Kitchen* for all of her tough love and wise advice. Thanks also to the website that I got the *Cryptic Jumbo* clue from – I'm very sorry I can't find you on *Google* anymore to provide a better reference.

Two excellent books helped me with my research and understanding of the *Mau Mau* uprising in Kenya: *Histories of the Hanged: Britain's Dirty War in Kenya and the End of Empire* (W&N) by David Anderson and *Britain's Gulag: The Brutal End of Empire in Kenya* (Pimlico) by Caroline Elkins.

Finally, thank you to my family for giving me the space, time and encouragement to write.

HCB, 2017.

About the Author

Hari C. Barnes lives and writes in a village near London, England. *Perfect Cadence* is Hari's debut novel.

29985250R10197

Printed in Poland
by Amazon Fulfillment
Poland Sp. z o.o., Wrocław